Out of Time Series

Sage

Debra Rard Ledford

Sage- Out of Time Series

Re-edited 1st Edition

Cover Design by Selfpubbookcovers.com/RLSather

Copyright 2016
Debra Rard Ledford
Ledford Publishing
ISBN: 978-0-9840777-6-2

Out of Time Series

(May be read in any order)

Gabriel

Sage

Emily
(expected publication soon)

Other Books by Debra Rard Ledford

Fructose Malabsorption: The Survival Guide

Fructose Malabsorption: The Shopping Guide

Oregon Brew Tour: Craft Beers...Microbrews, Nanobrews, Festivals, & Homebrew Info

Other Books by Ledford Publishing

Slowman Snowman
Written By Philip Egleston
Illustrated by Jayme Walter

Sage- Out of Time Series

1

With a soft puff, Sage blew on the bundle of tinder. Blowing harder, more smoke rose. Then, as though yielding to her will, with a whoosh, the bundle burst into flames. She laid the bundle on the snow, added the prepared, dry twigs, then smiled, enjoying the warmth it produced. Soon a respectable cooking fire burned hot.

A nod of approval from Phoenix added to her pleasure. Sage respected this amazing, albeit unusual, woman, who possessed wilderness skills far superior to those of anyone she had encountered; a worthy survival mentor.

Not that Sage would ever choose to live as Phoenix did. These weren't just classes for Phoenix; this was life, a primitive life. The yurt to which Phoenix welcomed them upon arrival was framed from materials gathered in the surrounding forest. She tanned the deer hides that formed the covering for the yurt. She used materials she gathered to construct everything inside. Its beauty surprised Sage. In this case, primitive was not a synonym for crude. The yurt demonstrated Phoenix's artistic talent. The talent of a tough woman. As Phoenix showed the small group the ice-edged creek flowing behind the yurt and explained how, along with collected rainwater, it provided all her water plus served as a bath, Sage gazed around at the snow-covered wilderness and shivered. Even more shocking—Phoenix's explanation of how she hadn't bought toilet paper in more than fifteen years. Instead, she showed them examples of the moss and leaves which served the purpose. Though grateful for the lesson on alternatives, Sage preferred toilet paper.

While she had no desire to take on a primitive lifestyle, the goal of self-reliance in any situation became an obsession. Dependency upon someone else for care or provision was not in the game plan.

When asked about her name, Phoenix explained that when she left her old life behind, she also left her old name behind, legally changing her name to Phoenix. No last name, just Phoenix. Like the mythical bird, she rose from her former self a stronger, more confident, self-reliant person.

Yes, Sage admired her.

Sage used two sticks, chop-stick style, to transfer hot stones from the fire to the water, which filled a depression she made and lined with the leather which held her first aid supplies. She soon replaced them with fresh hot stones, continuing the process until her water boiled ever so slightly. Adding fresh pine needles gathered from nearby trees and using a large, flat stone to cover her brew, she let it steep as she glanced around and listened to her classmates in various stages of their final assignment.

One attendee punctuated his attempts with very colorful language. Another student still struggled to start his fire. She guessed he selected two hardwoods instead of one hard and one soft. She wanted to offer aid, but that would defeat the point of the exercise. One student endeavored to get her makeshift pot to hold water. A sense of satisfaction filled Sage; she felt in control of her camp.

After the pine needle tea steeped, she removed the needles and lifted the leather, careful to keep the liquid inside the leather cup. Forming a spout, she sipped the brew. The flavorful brew and the warmth it created felt delicious. Sage reveled in the slight smile she received from Phoenix upon completing her task. She coveted this teacher's respect.

Once all six of the students completed their assignment, they hiked back to Phoenix's yurt, said their goodbyes, and then continued to where the road ended and their vehicles waited. Sage started the engine of her pickup and turned the heat on high; she looked forward to warmth. Though never feeling frozen over the last few days, true warmth had eluded her, causing a constant, exhausting chill. As the truck heated, she scraped snow off the windows, mirrors, and lights. Removing her outer coat, she climbed inside and relaxed as the warmth enveloped her.

Driving away, Sage smiled and waved at the other participants scraping snow, while waiting for vehicles to warm. All except one returned her wave. Rory did not. Guys like him were everywhere. You couldn't escape them, even in the wilderness.

Sage noticed him the moment he arrived. Everyone did. Some people garnered attention without trying, though Sage suspected Rory worked to be noticeable. Good looking and well built, his physique shouted many gym hours, rather than a lifetime of hard work. His straight teeth almost glowed white. He appeared to have just come from purchasing his entire outfit, pack, and gear from the outdoor store, all top name brands. Maybe that explained his tardiness. As he approached the group, his attitude bore an unmistakable note of superiority, giving an in-charge impression.

This created a comical contrast to Phoenix. The disparity was palpable. Rory, with his perfectly cut and combed hair, crisp new outfit, and superior manner as opposed to Phoenix's short dishwater blond hair that looked as though it had been cut with a knife and possibly not washed or even combed, buckskin clothing, and unassuming air.

He evaluated the members of the class as he approached, studying each participant with some unknown gauge until his eyes settled on Sage. He examined her in an insulting manner, flagrant in its sexuality. At the first opportunity, he sauntered toward Sage with the audacity to act as though their relationship were a foregone conclusion. Sage seethed. Rather than create a scene, her sharp glare said, "Back off." Then with obvious deliberateness, she spoke with another student. Her clear response lingered, even to the arrogant Rory. Unaccustomed to rejection, he spent the next three days attempting to make the accomplished Sage look incompetent. He only succeeded in making himself look like a jerk. His mediocre skills compounded this image.

The end of any possible association with him filled her with relief as she drove away.

Reaching into the glove compartment, she grabbed an energy bar. Living off the land for the last three days fed her, but it didn't fill her. Physically. It did, however, produce an extreme sense of accomplishment.

Of the three survival classes she had taken, this was the hardest, and without question, the best. The week at forest survival training last spring gave her basic

4

knowledge, but she came away feeling as though the instructor had just taught them everything he knew. Last year's week of desert survival classes was interesting and informative. But with much of it in a classroom, it left her sure she still would not survive long-term if stranded in the desert. The instructor seemed as though his knowledge came through book learning, with little-to-no practical experience and even less aptitude for teaching. Phoenix, on the other hand, amazed Sage, who had no doubt whatsoever of Phoenix's ability to survive the rest of her life in the wilderness. Besides her vast knowledge of the outdoors and survival, her proficiency as an educator was unquestionable. Sage learned more in the short, three-day winter survival training with Phoenix than she could have in sessions ten times that length with either of the other instructors.

She would return. Phoenix offered several survival experiences of varying lengths. Sage planned to take a few of the week-long classes and work her way up to the month-long primitive lifestyle course Phoenix offered each summer for more experienced students. While the timing may be delicate, Sage would adapt. After all, she chose this lifestyle for adaptability and the ease of moving around and experiencing life.

As she drove, Sage marveled at the scenery. While Phoenix taught classes throughout the country, and even internationally, she had selected the northwest corner of Montana as her home. Sage understood why. It was breathtaking.

After driving several miles in the warmth of her vehicle, the deep chill within her bones was finally dissipating. A quick stop at a small country market for a cup of hot tea helped.

At home, she unloaded her truck and stowed everything in her small, efficiency apartment. It suited her short-term needs. Though not advantageous for entertaining, that wasn't high on her priority list. After experiencing Phoenix's class, she may remain longer than she initially planned in order to take additional classes. The beauty of her lifestyle meant she wasn't restricted to the calendar.

After storing her gear, Sage undressed and stepped into the tiny, old, disgusting shower. While this particular shower normally left her appalled and feeling as though she needed a shower, this time it felt wonderful. After four, icy days, the hot water cascading over her slim, cold body felt glorious. Despite her desire to linger, she quickly washed her long, blond hair, applied the conditioner, washed her body, and rinsed the conditioner out of her hair, finishing just as the water began to cool. Without a doubt, this apartment possessed the world's smallest water heater.

Part of her lifestyle called for inexpensive rentals in order to save for her experiences. Most of the time, she achieved this and still obtained a decent place to live. But Montana's rental shortage left little choice. It was either pay high rent or lower her standards. She chose to lower her standards, but even this forced her into paying more than normal.

While drying her hair, her phone rang.

"Hello."

"Hey Sage, it's me, Rory. How about we grab us some dinner? I've been itching for some real food. I can pick you up in about twenty minutes."

"Rory? From survival class?"

"Yeah, so what's your address?"

Sage was thrown slightly off guard by his phone call. "No Rory, I can't. I was just about to go to bed. I have to be at work early tomorrow."

"Too bad. We would have had fun. Catch you next time."

Astonishing! She thought as the line went dead. *How could he possibly believe I had any interest in him whatsoever?*

As Sage entered her office the next morning, a full day loomed ahead of her, with back-to-back appointments. Becoming a drug and alcohol counselor gave her freedom she hadn't anticipated. With high turnover in the field, she could always find a position available with little search. There were far too many who needed help and a significant shortage of counselors.

Some of her clients participated in counseling to comply with diversion requirements for their legal problems and would return to their drug and alcohol lifestyle as soon as they completed diversion. But for some, the light bulb came on. She always knew when this happened. It wasn't just the client's attitude that changed; even the way they held themselves physically was altered.

Clients' backgrounds and stories of decline into addictive lifestyles varied as much as their ages and socio-economic backgrounds. Nothing provided immunity to the clutch of addiction. Not race, not status, not religion, not age, not beauty, not wealth.

7

Sage's goal was to help them find the strength and determination, plus the desire, to break away from the hold of dependence. First, though, she tried to determine what spawned the behavior. She saw the disorder as a symptom of a deeper problem: loss, depression, low self-esteem, sexual abuse, trauma, the list of possibilities was long. After determining the root of the problem, a difficult task since her clients often had severe trust issues, together they dealt with the resulting symptom of addiction and its consequences, with the long-term goal of staying clean and sober. Some did. More did not. Though good at her job, success depended on many variables having nothing to do with her skills.

After her last session, there was just enough time to change and rush to her job at Jed's, a local family restaurant where she worked as a server three evenings a week. Sage loved the contrast her jobs provided. She felt her degree in psychology helped her as a server as much as it did as a counselor. Understanding what motivated people helped add to her tips. She held the record for most tips during a shift.

She joked with a friend and fellow server that when someone ordered fries, she needed to restrain herself from asking, "And how do you feel about that?" But it was only a joke. She almost felt like two different people at her two different jobs. She really didn't take her counseling job to the restaurant any more than she would take her waitressing job to the counseling center.

Sage wanted to experience life. She wanted to see places and get to know the people in those places. She wanted to learn things. Not just academics, but ways of life, ways to survive, ways to create, ways to be. To Sage, learning to weave a basket had been as important as learning to fry a chicken. Learning to identify edible plants became as crucial as learning to mow the lawn. To learn self-defense as vital as learning to drive a car. Sage wasn't satisfied with watching life; she wanted to experience it, all of it.

To this end, she worked two jobs. As a matter of course, she would work for between three months and two years, saving every penny she could, then move on to her next adventure. Depending on the cost and length of that adventure, she would often be off work for as long as she worked. When funds ran short, she settled somewhere new. Somewhere that offered more adventure or more training, such as near Phoenix's survival workshops.

In addition to providing extra income, waitressing also allowed her to get a feel for the local people, both her co-workers and the regulars who frequented the restaurants where she worked. She wasn't picky about the kind of restaurant; she had worked everything from the local greasy spoon to a five-star resort restaurant. Though the tips were better at the resort, she acquired a keener perception of the locals at the greasy spoon.

Sage traveled a great deal to a wide variety of places. Though she indulged in relaxation, she was more inclined to hike, bike, dig, seek, learn, or some other activity. She wanted to experience the world and everything in it: foods, crafts, people, techniques, attitudes, cultures, history. These all interested her. Sage was driven to learn from all she saw and experienced.

Though some would find her lifestyle lonely, Sage loved it. She made friends easily, but didn't need the company of others. As a result, she developed a wide circle of friends within a short time of moving but had no problem leaving them when it was time to move on to a new adventure. The internet allowed her to remain in contact with many of her friends, while other friendships died the natural death that came with time and distance.

Despite her mother's insistence otherwise, Sage hadn't found it necessary to bring a man into her life. Though she dated and even had a couple of relationships, no one had come along who she cared for more than her independence.

2

Drastic variety influenced Sage's life. Her analytical mind questioned if perhaps this motivated her nomadic lifestyle. She liked change. She enjoyed trying new things. But this had not always been true.

Born in a commune, Sage's parents had been commune babies themselves. Not knowing any other way of life, they stayed and started their family. They worked within the commune community, rotating jobs as almost all members of the community did. Her mother's favorite job was gardening. She especially enjoyed the herb garden and chose her children's names from among its many plants. Boys: Thyme, Parsley, and Chervil; plus Sage and her sister, Chamomile.

Sage enjoyed life at the commune. Free to explore, learn, test, succeed, and fail as she wished, rules were few, with children encouraged in their freedom from a very young age, barely more than a toddler. Around that same age, expectations called for children to help with the work it took to keep the community going and self-sustaining. This was never questioned, it just was. Everyone did their part.

Her father included Sage and her sister in all the activities he introduced to her brothers. They were different but treated the same. A wide variety of abilities were encouraged for everyone. The community didn't promote restrictions. With their father's guidance, they learned to fish, hunt, trap, and track. He instructed them in the safety and art of many forms of weaponry, including archery, firearms, and knives. Learning to dress and preserve the meat followed. He also taught all five children about cooking, sewing, gardening, and other life skills as they grew. Of course, her mother assisted in the teaching, though she was more inclined to work alone.

These were necessary skills for the benefit of the community. Due to the pooling of worldly goods and finances upon joining the community, the commune purchased a substantial amount of land when land was still inexpensive. The members of the community reasoned that since it belonged to them, they could hunt, fish, and trap whenever they wanted. As with many of society's laws, the community determined they did not apply on commune land.

Sage's mother renamed herself Amaranth, after one of her favorite herbs. Sage and her siblings called her Amaranth and her father, Sky, following the commune's standard practice. The community abandoned titles of any sort as restrictive, unnecessary, and too establishment.

When Sage was nine, she accompanied Amaranth into town to a community market to sell produce and other items grown and made at the commune. Despite the community's self-sustaining lifestyle, cash income was still a necessity. Some things, such as salt and vehicle parts, could not be grown or manufactured within the community. Property taxes took a substantial portion of the community's cash income.

It was on this weekly outing that Amaranth met Lydia. The two women bonded immediately. As they shared their respective lifestyles with one-another, Sage listened with fascination. She had never known life outside the community. Meeting Lydia was only the third time Sage had been off commune property.

Years later, Sage thought, *I suppose the third time really was a charm*. That meeting became the catalyst which changed her family's lives beyond anything Sage, in her limited exposure, was capable of imagining.

After meeting Lydia, Amaranth continued to take goods to market. Sage enjoyed accompanying Amaranth on these outings. Soon, they visited Lydia's home after closing their booth. Though Sage found some of their discussions interesting, Lydia's children, their toys, clothes, and manners fascinated her more.

Then Amaranth insisted the entire family visit Lydia's church. Though Sky questioned the idea, he felt refusing would not be positive. Sky was all about positivity. So, at Amaranth's insistence, they all bathed, dressed in clean clothes, received a short lesson in conduct, and were off to church.

Sage and her siblings stared in wide-eyed awe as they entered the church and sat in the pew next to Lydia's family. Everything and everyone seemed elegant to children raised with little, despite the simplicity of the church and the humble clothing of the congregation.

As the weeks continued so did the family's church attendance. Before long, they also attended mid-week service. Amaranth joined a women's weekly Bible study.

Then everything changed. With the help of their new church, the family left the commune and moved into a house by themselves. Sky took a job on a construction crew owned by a member of the congregation. While the commune homeschooled their children, it was more unschooling than school. With the move, Amaranth conducted school on a regular schedule, with assignments due within a given time. Family devotions became a daily routine. Showers were also required each day.

Sage liked many of the changes. She enjoyed church and learning about Jesus, but did not enjoy some of the changes she saw in her mother. Instead of Amaranth and Sky, the children were told to call their parents Mom and Dad. Everyone had titles: mister, missus, doctor, pastor, sir, ma'am. Sage was okay with this. But with time, Mom became increasingly strict. For a child who had known few rules, this was difficult. No longer allowed to do "manly" things like fishing, hunting, building, or leading, Sage was required to learn the womanly arts: cooking, sewing, cleaning, caring for her younger siblings, and submission. She had ample opportunity to learn the art of parenting, since her mom had four more babies in the next five years, Samuel, Rachel, Matthew, and Luke. All named from the Bible.

The division of duties by sex confused Sage. She enjoyed doing all kinds of things, not just "womanly" things. She watched with yearning as Dad took the boys fishing. She missed helping him build needed items.

As a teenager, Sage listened to Amaranth explain how she must prepare herself to be a worthy wife and mother so she would be able to find a good husband to take care of her. This shocked Sage! She didn't want to be taken care of. She wanted to accomplish things. She had experienced two distinctly different ways of life and had since learned there were many ways to live. Her desire—her plan—was to experience life, to see places, and to learn about people and their lifestyles.

As Sage grew older, Amaranth became progressively more severe, and her adamancy that Sage's only option was to find a man to keep, protect, and care for her increased. With time, Sage's resentment grew. Resentment of Amaranth extended to her way of life, her faith, and her very existence.

Unlike Sage, her sister Chamomile had been young enough when they left the commune that her memories of the freedom it allowed were few. Chamomile's personality also differed from Sage's; she hadn't cared for outdoor activities, preferring instead to excel in homemaking skills, such as cooking and sewing. She loved caring for the babies.

Sage spent her teen years babysitting for family friends and friends of friends, saving almost everything she made. Though she hoped to find a regular job when she turned sixteen, Amaranth would not allow it, maintaining her stance that a decent woman should not hold a job outside the home. Instead, Sage continued babysitting, which Amaranth allowed, feeling it would prepare her for motherhood. As her reputation as a sitter grew, so did her clientele. Soon she was babysitting six days a week. She could not babysit on Sundays; it was the Lord's Day. Even during a time of emergency, Amaranth would not consent to it.

When Sage took steps for college, Amaranth was adamant that she would not go. By this time, Sage was eighteen and even more determined that she would.

After her homeschool graduation, which was held at the church and included other graduating members, Sage took a position as a live-in nanny. The upscale, professional couple had two school-age children. This provided for income, housing, and time for her education while the children were at school. This also exposed her to yet another way of life, an upscale life.

With her income as a nanny and virtually no living expenses, Sage paid all her expenses at the community college and even saved a small amount. When she switched to the university, the higher cost stretched her nanny income, but she still managed on her own. She rode her

15

bike to classes, so she did not need a vehicle, since her employers made one available for emergencies and transporting the children. Tutoring other students added additional income, which she saved.

Sky and Sage's older brothers attended her college graduation, but Amaranth would not allow the younger siblings to attend, nor did she attend. In tears, she told Sage, "You're defiant, willful, and prideful. I will pray for your soul."

By this time, Sage's goal in life was to be the opposite of her mother. With yearning, she remembered the kind, easygoing, loving mother from her young years, but her mother had grown into a controlling, judgmental, sanctimonious woman. While Sage respected her desire to give one-hundred percent to whatever she did and believed, her mother seemed to have forgotten the Bible states God is love. Somewhere along the way, Amaranth appeared to have lost the love, focusing instead on what not to do. Legalism had become her guide.

When introduced to the Christian faith, Sage had been fascinated by Jesus and quickly accepted Him as her Savior. As resentment of the restrictions placed upon her grew, she no longer wanted to call herself a Christian. Association with judgments and requirements did not seem to fulfill what Jesus taught. She still admired Jesus, still wanted to be like him, still believed in a corner of her heart, but her limited experience with others who called themselves Christians led her to avoid being grouped as one.

Sage was determined to be independent. She would not depend upon others for her well-being. She did not need, nor want a man, a god, or anyone else for protection or support. She was a capable human being who could handle herself in any situation or would be able to with proper training. To this end, she took classes: survival, gun safety, concealed carry, first aid, auto repair, basic carpentry, basic home repair, self-defense, anything to train her for independence. As a psychologist, she knew she was giving her self-dependence the same one-hundred percent her mother gave things, but it was what she needed, and did not affect others.

Ever practical, after her college graduation, Sage used part of her savings to buy a vehicle. Though inclined to purchase a small, economy car, for superior gas mileage, she chose a small pickup with a canopy instead, to allow hauling things when needed. After fluctuating between purchasing a four-wheel-drive for its accessibility and a two-wheel-drive for its economy, she determined the possibility of needing a four-wheel-drive was less than the need to save money on fuel. Two-wheel it was. She did not regret this decision. With no attachment to material things, she moved everything she owned in her little truck.

3

An early riser by nature, Sage woke to a dark room. At this hour most people turned over and fell back to sleep, but Sage coveted her early mornings. It gave her time in her busy schedule for a short workout followed by a quick jog, then a leisurely cup of tea, breakfast, and perusing the latest drug and alcohol abuse journals. Most of what she found in them was old news rehashed or ideas she considered more harmful than helpful, but the occasional gem she came across made it more than worth her time. This left half an hour to log-in on her laptop and catch up with friends.

She skipped the jog. It was her day off. She made it a condition of hiring as a waitress that she not be scheduled to work on her days off from the drug rehab clinic. She varied her activities on those days. Sometimes she visited or went out with friends; other days she did things on her own. She enjoyed volunteering wherever she lived. She dedicated a few hours one day a week to delivering Meals-on-Wheels, finding the most difficult part was to avoid staying to chat. For some recipients, the person who delivered their meal was the only person they ever saw. She often volunteered at schools' job fairs. Reading to children at the library's story hour was one of her favorite activities. If she could help to pass on her love of reading to children, their world showed endless possibilities. Such activities, which she enjoyed, felt like she was doing them for herself, rather than others, so she helped with community clean-up days. She hated picking up other peoples' trash. Her pet peeve—cigarette butts. Seeing cigarette butts on the ground sparked anger in a person not prone to anger. So disgusting! *Why do people litter?* Some of the trash she helped gather was probably blown away by the wind, but someone tossed most of it. So, she helped. She volunteered for a duty she despised. *Who knows*, she reasoned, *maybe it will make a better person of me.*

Occasionally, she stayed home and read. Reading pleased her. It relaxed her. It educated her. She enjoyed a wide variety of books. She read self-help, how-to, survival, and trade journals for information. Mysteries and crime dramas fascinated her. She loved the detailed descriptions in works such as the *Scarlett Letter, Lorna Doone,* and *The Lord of the Rings.* With science fiction, the imagination of authors seemed to sprout wings and soar. Good historical fiction made her want to delve into historical journals. Even children's picture books thrilled her. Most relaxing to read were young readers' series, such as *The Boxcar Children, The Little House on the Prairie, The 39 Clues,* and *Encyclopedia Brown.* Ancient literature fascinated her; *The Epic of Gilgamesh, Beowulf, The Iliad and the Odyssey* were among her favorites. These helped to increase her vocabulary and understanding of society. Then, there was the pure fluff, romance novels. She couldn't help it; she enjoyed them, though she thought vivid sex scenes qualified as pornography and avoided the trashy romance novels. But even some of the best romance novels had an occasional sex scene. Rather than toss the book when happening upon such unnecessary drivel, she skipped it.

She rarely purchased books. Some might call her cheap, but she preferred to think of herself as thrifty. Why buy a book she would read only once when she could check it out for free? Utilizing the local libraries soon found her on a first name basis with the staff. Several became friends. There were only two types of books she bought, books to survive and indie author books. Survival books included a *Chilton's* for working on her pickup and a first aid book, just in case. She loved books by independent authors. She loved the spirit that kept the authors going, despite the odds against them. Plus, she found amazing stories hidden in these books. She liked encouraging budding authors. Then, after reading them, she always donated them to the local library, allowing others to become familiar with talent otherwise unknown.

On this day off, she decided to go for a hike. Thinking of the return trip from her class with Phoenix, Sage remembered a park which included hiking trails. Though many might find her odd for hiking in the snow, she enjoyed the weather, with its variety, change, and wildness. The quiet of the snowy woods drew her.

Walking in the rain had been a childhood favorite–one her mother never understood. Storms fascinated her. She loved watching, listening, smelling, and feeling the fierceness of a storm. After moving to Montana it had taken several snowstorms, which didn't seem to materialize, for her to understand that when they predicted a snowstorm, it meant to expect a lot of snow. It didn't necessarily mean harsh winds.

After filling her daypack with the necessary survival gear—she never went hiking without being equipped for basic survival, especially in winter—Sage headed for the door. Just as she reached for the knob, her cell phone rang.

"Hello?"

"Sage! Hi, it's Wanda." She sounded rushed and desperate. "Hey, look, my son is sick; I got Bev to cover my shift today, but I need someone to cover it tomorrow. Can you help me?"

"Sure, what time are you scheduled for?"

"Oh, you're a lifesaver! I can't thank you enough. Six to two."

"No problem. How's your son?"

"He seems to have a mild case of the flu. I'm hoping it stays mild and that I can keep from getting it. Anyway, thanks again. I'll have them mark the change on the schedule at work. Bye."

Wanda hung up before Sage told her goodbye.

She thought over her plans to go hiking. She didn't like to rush her hikes, and she needed to get home so she could get to bed early for a six A.M. shift. *How silly, this time of year in Montana it turns dark well before five o'clock.*

Grabbing her pack, she headed out the door. Sampson, the neighbor's cat, sat on the railing of the second-floor walkway outside her apartment and meowed as she closed the door. Sage stopped to pet the fluffy giant of a cat. He looked much like a big orange pumpkin with his long, tiger-orange hair. He lazily nuzzled her hand as she stroked his soft fur. *Such a sweet guy,* she thought. *I would love to have a cat or even a dog, but that would make it difficult and possibly more expensive to find a place to live. Though I could have one here, who knows about the next place. Oh well, I'll enjoy Sampson for now.* Giving Sampson one last scratch and pet, Sage headed for her pickup.

21

What a glorious day! She put her supplies in the passenger seat beside her. *I think I'll stop at Ye Old Crock and get a thermos of soup on my way out of town.* Locking her truck, she ran back up the stairs and unlocked her apartment door, leaving it ajar as she rushed to the kitchen to retrieve her soup thermos. She rarely left her pack unattended in the pickup, but her eyes were only off it for a moment.

As she locked the door, she saw Sampson on the windowsill inside her apartment. Glancing first at her pickup, she unlocked the door once again and picked him up. "You're a sneaky old guy, aren't you?" Sampson purred, rubbing against her hand as she sat him down outside the door and then re-locked it.

Sage breathed in the luscious bouquet as she entered Ye Old Crock. The yeasty scent of fresh baked bread combined with a concoction of scents from today's various soups tickled and teased her, causing her mouth to water and her stomach to rumble. She chose her favorite, clam chowder, for her thermos. She ordered a cup of the pureed cheesy broccoli cauliflower to drink as she drove. Unable to resist after the mouth-watering aroma, she added a small loaf of sourdough bread to her order.

As she returned to her truck, her phone rang. *Wow, two calls in one early morning.* She didn't recognize the phone number of the caller.

"Hello."

"Hey, Sage! How's it going?"

"Good. Who is this?"

"Rory. Hey, it's been a while, I know. Wanted to call you back sooner, but, well, I'm in demand, you know."

"Rory?" Sage rolled her eyes and looked to the sky.

"Yeah, Rory. Like I said, sorry for taking so long to get back to you. Anyhoo, with the way we clicked at the survival class, I knew you would be a great skiing partner. So, just let me know where you live, I'll be there in a flash, and we'll head out cross-country."

"Rory. Hmmm, I meant to ask, how did you get my number?"

"Class list. Good thing I kept it, huh. So, what's your address?

"No. I will not be going skiing with you."

"Bad timing huh. What you up to today? Maybe I can join you."

Flabbergasted, Sage stared at her phone before saying. "Rory, I don't wish to be mean, but no, we did not click at all. We will not be skiing or anything else together. Please, do not call me again. In fact, lose my number."

"Hey babe, I'm not sure what I did to get you so pissed off, but..."

"Rory, let me make this abundantly clear," she interrupted him, speaking calmly and clearly, "I'm not angry, but I will be if you contact me again. I have no interest in you at all and do not wish any further association with you."

After a derogatory remark, Rory disconnected the phone, hanging up on her.

"Wow! Unbelievable. I hope he got the message this time." Sage looked at her phone, put it away, and climbed into her pickup.

She usually avoided such bluntness, but Rory made her skin crawl. There were few people she disliked. In fact, she liked almost everyone. She believed all people offered something unique, if you looked deep enough. This made her a good counselor. But people like Rory couldn't get past their egos long enough to allow her to find that sweet spot. Attempting felt like a waste of time.

After last night's snow, she gave thanks for her snow tires. As she parked, she noticed only an SUV in the lot. She wondered if it was a winter picnic or another hiker.

While she had assumed people in Montana would be involved in winter activities: skiing, ice skating, snowmobiles, and ice fishing, it surprised her when she first realized they still had picnics and other outdoor activities in the snow. She should have expected it in an area where snow's on the ground up to six months of the year. She loved living in different sections of the country rather than just visiting for a short time; she learned so much.

Sage put on her coat and her backpack, to which she attached her snowshoes, just in case. Taking her pistol from the glove box, she verified the chamber was empty before shoving it in her coat pocket. While her extensive training and practice had taught her not to fear guns, she always erred on the side of caution by double checking everything involving safety. Despite verifying the empty chamber before putting it in the truck, it never hurt to check it again before transferring it to her pocket. On impulse, she grabbed the four ammo clips from the glove compartment and stuck them in the other pocket before closing and locking the pickup and putting on her gloves.

Sage used her phone to take a few photos of the landscape as she hiked through the snow-covered forest. The crunch of her footsteps and an occasional caw of a crow were the only sounds she heard; the thick, fresh blanket of snow absorbed the sounds, preventing them from carrying far. Breathing in the cold air, Sage relaxed and looked around her. *So beautiful,* she thought. *It seems like another world, so disconnected and peaceful.* The snow, not yet deep enough to require snowshoes, flew like feathers around her with each step.

Soon after Sage arrived in Montana, it snowed the first snow of the season. Pleased to see a six-inch accumulation, enough to build a snowman, she headed for the parking lot. On the rare occasions it snowed when she was a child, she always built a snowman. However, she soon realized she needed a new instruction manual for building snowmen in Montana. Every time she tried to make a snowball it disintegrated in her hands. After many frustrating tries, she stared at the uncooperative snow in her gloves and thought about it. Beautiful, dry snow. Too dry. It needed moisture to stick together. Going back to the apartment, she grabbed a nearly empty spray bottle, dumped the contents, rinsed it well, filled it with water, and headed back outside. A squirt of water on the snow and she was in business. In no time, she not only built a snowman but cleared the apartment's parking lot of most of its snow.

Now, she reveled in the sight before her. The tiny dry flakes formed a blanket of sparkling crystals on the landscape before her. She wished she had the knowledge and gift of photography to capture the sheer beauty surrounding her.

Ah-ha! She thought, *I will sign up for a photography class as soon as possible. I may not be gifted, but that's never stopped me before. Education and determination can often overcome a lack of talent. After all, I'm not trying to be an artist, just happy.*

Something about this beautiful state seeped into the very center of one's being. Sage wasn't sure whether it was its beauty, its wildness, its people, its wildlife, its weather, or maybe a combination of all, but she loved this place called Montana. She might leave it, but it would never leave her. When she left, she would return. Of this, she knew.

She sat on the trunk of a fallen tree, sipping her water and watching the birds flit from tree to bush, in their constant quest for food. Reaching into the side pocket of her daypack, she pulled out a container of granola, throwing a handful on the snow a few yards in front of her, and then snacking on some of it herself as the first cautious bird investigated the offering. Soon, a variety of birds joined in, happy for such easy pickings. Sage tossed another handful to the grateful crowd and then put the remainder back in her pack.

After another drink of water, she continued on her way.

Though it appeared to be snowing under the trees, the light falling of flakes was just a scattering of dry snow falling off the limbs. No noise. Silence all around her. Just the light falling of snowflakes. Such peace.

The snow grew deeper as she ascended the trail. At the top, she sat on a rock and took out her thermos of soup, sourdough bread, and her bottle of water. Above the tree line, she now beheld a splendid view of the breathtaking vista as she ate.

Wish I could make chowder like this. It's better than any I've eaten, even on the coast, she thought to herself as she took another spoonful. *The bread is as good as the chowder. I should learn to make sourdough bread. I'll put it on my list.*

Sage kept a list. She loved the excitement of adding new adventures to the ever-growing list: places to see, things to learn, and things to do. Even more, her excitement at crossing accomplishments off the list nearly equaled the accomplishment itself. But not quite. She kept her list in a small, colorful book she found at a garage sale at the age of sixteen. Though it said *Journal* on the front, it worked well for her lists. Measuring only five by seven inches, it was large enough to allow plenty of entries but small and thin enough to carry with her at all times. It fit perfectly in the secret pouch of her daypack. With it, she kept extra cash and two pens, just in case.

She took it out and added *Learn to Make Sour Dough Bread* and *Take Photography Class*, in neat printing. She originally planned to divide the journal into several lists by category but decided against it. One long list required her to search for items she needed to cross out, using a single straight line. This helped to remind her of all the adventures yet to come, while still allowing her to read where her journey had taken her.

After tucking the small book and pen away, Sage continued her hike. The trail made a curve and headed back down the hill. She was thankful for a loop. Though having to return the same way she came always gave her a different view it didn't provide the same thrill as a circuitous route.

As she walked from beneath the protection of the forest canopy into the bright sun, she pulled her sunglasses from her pocket. Rounding a corner left the forest on one side of her with a flowing river on her other side. The ice along the edges of the water created a beautiful scene.

Crystal clear water allowing views of the rocky bottom came in shades of both blue and green which created a striking picture. Wanting a better view and perhaps a few photos, she headed for a large boulder jutting out over the water. This allowed her to photograph the river from an angle which made it appear as though she were on the water.

Removing her phone from her pocket, she snapped a few shots from the center of the rock looking across the river. As she glanced upstream, she saw the perfect shot. The water was such an extraordinary blue-green color. The ice at the edges seemed to form matting with the snow on the bank being the frame. She just had to get this shot. Standing at the edge of the boulder allowed her to look upstream from where it jutted out over the water. As she lifted the phone, she adjusted her feet to better her angle and realized at once she had made a fatal mistake. Her feet slipped from beneath her on the rock's ice-covered edge. She struggled to regain her footing as the phone dropped into the water below. For a brief moment, she thought she would win the struggle, before falling backward toward the icy water.

The splash into the frigid water stunned her as if thousands of needles hit her simultaneously. Upon hitting the water she gasped in a large breath of air from the shock of it, which allowed her plenty of oxygen in her lungs. Pulled down by the heavy backpack, a thought crossed her mind, *Wouldn't it be ironic if the very thing meant to save me becomes the cause of my demise?*

Then she felt the whirl. She was spinning. *I'm caught in a whirlpool!* Letting out just a smidgen of air, she told herself, *Don't panic, stay calm.* As a certified lifeguard, she had trained for this. She knew what to do. She attempted to swim with the current and slightly out of it, but her backpack and the strength of the vortex prevented her movement. Attempting to remove the backpack proved futile.

Pulled further and further down into the vortex, unable to combat the swirling mass of dark, icy water, Sage continued to fight. She used every technique she knew and when they failed, tried whatever she could think of. Her lungs screamed for fresh air as she let small amounts of air out of them. In desperation, she attempted to put her arms above her head and form herself into a thin bullet-like person, hoping to drop to the bottom of the vortex, something to be avoided, because of depth, but she calculated the river couldn't be too deep. She was desperate. This technique only increased her rate of spin.

Think, Sage, think! She screamed in her head. *You can do this.* She continued various techniques as her lungs burned more and more. The constant spinning brought about both nauseousness and light-headedness. *If I vomit now, I'll die for sure.* She pushed the idea from her mind and concentrated on any possible way to extricate herself from this nightmare funnel.

Then she shifted. Something pulled her to the side. Hope flooded her as she renewed her efforts at escape before finding herself in extreme darkness. The pain was intense as her body scraped the sides of something hard. Her lungs felt as though they were going to explode. Realizing she was surrounded by hard scraping, she sensed that she was being propelled through an underwater cave. If only she could hang on long enough, maybe at the end she would have control again and find oxygen.

Sage's head spun for want of air. *How long, how long*, she thought as she blacked out.

4

The melody of birdsong penetrated Sage's deep sleep. A slight smile graced her lips as she listened to the enjoyable twitters and tweets melding together to form a symphony of joy.

I must have left my window open. As the fog of sleep lifted, awareness of pain pierced her consciousness. She hurt. Everywhere.

Why am I so sore?

Struggling to dispel the cobwebs of sleep, Sage attempted to open her eyes, but her body refused the command. Instead, she moved her fingers, then her hands, followed by her arms. She rotated her head. With a deep breath, she endeavored to roll from her side to her back. *No, there's a pillow. It's hard.* She shook her head.

Why can't I wake up?

Trying a new tactic, she wiggled her toes. *I still have shoes on. What...?* Moving her legs, she roused. She tucked her knees and rolled to her stomach, resting on her elbows and knees. She maintained the position and took a few deep breaths then rubbed her eyes and slowly opened them.

"What in the world!" She sat up and looked around her. Nothing was right.

Then she remembered. "I'm alive!" Puzzlement filled her features. *How did I get out of the whirlpool? I'm dry. How long have I been out? Better yet, where am I? Where's the snow? The River? Could I still be asleep? Maybe I'm dreaming. No, I'm definitely awake.* She

31

chuckled. "I wanted adventure! I must have found it." A note of concern crept into her voice.

"Okay, Sage, you've trained for any emergency. While this may not be an emergency situation, it's," she paused, searching for an adequate word, "definitely a situation. So handle it as you've been trained."

Discovering the pillow at her back was actually her daypack, she pulled it off and placed it next to her. She stood and caused many of the aches in her body to become pains. She moved, wiggled, and stretched. Though sore, no indication of serious injury showed itself. Her face stung. Sitting cross-legged next to her pack, she used the small signaling mirror to check her reflection. Several scrapes, scratches, and bruises covered her face. A gash on her forehead, which she assumed came from the small, remaining piece of her snowshoe, ran along her hairline. Her swollen right eye showed discoloration, as though she had been punched, but saw nothing needing actual medical attention. Taking the first aid kit from its pocket in her pack, she cleaned and applied antiseptic ointment to the gash. The rest she would watch.

When she returned the mirror to its place in the pack, she pulled out her water bottle and took a long drink. *You would think I had gotten enough in the river*, she thought, then took another drink and put it away.

Now, where am I? No snow. Weird. Montana is covered with snow. I don't recall a thaw in the forecast. In fact, "it's hot!" She peeled off her gloves, hat, coat, and snow pants. Still warm, she removed her wool sweater, pulling it over her head. Off came the flannel shirt. Next went the polypropylene, long-sleeved thermal shirt. Down to a sleeveless t-shirt, what some would call a wife-beater, she felt better. Still too warm, she unzipped her hiking pants, removed them, pulled off the thermal underwear, worked the zipper at the knees of her pants, removed the bottom part of the pant leg from the knee down, and pulled on the pants-turned-shorts. Her heavy hiking boots might look somewhat odd with the shorts, but she wasn't here for a fashion show, and they were all she had. She stuffed what she could of her clothing in her daypack and connected both the hanging loops on her pack and coat with a carabiner, since the coat wouldn't fit inside.

The sudden realization of the capability of learning her exact location made her feel a little foolish. She reached into her pocket for her phone but found it missing. She squinted and then remembered; she was taking a photo of the river when she slipped. Her phone was in the river—wherever that was.

Taking the compass out of her pack, she got her bearings. *Now I know the directions. What am I supposed to do with them? I have no idea where my truck is or anything else for that matter, including me.* A glance at the sun told her it should be about 1:30 P.M. *Odd, it's too high in the sky to be winter. I would guess somewhere between August and October. This is getting stranger by the minute.*

With mountains on both sides, she followed the valley in which she awoke, hoping to locate a river. Though her location plagued her, she chose not to think about it, knowing such thoughts would waste energy and keep her mind from concentrating on what needed done.

Just another hike, she told herself. As she walked through the tall grass, she felt, rather than realized, her error. Stopping, she pulled the bottom of her pants out of the pack and zipped them into place. *Better hot than scratched and itchy legs.*

The area was picturesque. Several varieties of trees graced the valley with an artistic mixture of conifer and deciduous, creating an array of green mixed with a palette of oranges over the golden, dried grasses. Somewhat arid, plenty of pines added to the mix. The close mountains consisted more of rock than trees.

Where am I and how did I get here?

The faint sound of water reached her, requiring an ever-so-slight adjustment in direction to head straight for it. Happy to find a water source, she thought, *That's progress.* Walking toward the water, something about this place looked familiar, but she couldn't place it. The astounding beauty and the walk were enjoyable, despite the bizarre circumstances.

Hunger gnawed at her. *When I reach the water, I'll eat. I need to keep up my strength.*

At last, she reached a beautiful river. She sat on a rock and took the thermos and remaining bread from her pack. Still somewhat warm, the soup tasted good.

Golden mantle squirrels and chipmunks frolicked among the rocks. Down river, a group of mule deer drank their fill. Wherever she was, it was beautiful. She loved the sounds: the wind through the trees, the birds, others she assumed were bugs of some sort, perhaps grasshoppers. The number of butterflies astounded her. They weren't something she saw often.

She pulled her pistol from her coat pocket to check it. Odd, no signs of having been wet. In fact, nothing showed any sign of having been wet. Holstering the pistol in her belt, she retrieved the first-aid booklet from her pack. Dry, without a single crinkle. She took another bite of bread. It should have disintegrated in the water; it was only wrapped in paper, yet it tasted as fresh as when she bought it.

This keeps getting stranger. But you will not figure out what happened by sitting here, so get up and go, she told herself as she gathered her things.

She froze at the movement downstream and watched in fascination, glad her pistol was close at hand, just in case. While her heart ached for the beautiful deer, the fascinating display of the natural order of the wild was still grim to witness. The short-lived screams of the deer subsided; the massive grizzly didn't take long to kill her.

Sage well knew of the dangers of grizzly bears and how fast they could move. The wind blew from the bear to her, so it shouldn't catch her scent, but if the wind changed and the grizzly got her scent, she could be in trouble. The creature may see her as a threat to his meal. As the bear turned its back on her while positioning the deer for better eating, Sage slipped behind the boulder she had been sitting on and pulled the pistol from its holster. If attacked, her shot must be true. Killing a grizzly with a handgun was not easy, and unlike a black bear, they didn't necessarily scare off, they just got mad.

She willed herself to remain calm and relaxed. If the bear attacked, high levels of anxiety could mess with her aim. Though a good shot, she had never shot at an attacking animal. She hoped the deer filled the bear's stomach enough that if it saw her, it would continue on its way and not bother with her.

Cramped and uncomfortable in her rock hiding place, Sage didn't dare risk the noise adjusting her position would create. The bear was in no hurry. She gauged the likelihood of sneaking off without the bear noticing. No, grizzlies had excellent hearing, better to stay hidden behind the boulder. From here, the bear was visible between the boulders, while making her less visible. She counted on the grizzly's poor eyesight, the wind not changing, and her silence. Just wait for him to finish his meal.

After what felt like hours, the bear left the remainder of the deer, ambled to the river, walked into it, and drank his fill before continuing to the other side. Happy to see it walk out of sight, Sage relaxed for the first time since seeing the magnificent creature. *Well, that was exciting.* She grabbed her pack, put it on, and continued on her way, pistol still in hand.

Despite the puzzling circumstances, Sage enjoyed the hike. Some idea of her location would make it more enjoyable, but hey, she craved adventure. This qualified as a ten on the adventure scale.

Unable to stop the nagging sensation of familiarity, Sage looked around her. She knew this place. In the higher elevations, the trees were changing color. Fall would soon be here. *How could I go from mid-winter to fall?* Sage pondered the question as she walked. No viable explanation came to mind. Perhaps she had awakened from a long bout of amnesia. As silly and cliché as that sounded, it seemed as though it could be a credible possibility, until she remembered the sourdough bread and clam chowder from Ye Old Crock was still in her pack. While she could have ordered more for this hike, the bread still had the odd edge she had removed to feed the birds in the snow. No other plausible idea came to mind.

The sun sank lower in the sky, and the temperature cooled. *I'd better keep an eye open for a good campsite. I must not be caught unprepared, especially with a grizzly in the vicinity.* She searched for a location near the river which included a tree for suspending her pack, with an open space away from both the river and tree for sleeping. The tree needed to be between her and the water, in case a bear or other animal came to drink and decided to investigate her pack hanging from the tree. She didn't want to be caught on the path between the two.

While not yet dusk, but close to it, Sage found the area she searched for. Taking the length of Paracord from her pack and attaching it to her Leatherman for additional weight, she slung it over a high branch, allowing plenty of space between the rope and the trunk of the tree. Then she pulled on the Leatherman until it was near the ground.

With that job complete, she took the peanut butter and jelly sandwich out of her pack. It had been her original lunch plan. Coupled with an apple, they made a nice dinner.

After eating, Sage took her supplies to the river and washed the containers and her hands to remove any smells which might attract unwanted guests through the night. She put the containers back into the pack and removed her space blanket and wool sweater. Unsnapping her coat from the pack, she laid it with the other supplies before removing her survival knife and flashlight from their places on the outside of the pack. With her night supplies set, she attached the backpack to the rope and hoisted it up high in the tree, securing the remaining rope around the trunk of the tree.

Away from the backpack and the river, Sage chose a level, rock free spot of ground. Laying her coat on the ground, she unfolded her space blanket and placed it over the coat. *Well, at least my timing is good,* she thought, as the last of the light faded from the sky.

Already chilly, Sage assumed it would get colder, so she put her sweater on before lying on top of her coat forming a makeshift pillow with the hood. She pulled the space blanket over her and made sure her knife lay next to the improvised pillow. Holding the pistol on her chest, she looked at the magnificent sky. While she had slept outdoors many times, this was the first time she knew of a grizzly's presence in the vicinity. She wanted her weapon in hand if he decided to make her his next meal.

The stars came out in force. She had never seen such a display. Locating the Big Dipper, she smiled at the sense of security it always gave her. Though she knew and could identify many of the constellations including the full Ursa Major, the prominent portion known as the Big Dipper held her heart. She thought perhaps it had to do with it being the first asterism her father had shown her. She was small, probably three years old. He had held her, pointed to the stars, and told her the story of the bears. Or perhaps it was because of its identifiability. Regardless of the reason, it was like finding an old friend. In all this strange confusion, that felt good.

Morning dawned with Sage still lying on her back, holding her pistol on her chest. She slept well, under the circumstances. She glanced around, verifying safety before inhaling the wonderful aromas of awakening outdoors.

Gathering her things, she lowered her backpack and returned each item of equipment to its prescribed place. She removed her toothbrush and brushed her teeth, using the last of her water. Going to the river, and taking out the packet containing water purification pills and a cotton cloth chosen for filtering water, she placed the cloth over the open water bottle, grasped it with her hand, and dipped it into a rapidly running section of the river. When full, she repeated the process with the second bottle. After rinsing the cloth and hanging it from a clip on her backpack, Sage dropped two tablets into each bottle, closing the lid. As the bottles sat, she washed her face and hands in the river, then took her folding brush from her pack and brushed her long blond hair, securing it into a ponytail. Replacing the brush, she picked up both water bottles and shook them for several minutes. When finished, she placed them into her pack to work their purifying magic and then put the pack on her back and continued on her way.

Sage rounded a bend. Shocked at what she saw, she stopped. There could be no mistaking it. She turned, and sure enough, there it was, the unmistakable dried-up falls. But how could this be? There's no other place like it. It has to be. She looked again, noting the reflection in the river. Her mind struggled to comprehend the sight before her. It left no doubt. No other place on earth looked like this. Her knees buckled. How did I get here? Puzzling the question in her mind, she stared at the sight before her.

She had been here before, camping and hiking for three long months. It was a glorious place, unlike anywhere in the world. As she gazed upon Half Dome and its reflection in the Merced River, she said aloud, "How did I get to Yosemite?"

5

"Well, at least I know where I am." Sage threw her hands in the air and chuckled at the insanity of the situation before continuing on her way. She followed the Merced River for a short distance before cutting across the valley to Yosemite Creek, only to find herself alone.

Stunned, Sage looked around. *Where is everything? Where's the Village? The people? There should be hordes of people here. There should be several buildings, a store, a visitor's center, all crowded with tourists. There should be roads!* She continued walking, headed for landmarks she knew. They were there. They were all there, except for any sign that people had ever inhabited this place.

"Okay, this is even stranger than I thought."

Sage sat on a nearby boulder. For a brief moment her mind went blank. Whatever was happening, she was unprepared for it. This frustrated her. Her goal was to be prepared for anything. She had lost control.

Then she realized her thinking had gone awry. Her goal was not to control all situations; it was to be prepared to handle any situation. Though she may not understand the circumstances, she could handle this. She possessed the tools she needed, both physical tools and tools of knowledge.

I know where I am. How I got here does not matter, for now. She put her pack on her back, and continued walking. *Sacramento. It's the closest large city and I should find something or someone before then.*

The grueling hike took time. With no roads, the only trails were game trails. The rough terrain slowed progress. By the end of the second day, Sage looked down into the Central Valley, but no roads, buildings, or any other sign of human life caught her eye.

Shaking her head in wonder, she made a more thorough assessment of her situation. Though she picked and used edible plants along the way to stretch food supplies, a more aggressive approach was required. She had expected to be on a day's hike, so, as was her custom, she packed a generous two-day supply of food. Now, three days into her adventure, food was running low. Though she always reserved the separate, small, bottom portion of her pack for as many freeze-dried meals as would fit, they wouldn't last long and she preferred to reserve them for emergencies. This called for some serious food gathering, which would require time and slow forward progress.

Before heading down the mountain into the valley, Sage took a compass bearing. While not positive of the exact location of Sacramento in comparison to her current position, she was reasonably sure she could find it. If she didn't find anything or anyone before then, reaching either the American or Sacramento River would lead her right to her destination.

Then a thought occurred to her, *What if Sacramento isn't there?* She shook her head. *Now you're just being silly. Besides, don't borrow trouble, as grandma used to say.*

She gathered food as she walked: roots, berries, pine needles, cones, and whatever else she ran across, but something more substantial would be needed. She watched a small pool of water. *Yes.* The pool of water teamed with frogs. Catching frogs had been a favorite childhood pastime, and they tasted good. Debating whether to use a forked stick, which she would need to take the time to find, or to remove her shoes and go catch them by hand, she opted for the old-fashioned way, pulling off her hiking boots, socks, and unzipping the bottom of her pant legs.

Soon, she held a good sized frog, but hesitated. An endangered species, she had read about the yellow legged frog and enjoyed looking at a few during her stay in Yosemite two years ago. *I can't kill endangered animals.* Then it occurred to her*, I saw a grizzly bear in Yosemite National Park! The last of California's grizzlies was killed back in the early 1900s. What is going on?*

She stared at the frog. This qualified as extraordinary circumstances, which called for survival mode. Not wanting to be an endangered species herself, she must take only what she could eat. This pond was full of these cute little guys.

Soon, she had a "mess of the little fellers," as grandma would have said. Using a nearby rock, she took out her knife and prepared them for cooking. Finding two sturdy green sticks, she used her knife to remove the bark from the ends. Filling the pot included in her mess kit with fresh water, she tossed in some pine needles, wild onion, and dandelion leaves. After starting a small fire, she placed the pot of water on a rock at the edge of the fire, secured each frog end to end on the sticks, and held them over the fire. When the frogs were cooked, she put them on the mess kit plate to cool and threaded more of the prepped frogs onto the sticks.

All the while, she kept a wary eye around her, hoping the smell of cooking food wouldn't encourage unwanted guests. Just in case, her pistol lay on top of the pack beside her.

She tore off a frog leg and tasted it. "Needs salt," she said aloud, before reaching for the salt she kept in her pack. She also added some to the pot. After eating a few legs, she deboned some of the meat and dropped it into the pot, reserving a few more legs for eating. When full, the rest of the deboned frog meat went into the pot. She placed the lid on the pot to simmer for a while to distribute the flavors.

Despite the odd situation in which she found herself, Sage enjoyed this. She liked camping and backpacking and was delighted to put her skills to use. While it would have been nice to have a full pack with her, what she carried worked. The multitude of wildlife excited her: mule deer, birds, an occasional rabbit, squirrels and chipmunks. Despite dinner's main course, she enjoyed watching the frogs. *I just hope Yogi and the local kitty cats don't come calling, though I wouldn't mind bumping into Ranger Smith. I've got a few questions for him!*

Lifting the pot, she poured the soup into her thermos and replaced the lid. Once again, she was thankful she had decided to stop at Ye Old Crock before her hike. If not, she wouldn't have her thermos with her.

She placed gathered pine cones in the dry pot and covered it. The heat would allow them to open and release their pine nuts. Though few, on a limited foraging diet they would provide added nutrition. When they were done, Sage placed all the pine nuts in with her small container of nuts and poured water in the pot to heat for refilling the water bottles and for cleaning the mess kit before putting it away.

Hiking through the Central Valley left Sage baffled. She knew this area. It was criss-crossed with roads. Four days of hiking and she had not yet come across a single road. On the other hand, it was beautiful. Unspoiled. Abundant with wildlife. She encountered no problems locating food. Fish, frogs, plants—all were plentiful. Everything except people. And towns. She had not yet run across a single town, city, or even house. It was as though she had been dropped into California pre-settlement, but that was impossible. She had even seen a few more grizzly bears. So far, she managed to avoid their detection, but the craziness of the situation stumped her. There were no grizzlies in California, or at least there hadn't been for over one hundred years.

She kept telling herself Sacramento would be there. It had to be. While she knew how to take care of herself and enjoyed being alone, this was extreme. She felt like the only person left on the planet.

After spending many hours pondering the questions of how she came to be in California when she was supposed to be in Montana and how she went from winter to what appeared to be either late summer or early fall, Sage decided it was not answerable. At least not at this time. Thoughts about the whirlpool and how she had not drowned, but instead found herself here, had her perplexed. *Just be thankful and patient,* she told herself, *answers will come.*

This brought her father to mind. When she was young and still able to go hunting and fishing with him, before her mother had determined it was not ladylike, he told her repeatedly, "Just be patient and wait." Patient she could handle; waiting was problematic. She wanted to take control; she wanted to find it, do it, help it, fix it. Once she was in command of the situation, she had infinite patience. *Perhaps I'm more like Mom than I care to admit. I have this need to know. I need to understand what is happening. It doesn't matter what it is, I can handle it, but it drives me nuts not knowing what has happened.*

Sage stopped walking and looked around. She chucked. "So much for being thankful and patient."

Finally, she came upon what she was sure was the American River and followed it downstream. "Soon. Soon I'll be in Sacramento and able to determine what has happened. I hope."

When Sage saw where the American River met the Sacramento River, for a brief moment she sighed with relief. Then reality hit; if she could see the confluence of these two rivers, she should be standing within Sacramento. She saw nothing. Turning, slowly looking around her, she stopped. There, not far to the southeast, on a small knoll, was a structure.

"Well, at least it's something."

As she drew nearer, shock registered. "Sutter's Fort?" Sage swallowed. She couldn't believe her eyes. She had toured the restored fort when visiting the area, with its guides in period dress demonstrating life in the 1840s, but this looked different. Similar, but different. *Could it be?* Sage continued to stare. *No, it's impossible.*

Determined to discover information which would lead to answers, Sage headed for the Fort.

6

Sage felt the stares as she walked toward the fort. Several Native Americans worked around the fort. They didn't look happy. She remembered reading that John Sutter didn't treat them well. They seemed to be watching her without looking at her. There were also Hawaiians and Mexicans. Neither looked too happy. The white men were different. *They look at me as if I were from Mars, and some of them look at me more like I'm a Mars candy bar they would like to eat.*

When she arrived at the open gate of the fort, a guard stopped her.

"State your business." Growled a rough-looking, unkept man.

"I need to speak with the person in charge," Sage said with as much authority as she could muster.

"We'll see about that. Wait here." He turned and walked away.

Not to be deterred, Sage followed him. She was surprised by the number of people and amount of activity at the fort. As she followed the guard it seemed as if every eye in the fort was on her. When he reached a doorway and was about to open it, he noticed her behind him. "Thought I told you to wait at the gate."

She gave him a rather condescending smile. "I thought I'd save you an extra trip."

"Humph. This time, wait here!"

As Sage awaited his return, she wondered what she would do if he came back and said to leave. *Surely, they wouldn't,* she thought, *curiosity alone should gain me admittance in a place like this.*

Moments later a middle-aged man with a heavy mustache and thinning hair greeted Sage. "John Sutter, pleased to make your acquaintance."

Sage gasped. He looked just like the pictures she had seen when visiting the fort replica. Could it be? Realizing she must say something, she extended her hand. "Mr. Sutter, Sage Brooks. Thank you for taking the time to meet with me."

"No trouble at all, Miss Brooks. What is a lovely lady such as yourself doing here in Helvetia and how may I be of assistance?"

Noting the use of Sutter's original name for the area, Sage paused. "I suppose you could say I've been doing a bit of exploring. Beautiful country here."

"Yes, yes it is. But surely a woman such as you is not here alone. Where are your people?"

Unsure of the wisdom in admitting to being alone, she decided to rudely shelve the question. "You have such a wonderful place here, Mr. Sutter. Have you been here long?"

"Why thank you; I enjoy it myself. Please, Miss Brooks, have a seat."

By this time Sage recovered enough from her initial shock to look around the room. A handsome, yet somewhat rough room, it included a sturdy desk, topped by a lamp, an inkwell, what appeared to be a feather pen, and several papers. He had been writing something when he was interrupted. In addition to the chair behind the desk, there were four other chairs in the room as well as a bookcase and a small table. She sat in a chair in front of the desk.

Diving right in, Sage asked, "Mr. Sutter, can you tell me the date, please."

With a chuckle, John Sutter said, "Easy to lose track out here, isn't it? I myself keep a running calendar. Today is Sunday, Miss Brooks, Sunday, the 27th day of September."

Sage quickly calculated and discovered she had found herself in this odd situation on September 19th. "And the year, Mr. Sutter?"

"My, my, you are disoriented, aren't you? Why, this is 1847, of course."

Sage felt the blood drain from her face. She closed her eyes and inhaled, letting the air out slowly. Thoughts flittered through her mind, *1847. The whirlpool. Could it have been? It's not possible! But it would explain. No roads. No people. No buildings. No Yosemite Village. No Sacramento. Nuts!* She raised her hands, splaying her fingers along her forehead with her eyes closed. Then, forming her hands into fists, she butted them against one another with her thumbs against her lips. Her eyes remained closed.

"Miss Brooks, are you okay? Are you going to faint? Can I get you some water?" Her host seemed flustered by her response to the date.

Willing the array of somewhat disjointed thoughts flashing in her head to slow and form a comprehensive and plausible analysis of the situation, Sage looked at her host. "You're sure about the year. In reality? This is not a reenactment?"

"I truly am sorry, Miss Brooks, but I am not quite sure of your meaning."

"This is actually the year 1847?"

"Of course. Are you not well? Can I get you something?"

With the knowledge that she must gain control, Sage gave a slight smile. "Thank you, Mr. Sutter, I am quite well. I apologize for my momentary lapse; the events of late have been quite bewildering. I suppose I will require a bit of time for adjustment."

"Perhaps a morsel of nourishment will help." John Sutter rose, opened the door, and turned to Sage. "You relax and gather your wits, in no time we'll have a bite to eat."

"Thank you, sir, that would be very nice."

John Sutter left the room, and Sage attempted to organize her thoughts. *Is it possible? Could the whirlpool somehow have catapulted me back in time? While not plausible, there doesn't seem to be a more convincing explanation for what I've seen, and for that matter, haven't seen. If it weren't for having seen Yosemite, I couldn't possibly consider time travel, but...*"

John Sutter's return interrupted her thoughts. "You appear to have recovered some. I brought you some water."

"Thank you. Yes, I am better. I'm so sorry to have caused you trouble."

"No trouble at all, my dear. You just relax and we will soon have a nice meal. I have one of the best cooks in all of California."

He was correct, the meal was wonderful. Especially after eating trail food for over a week. John Sutter fascinated Sage. She wasn't sure she had ever met a more gracious man. Oddly, his affability seemed a harsh contrast to his reputation for racially based abuse of his employees.

During their dinner conversation he alluded to a couple who had been members of the Donner party. Sage was momentarily baffled by the reference he assumed she would know, until she made the connection, John Sutter had played a key role in assisting the Donner party. "Their trek was such a tragedy. Your generosity in their assistance was widely publicized. No doubt they and their families think very highly of you."

"They had been through a great deal and the misfortune of their crossing, I fear, will forever haunt them. I only did what any civilized man would do."

Awareness of sitting there speaking to this man as though he really were John Sutter stunned Sage. She thought back to Yosemite, devoid of any vestige of human life. She pictured the Central Valley with nothing modern, no improvements, and no people until Fort Sutter. Here, Fort Sutter—not the mostly reproduced fort she had toured—but the authentic fort, free of the encircling city of Sacramento, filled and surrounded by the very people Sutter employed or enslaved.

Is it possible? Could that whirlpool in Montana somehow have transported me to the Yosemite Valley in

1847 California? Might this actually be John Sutter? To even consider some truth in any of this seems crazy, but what other feasible explanation could there be? Feasible? Sage laughed to herself. *I'm calling time travel feasible! Have I totally lost it?* She raised her hand to her head, running her fingers through her hair. *No, I'm quite in control of my faculties.* As the truth of her circumstances dawned on her, she felt as though it washed over her, as though something had just run throughout her entire body from head to toe. She looked again at the room in which she sat. Awed by her surroundings, she felt a tingling sensation. Then Sage looked again at her host. *Wow!* With a shiver she thought, *Now **this** is an adventure!*

Sutter observed Sage as she worked through the situation, remaining silent.

"Mr. Sutter, this is a wonderful meal. Please accept my appreciation for your kindness."

"It is indeed my pleasure, Miss Brooks. Tell me, what plans would a young lady, such as yourself, have in California? May I assist in any way?"

"Plans…" Sage thought for a moment. "Now that I'm here, I would like to take a day or two to solidify my plans. In the meantime, I would like to look around your fort. If you have no objections, that is."

"Certainly! In fact, I would like you to be my guest. I will arrange for a room and you are welcome as long as you need."

Overwhelmed, Sage thanked him.

It was Sage's second day at the fort and she was enjoying herself immeasurably. To observe life in 1847 first-hand, to witness the making of tools, food, clothing, everything needed to sustain life was an honor beyond description in Sage's way of thinking. However, the treatment of the Natives, the Hawaiians, and the Mexicans Sutter employed or enslaved distressed her and she wondered how an otherwise gracious and generous man could treat other human beings so poorly.

She considered her predicament for some time. While thankful for the survival skills she possessed, she needed to do more than just survive; she needed a way to make a living. When the solution occurred to her, she was shocked it had taken so long. She was now in the month of September, of the year 1847, at Sutter's Fort. Within a few months, James Marshall would approach Sutter with his discovery of gold at Sutter's Mill on the American River, about fifty miles east of the fort at what would become the city of Coloma.

For those who arrived early, gold had been available. Not only could she beat the rush, she could beat the discovery. She only needed to keep it quiet until after the world knew. She would go to Coloma, downstream from Sutter's Mill, and get her fortune, her grubstake!

7

Sage found her time at Fort Sutter interesting, relaxing, and very educational, but looked forward being on the trail again. With an abundance of time to think and plan, she developed what appeared to be a solid and sagacious plan. It hinged on only one thing. While timing and tenacity were on her side, it was the only thing left to chance. Well, chance and hard work.

Sage traded an extra LED flashlight with spare batteries for supplies. Hoping not to take advantage of Mr. Sutter, it was the only item she felt she could do without. John Sutter had been so fascinated by the "magical" item, he allotted her enough in trade to purchase adequate supplies. She chose salt, a gold pan, a shovel, a tent, two wool blankets, some towels, a couple pairs of socks, a journal, a bow with a quiver of arrows, a few bars of lye soap, and some food supplies, including pemmican, a Native mixture of dried pulverized meat and berries mixed with fat. With some minor modifications and by hanging items on the outside, Sage made her daypack work for carrying everything.

When leaving the fort, John Sutter said to be sure and stop in if she found herself that way again. Sage doubted she would. She planned to head straight to San Francisco when her mission was complete. No unnecessary stops. However, she didn't wish to get ahead of herself. First things first.

Heading east up the American River, excitement coursed though Sage. Maybe it was the idea of panning gold for real. On one of her trips she had tried it at a tourist stop and it seemed easy enough. But that wasn't real life. However, it had stimulated an interest. The internet and a couple of library books had been very informative. The tourist stop panning had provided the basic knowledge of how to work the pan, but she hadn't needed to dig out of a cold stream. She looked forward to the real life experience. Plus, it provided opportunity to cross an item off her goal list. Refusing to succumb to the idea that she had been struck with gold fever, she set a date limit, February first. On February first, she would take whatever gold she found and head for San Francisco.

After a great deal of thought, Sage decided to pan down river from Sutter's mill. To risk changing gold-rush history was unacceptable. Her original plan had been to go upstream from there, but she had visited Coloma on the same trip she had stayed in Yosemite and knew the terrain gets mighty rugged upriver. Also, her movement in the river must not prevent Marshall from finding the gold nugget.

To avoid being discovered, Sage decided to work on the opposite side of the river, far downstream from the mill, where she would construct a camouflage camp. She would first erect her tent and then build a brush shelter around it. This would prevent detection and aid in warmth. Though she was almost sure winter didn't get too cold there, she wanted to be prepared. She wasn't keen on being cold.

Climbing the hills, Sage appreciated the beautiful scenery. Despite her excitement, she took her time, spending time gathering food, enjoying the raw, unspoiled landscape, and watching the abundance of wildlife. The late September weather was perfect, and she felt well prepared. A camera would have been a plus, or at the very least, a talent for drawing, but neither were to be had. Though she may not be able to draw or photograph her surroundings, she could certainly write about it in her journal.

At last, she found a location to make camp. In her inexperienced mind, the river appeared good for gold and the undergrowth provided excellent brush for hiding her tent. First, she must confirm the location.

While researching gold, Sage had learned to watch the water: find inside curves; sandbars-before, during, and after; undercuts; gravel bars; opposite fast moving water; and behind and under large boulders. Though sure there were other indicators, these were all she remembered. This spot seemed to have a good variety of each nearby.

Pulling the gold pan from her pack and the shovel from its attachment on the outside, Sage left her pack next to the river, holstered her pistol securely on her belt, and waded into the edge of the water. After a few tries, gold! *Only a few flakes, but I'm on my way.* Soon, she realized her biggest struggle wasn't the cold water, it was fighting her hair, which kept falling in front of her as she worked. A quick trip to her pack produced an alligator clip, which soon held her long, blond locks tightly out of the way, allowing the fun to proceed with a full range of vision.

Sage worked at panning the gold for a few more hours before stopping to set up camp.

She enjoyed panning gold. It reminded her of a new toy; she didn't want to put it down and stop playing with it. It had been going well. After transferring first aid supplies to an exterior pocket of her pack, she half-filled the small stuff sack with the gold. The gold consisted of everything from dust to flakes, to nuggets. Pea sized or less, they were still nuggets.

Waking up sore and achy days later, Sage needed to spend some time gathering food before her supplies were exhausted. Pistol securely holstered, bow in hand, and a quiver of arrows on her back, Sage headed up a game trail. If she didn't find any game, she would forage for food on the way back to camp.

This reminds me so much of when I was young at the commune. Sky never hesitated to take me with him. The lessons he taught will serve me well in this time and place. He would love this!

Unaware of it, Sage always thought of her parents by what she called them at that time of life. If she referenced the commune days, she referred to them by name. If she thought of them post-commune, they were Mom and Dad. It was as though she had lived two lives with two sets of parents. But she could still find Sky in Dad. Amaranth seemed to have disappeared with the arrival of Mom. Sage missed Amaranth. She was a happy person; Mom just seemed critical.

Sage followed a game trail up a steep hill. The view was awe inspiring. It saddened Sage to think that within a few years gold-hungry miners would change this beautiful country considerably. Even the course of the river would be changed. Coming changes would transform not just the landscape, but many lives, including the local Natives. *Do I really wish to be a part of this? Yes. This is history in the making. I will see and know firsthand what some have only guessed at and many have attempted to reconstruct though letters and journals. I'll be a part of it!*

On the trail ahead of her, Sage saw a small doe. Though she preferred a buck, the difficulty of getting an animal of that size and weight back to camp meant a doe was preferable. The doe presented enough challenge. *It's not like the law forbids killing a doe in 1847.* She nocked the arrow on the bow string. Drawing back on the string till her fingertips were beside her cheek, Sage stopped breathing as she took aim. Determined her aim would be true so as not to create any unnecessary suffering for the doe, Sage let the arrow fly. The doe had a shocked look, took two steps, and fell over.

Walking to the backside of the deer to avoid the sharp hooves in case it lashed out, Sage quickly reached down and sliced her throat to assure the doe was dead, as well as to drain the blood. After removing the arrow, she gutted the deer then heaved the carcass across her shoulders, holding onto the legs, before heading back down the game trail to her camp. This presented the most dangerous element of her hunt. Should a bear be downwind, the smell of blood would be enticing. Loaded down with deer and equipment while descending the steep trail would not be the time to encounter Yogi.

When she had dressed the deer, she laid the hide aside to tan, put some of the meat in a pot for stew along with a couple of broken bones for a good broth, and cut the remaining meat into strips to salt and dry for jerky. She didn't have the time or means to preserve it any other way.

The day grew long. Sage spent well into the night processing the meat and salting the hide for later. As she worked, she gave thanks for Sky's early teachings as well as her survival training. She couldn't help but wonder how she would have survived without the knowledge she possessed. *More what ifs!* She thought with irritation. *Why do I always wonder about the "what if" scenario? Why can't I just be thankful for things as they are? I've always done this. It's probably one of the reasons why I started training so hard to be independent. That and Mom's attitude about me needing a man to be happy.*

From there, Sage's mind wandered. There had been a time when a man made her happy. At the beginning of her final year of college, she was waiting to speak to her advisor regarding her senior thesis and in walked a man who took her breath away. He was tall and slim, yet muscular, like a swimmer. Thick, wavy, blond hair was accented by brilliant, sky blue eyes. Finding the advisor's door closed, he took a seat near Sage. When he looked at her and smiled, it was as though the sun rose and the stars came out at the same time. She mentally scolded herself for such a silly reaction to a stranger. Then he spoke. She could still hear him speak with a low, slow, sexy voice that seemed to mimic music.

When the advisor opened her office door to call on Sage, she noticed the Adonis and motioned him in instead. Within a couple of minutes he was back and Sage was summoned. He was still waiting when Sage finished her meeting almost half an hour later. She smiled at him as she headed toward the building's exit. Her breath caught as he smiled back. Reaching to open the exterior door, a hand pushed ahead and opened it for her. His nearness made tingles flow up her spine through her neck and somehow down her arms to the tips of her fingers.

He walked beside her. Nothing was said for at least two blocks, and then he introduced himself. Elliot Swenson was a grad student finishing his MBA. Over coffee, they talked. They walked and talked. They went to dinner and talked. They held hands and talked. Throughout the remainder of the school year Sage and Elliot were together whenever time allowed. On Sage's days off, they went hiking or biking. Many times they just studied. Anything to be together.

When graduation day came, Sage looked forward to introducing her dad and brothers to Elliot. Though she hadn't said anything to her family about Elliot, she did tell him all about her family. After scanning the crowd endlessly, she finally saw him talking to people she presumed were his parents. Excusing herself from her family, she hurried to Elliot. When she finally made her way through the crowd to his side, she smiled and said, "Elliot, we made it! Congratulations." She saw him stiffen.

Her blood ran cold as he shook her hand, thanked her, congratulated her, and turned his back on her, taking his parents arms and leading them away. She heard his mother ask, "Elliot, who was that young lady?" Then Elliot's reply, "Nobody, mother. Just an undergrad. We had the same advisor."

Her heart was broken. Just the day before they had whispered words of love. She didn't understand. What had happened? As she walked back to her family, Sage determined to be as cold about this as Elliot had been. With this steeled determination, she made it through dinner. Then she made it through the congratulations, gift, and her last evening with the family for whom she worked and children she had nannied for four years. She sobbed throughout the last night in her bedroom at their house. By morning she was all cried out and resolved to never shed another tear over Elliot or any other man. From then on, she guarded her heart with walls of unwavering control. Elliot never called.

Sage admonished herself for allowing her mind's wanderings to go there. It had been a long time since he had invaded her thoughts. Refusing to admit he had anything to do with her independent ways, she proclaimed aloud, "I had these plans before I even knew him!"

Pushing all thoughts of Elliot away, Sage focused on the job at hand. Concern about the wafting odors from the drying meat was ceaseless as she finished affixing it to the drying frame. After a reassuring pat, noting the pistol was at the ready in its belt holster, Sage finished laying the fire for drying the meat. She used green fir branches to build a smoking hut around the drying frame before lighting the fire. *Okay, now I need the hut not to catch fire and the smoke not to attract attention.*

The quest for gold progressed well. Sage moved up and down the stream on a regular basis, but stayed within proximity of her camp. She used some of the tanned buckskin for pouches to hold the gold, which she placed in a cache dug and concealed near the tent. With the increasing cache, Sage considered how to transport it to San Francisco.

As the weather grew colder, panning became more and more difficult. Sage stood in the icy cold water for hours at a time. This was not for sissies. It would have been easier and faster to name the spots on her body that did not hurt than to name all the parts that did. Thermal underwear served as a change of clothes when she finished in the river each day. When she felt she couldn't tolerate the river another day, she worked in one of the spots that allowed her to stay out of the water. But this created a trade-off; it caused more back pressure, but the constant cold of the water made her back tense, so it hurt anyway. At least she could stay warm for a day.

To fight the fatigue the cold brought on, Sage dug a shallow pit the length of her body in her tent. Each evening, she heated several large rocks and placed them in the pit, covering them with a thin layer of dirt before placing a wool blanket on top of it. On this she would lie down with her other wool blanket, a coat, and her space blanket on top of her. It helped.

After working non-stop for weeks, Sage needed a break. She needed to forage for food and make a stew. Then she planned to sit back and do nothing all day. While she thrived on activity, everyone needed an occasional break now and then.

Enjoying a rare treat of taking a simple walk, she spoke to the few animals and some of the plants while passing by. Though alone time had always been precious, this was extreme. She giggled at the thought that many would say she was losing her mind talking to the flora and fauna, but an odd desire to use her voice seized her. Plus, it was entertaining to watch the fog her warm breath created.

There wasn't much food to find; the animals had stored away or eaten much of it, but a strong familiarity with wild edible plants helped. Despite the work and potential danger from bears, cougars, and man, she gave thanks for the dried venison. Not only great for snacking, broken into small pieces it worked well in soup. Adding plant matter enhanced both the taste and the nutritional value of the meals.

Forgetting food for the moment, Sage stopped and drank in the beauty of the scenic area. Though the brown of late fall seemed to encroach on the green of the many conifers, this place still amazed her. She was pleased with her plan. By summer, word about the gold would have spread and she should be set.

When Sage awakened the next morning, summer seemed a long way off. It was cold. Even through the tent and brush surrounding it, the light held that certain look, that certain glare, which spoke of snow. Peeking out, Sage shivered at the sight. Not deep, but it looked cold. The water couldn't be that much colder than it had been, but somehow, surrounded by snow, it seemed like it should be colder.

"No slacking. You took yesterday off, so it's time to get back to work. Besides, this time of year, the temperature is only going to go down and the snow will probably just get deeper."

In the water, Sage worked extra hard in hopes of producing additional heat. The theory may not hold true, but a great deal was accomplished. It turned into one of her most productive days yet.

The snap of a twig alerted Sage to the presence of a being. Glancing around, with a solid grip on her pistol, she drew and came to ready when she saw movement in the trees. Something was coming her way. The slight breeze carried with it an offensive smell, even at considerable distance. *Bear?* Drawing nearer, Sage saw an ill-kept graying man. Wearing a bear-skin coat, his hands were bound with what looked like rags and there was a raccoon skin covering his head. The sneer on his face did not give comfort.

"You must be gettin' gold outa that there river to be standin' there freezin' in it." He shouted.

"I wish. I've tried this in every river I come across. Can't say it's achieved much yet."

The man drew nearer. Everything in Sage grew alert as her mind processed the best way to handle this.

"I've got some stew on the fire. Care to join me? I'm getting nothing but cold in this river," she said as she dropped her left hand and the pan into the water, releasing the dime sized nugget nestled in it as she did.

"Sounds mighty fine. What's a pretty thing like you doin' out here all alone anyway?"

Sage ignored the question. She wanted to change clothes, but had no intention of cluing him in on her tent. Instead, she added wood to the fire while not taking her eyes off the unwelcome guest or releasing her hold on her pistol.

"Grab a log and have a seat. The stew is hot." She filled her bowl and handed it to him, wondering how she would manage to sterilize the bowl when he left. Having only one service was an excellent excuse for waiting to eat. This was maddening, she didn't want to eat; she wanted to be in that icy river panning. But with this guy around, she dared not.

"I'm Sage," she said, looking pointedly at the man as he slurped, gulped, and smacked the soup.

Her guest did not respond. Either he was raised with no manners or he had no wish to disclose this basic information.

"And you are..." she prompted.

"Humph," he grunted.

Her patience was growing thin. "While I am more than happy to share my soup with a fellow traveler, I prefer knowing who I'm sharing with. I assume you have a name. What is it?

The glare she received in response spoke volumes.

"Mister, you either need to show a smidgen of common courtesy or put my bowl down and be on your way. I've made it quite clear I'm willing to share, but only if you can show some basic manners. What is your name?"

"Who do you think you are, woman!" It was not a question. "I'll eat whatever I please and do anything I please when I'm done. You sit your pretty little self down and I'll take care of you as soon as I'm finished." He shoved the bowl toward Sage. "More soup first."

Sage had heard enough. His implications were clear and she had no intention of tolerating him. "You leave, now."

The man laughed. "Darlin' you and me ain't yet had our fun."

Sage pointed the pistol she still held straight at the lowlife piece of trash.

He continued laughing. "You think that little toy is going to scare me. I ain't stupid, woman. You ain't scarin' me with that thing."

Hating to waste any of her precious ammo on this scumbag, she aimed at the man's canteen he had thrown on the ground next to him and shot, putting a neat hole right through it.

The shock on his face was soon replaced by cockiness. "Whoa, I's just funnin ya, no need to get mean.

66

You went and ruined my canteen. How am I supposed to carry water now?

"I don't care. Get out. Now!"

"Aw, honey, I didn't mean nothin'. I's just playin' with you. Name's Nelson."

"Well, Nelson, you can pick up your things and be on your way. Now."

He grabbed his things and started on his way before looking back at Sage, who still pointed the pistol at him. "See you soon, sweetheart." His sneer spoke volumes.

Sage watched as he walked at a pace which said it would be a long day and he had all of it to get nowhere. The heedless stroll, despite the gun targeting his every step, made Sage's skin crawl. *No doubt this will not be the last of Mr. Nelson. Revenge is sweet and he has a score to settle,* she thought with dread. *This is one experience of which I would rather not partake.*

When he was long out of sight, Sage finally holstered the pistol. Never before had she pointed any weapon at a human and didn't care to make it a habit. Despite his being a loathsome creature, she wanted to believe there was good hidden deep within, which would require only an appropriate catalyst to be released. However, aiming at him had been an indication of her preparedness to shoot, if necessary. After all, one should never point a weapon if not prepared to use it. Training had taught her to remain calm and detached, but now that the incident was over, she was a bit shaken.

In an attempt to settle her disquieted nerves, Sage grabbed the bowl and headed for the water's edge.

Scouring it with sand and water, yet alert to all around her, she ached to do the same to herself. Despite the iciness of the water, the thought of bathing held a peculiar appeal. His lingering stench had assaulted her olfactory system. But she dare not, so continued washing the bowl, filled it with water, and placed it on the fire to boil and sterilize.

While it heated, she took steps to make the camp look deserted. The tent was already well camouflaged, but the rest of the sight had taken on a lived-in look. This would not do. If he returned, it must look as though she had turned tail and ran. This plan would generate extra work on a daily basis, not to mention disrupting an incredibly effective routine, but as a safety precaution, could not be avoided.

That evening, she lay down on top of the warming rocks, under her covers, pistol and knife close at hand. The rest of her camp did, indeed, look deserted. Despite preparations, the relaxed feeling of contentment she had known previous to today eluded Sage.

She mulled over her options. *The prospect of moving to another place could pose more danger than remaining here. At this point, this tent and both my food and gold caches are secret, but traveling could expose all three. Furthermore, traveling while weighted down with food and gold would put me at a distinct disadvantage if I needed to defend myself. However, Nelson currently knows the precise location of this camp, leaving me vulnerable. Due to the general topography of the area, it would be a simple matter to observe everything I'm doing, once again leaving me and all I've accomplished at risk.*

8

Sleep eluded Sage. The decision weighed heavily, preventing her from relaxing. This irritated her. Despite the potential dangers and resulting precautions required, until now this had been an exciting adventure. Not only had it now become very real, but the need for security cut into her goal by consuming time and energy, not to mention sleep.

Late into the night, she listened to the river flowing past as the tension diminished. She had a plan. *It seems so simple, why did it take me so long to reach such a basic conclusion.*

Most of the items from her backpack remained inside the tent. Sage placed her gold pan, a few empty deer-hide bags for gold, the shovel, her snow pants, a thermos of stew, dried venison, and the two bottles of water in the pack. Scanning the camp to assure it looked deserted boosted her confidence. The cold fire ring added to the deserted appearance.

Assured, she headed down river. With little more than a dusting of snow on the ground, the easy hike rejuvenated her. After spending so much time panning, she missed hiking. Maybe this deviation would turn out to be a good thing.

Though captivated by the continuous changes in the river's mood, she remained ever alert, aware the river's noise could mask an intruder's approach. While stretches of rushing water framed by snow were picture perfect, she continued to search for a quiet spot which also suggested good gold production potential.

The weeks and months spent in the numbing water had taught her a great deal about prospecting, but she knew there was much more she could learn, if she cared to invest the time and attention. However, she had other ideas.

There, near a huge, old tree, the perfect cut called to her. *Some sort of elder*, she thought, though she wasn't knowledgeable enough to determine with the leaves gone. *I've hiked at least two miles from my camp; that should be far enough.*

Sage snuggled in the warmth of her coat before removing it and placing it on top of her pack at the edge of the water. Touching a reassuring hand to her belt-holstered pistol, she paused at the water's edge before wading in. An involuntary shiver coursed through her body as the icy needles of water stung her skin. Steadying herself from the shock, she sloshed through the hostile water to the cut.

All thoughts of temperature left her mind after panning the cut for only a short while. She wanted to shout as each pan rewarded her with several nuggets. This was a virtual treasure trove! Excitement built as pan after pan displayed the sought-after mineral. These were not merely the dust, flakes, and pebbles she had stashed away at camp. As Sage picked the marble sized golden rocks from the pan, her pulse raced and her eyes sparkled. Consumed with this remarkable find, she continued digging, panning, and plucking the precious pebbles, oblivious to the time.

"Oh my..." was all the farther she could get before a deep intake of breath took over. There, before her eyes, lying in her very own pan, was an odd shaped, golden stone far larger than the pebbles she had collected in previous weeks, larger even than the rocks she collected today. In the gold panning world, this was a bolder! Picking it up, it lay in her open hand, covering almost all of her palm and fingers.

Too large for the current bag in her pocket, she waded out of the water and knelt at her pack. Reaching in, the realization that all the bags were full shocked her. She looked at the rock which still lay in her hand, placed it in the backpack along with the bags of gold and changed out of her cargo pants into her snow pants.

The dry warmth felt good. If only she had a dry pair of boots. As the adrenaline of the day began to wear off, she shivered so hard she struggled to pick up her coat. While the warmth helped, she needed more, and knew it. She considered building a fire before returning to camp, but that still left her in wet boots with no shelter.

Then the sun's position caught her eye. Afternoon, late afternoon! She hadn't stopped or eaten all day. She must hurry, or the dark would beat her home.

But the cold made moving a struggle. *Food. I need food for energy.* Pulling the thermos from the pack, the soup retained some warmth. While hot would have been preferred, warm was an improvement and much appreciated. She gulped the warm concoction, stowed the thermos back in her pack, grabbed a few pieces of jerky, and forced her stiff body to walk. The trip was slow and painful. Her wet feet felt like cubes of ice. Each step of the trip screamed slow and painful.

With each excruciating step, she grew more and more irritated with herself. *I was so unaware, she thought. Anyone or anything could have easily overtaken me. At a time when I need to be extra vigilant! I allowed myself to become hypothermic. How could I have let the allure of gold numb me to my surroundings to such a dangerous extent?*

Sage continued with the diatribe of self-recrimination for a full mile. Then she made rules for herself. This would not happen again. By the time she returned to camp, there was no doubt in her mind that she would not be seduced by the wonder of the gold again. This provided a means to an end, nothing more.

Darkness closed in on her as she hobbled around the last bend of the river leading into camp. Thankful she had left her remaining little LED flashlight in its pouch, she performed a careful sweep of the area. No footprints, no signs of company either in or around camp. Once assured the camp remained empty, she placed the day's haul in the now crowded gold cache. *I need to make this larger*, she thought before realizing she had all her eggs in one basket. *Tomorrow, I will dig a second cache.*

Chilled to her bones, she determined to use one of her precious lighters to start the fire instead of flint and steel. It took all her control to insist her fingers flick the lighter. With the fire going, she made her way into her tent, removed her boots, wet socks, and snow pants. Her body's stiffness made the process both painful and challenging. At last she replaced her wet things with the two pairs of socks from Fort Sutter and thermal underwear, which she pulled the snow pants over. She donned all of her top layers, added the rough attempt at moccasins she made from the remainder of the deer hide to her feet, and headed for the fire.

She needed to warm her body before hauling the sleeping rocks to the fire. To this end she pulled the pot from her tent and plodded to the river. Carrying the water created more pain; it was a relief to place it on the flat rock at the edge of the fire.

Reaching in the tent, she grabbed her space blanket. The ground seemed to have moved farther down as she sat on the woven reed mat she pulled from the tent. Wrapping the space blanket around her back and holding it open at the front, she formed a reflective oven in which to warm herself.

The pain she felt was well deserved. She had been foolish and careless. While thankful for the day's haul, she remained quite angry with herself.

Though tempted to poor water for tea as soon as it warmed, she waited for it to boil and purify. As the warmth of the fire thawed her feet, a burning, prickling sensation reminded her of her foolishness that day. By the time she finished preparing the water for drinking and filled her water bottles, she felt capable of hauling her sleeping rocks to the fire. The thought of cuddling up on them and sleeping sounded wonderful.

9

Upon waking the next morning, Sage again felt the foolishness of the previous day's behavior. Everything ached. Movement only emphasized the pain. *Okay, suck it up, buttercup. Time to get some work done,* she thought as the cold air slammed into her while forcing herself from bed. Tempted to crawl back under the warm, wool blankets and spend a very lazy day, she persevered. After yesterday's fiasco, this day commanded responsible behavior.

Before exiting the tent, Sage listened for any unusual noises, indicating company. Hearing none, she stepped out, implementing great caution to avoid revealing the hidden shelter to anyone who may be observing the camp. After a brief detour away from the camp, she circled around, approaching it away from the tent. This provided the opportunity to ensure all remained clear.

Reassured, Sage retrieved the shovel and went in search of a separate, second cache location. It still needed to be near the tent, yet not. Finally finding the perfect location near a boulder, but concealed with brush, she dug. Then she covered it, placed a few large rocks over it in a haphazard fashion, and checked to verify the brush looked undisturbed. After filling the new cache with more gold, she would be ready for the next step of her plan.

Later that day, while walking the other side of the river on her way to the same spot which yielded such treasure the previous day, Sage spotted a snowshoe hare. High hopes plus extra precaution prompted the inclusion of the bow and quiver of arrows in the day's supplies. Nocking an arrow, leveling with a smooth draw, exhaling evenly, and letting it fly, the beautiful hare fell. After tying a cord to its legs, she hung it from her pack. If anyone happened along, the hare served to provide an explanation of her location. Even if caught panning, it could be nothing more than a diversion.

This time, she steeled herself against the mind-blowing buildup of gold. With constant awareness of her surroundings, she listened as she worked, and after every pan, glanced around with keen eyes. Determined to be safe, she picked a selection of pretty and unusual rocks from the pan and dropped them in her unused, left cargo pocket.

Stopping with plenty of time to return to camp, Sage topped the half-full bags of gold with the pretty rocks she found. If accosted, the loot would appear as nothing more than pretty rocks, unless the robber dug deeper. Before placing the bags in the cache, she would remove the decoy rocks to use each day. Cautious of the surroundings, she headed home.

After an uneventful hike to a clear camp, Sage stashed the gold, put on dry clothes, started a fire, and prepared the rabbit. Fresh meat sounded good.

While enjoying the fire, she spent the evening working on the rabbit hide. Sage anticipated turning it into something wonderful, maybe a small pillow. The feel of the soft white fur produced thoughts of comfort, something missing on this adventure. *Odd, I hadn't given consideration to modern comfort before now. It's been the quest, the learning, the experience, the excitement of discovery. I've been so caught up in this, so enjoying the wonder of this mind-blowing journey, thoughts of what I left behind—or should I say ahead?—hadn't even occurred to me. Have I been so disconnected from my family for so long it's taken me months to consider this means they are lost to me?*

The contemplation stirred reflection. Despite her propensity to look forward in life, rather than back, she loved her family. Her father was an amazing man, if a bit submissive. Although their difference in opinion of a woman's place in the world had caused a rift, Sage admired her mother's ability to immerse herself in whatever she believed. She loved and respected her siblings. As it came to mind that her family was forever lost to her, Sage felt as though all the blood in her body drained, numbing her. Tears slid slowly down her cheeks.

As sensation returned, she said, "It's been months, actually years since you've seen them. They're fine. Things will go on as they have before. It's okay."

With the shock of the reality of her situation subsiding, Sage thought again of the opportunities before her. *I'm on the ultimate adventure! Not only do I get to see history being made, I get to be part of it! Who knows, I might even make it. Looking around, she smiled and nodded, content with her life.*

Weeks later, it was nearly time to begin her trek to San Francisco. The original gold cache was nearly full again and the anticipation of seeing 1848 San Francisco was spurring restlessness. One more day spent panning should fill her stash.

Fresh snow covered the bare ground as she took a circuitous route to the river from her tent to avoid making tracks around her camp. Hoping to spot fresh game, with slow and methodical movements, her bow and an arrow in hand, she made her way to her panning spot. While using her pistol would have been easier, a shot would attract unwanted attention. Also, her ammo was limited. When it was gone, it was gone. She would only use it if absolutely necessary, for protection. She wished she had taken the time to learn to reload ammo.

The crunching of the snow as she walked made it difficult to sneak up on game. Nearing a bend in the trail, a covey of quail prepared to take flight. After previously spending many hours practicing her archery skills and several missed birds, she quickly nocked the arrow and let it fly just as the birds took flight. One fell. Amazed, Sage let out a joyous, "Yes!" And dropped her pack.

Just then, strong arms gripped her from behind. The stench left no doubt who held her entrapped. "Got you now, girly. You an me's gonna have us some fun!"

Spreading her feet and bending her knees, Sage lifted both hands, then swiveled her hip to the right side, allowing her left leg to pass behind her assailant's right leg. Reaching down and grabbing him behind the knees, she squatted slightly so her hip level was below his. Rapidly standing and lifting her arms, releasing him at the top of the arch, he flew over her shoulder, landing hard on the ground.

The shock of the landing and the defense move stunned him, giving Sage time to draw her pistol. "You're right, that was fun," she said.

The smirk on her face angered her would-be attacker. "Why you…"

As he spoke he rose and pulled an ancient pistol from his belt, raising it toward Sage. The shot she fired knocked it from his hand and blood erupted.

"My hand! You shot me!"

"You better be glad it's only your hand. Step back."

He didn't move.

"Now!" She pointed her pistol center body mass.

With a glare, he moved back.

"More."

He retreated a few more steps, watching her through fierce slits.

With her eyes fixed on Nelson, she kicked his pistol several yards away. "You should wrap something around that hand to stop the bleeding."

An angry stare was his only response to the concern she showed him.

"Okay, don't. Get down; on your stomach." After receiving a defiant stare in answer, she moved her finger back to the trigger, and commanded in a no-nonsense tone, "Now!"

This time he followed orders. Then, with a look to the side, said, "Git her!"

A quick glance revealed a filthy, skinny, German Shepherd. The dog cocked his head and looked at her.

With a snicker, Sage said, "I don't think he's inclined to help. You didn't have a dog before, where'd you get him?"

"Ain't none o' yo business,"

Keeping aim with her right hand, she patted her thigh with her left. "Come here, boy."

Wagging his tail, the dog did as commanded.

"Good dog, now sit."

The dog sat, his tail thumping the snow as he flopped it back and forth.

"Nice dog. Too nice for the likes of you. Did you steal him?"

"I inherited him! I ain't no thief."

Sage caught the implication, he had his standards.

"Well, Mr. Upright Citizen, what am I going to do with you? I should just kill you and be done with this, but that would be your style, wouldn't it? Is that how you inherited the dog?"

"I wanted me a dog and that old coot wouldn't give him to me. I ain't no thief, I weren't about to steal him, so when he died, I inherited him."

"When he died? Don't you mean when you killed him?"

"Same thing."

"The difference between you and me, Nelson, is I value life. Although you've surely asked for it, it's not my place to take yours. You get up and head out. I'll just sit here with you in my sights. And remember, next time, I won't hesitate."

Rising, Nelson headed for his pistol.

"No. Leave it there."

With a glare, he turned away. Then, with a rush, and a ten-inch Bowie knife in his hand, he came at her. She shot. He fell. Blood poured from his chest.

Sage attempted to control the bile rising to her throat. As his eyes closed and his chest stopped rising, she turned and became violently ill. It seemed she would never stop throwing up. Finally, stomach empty, tears rolling down her face, she sat on the ground and focused on breathing. All the defensive shooting, training, and discussion of the emotional aftermath: the self-doubt and self-talk, telling yourself you are a good person, you had no options, it was necessary for your very life, could not really touch the visceral effect of taking a life, even in self defense.

Feeling a nudge, she turned to see the dog place his paw on her arm. "Hey, buddy. I didn't want to do that. I tried to get him to leave. Why didn't he just go?" The dog nudged her with his muzzle and she reached up to pet him. Looking at the man she had not wanted to kill, she said, "I guess we have a grave to dig."

A couple hours later, she threw the last shovel of dirt on top of the grave. Having no idea how the situation should be handled legally in this time and place, she wanted to do right by the man whose life she had taken. Circling the area, she gathered rocks and laid them on top of the shallow grave, to prevent animals from digging at it. Feeling she should, she said a few words over the mound, and then gathered her things, adding his pistol and knife to them, along with the knife sheath, a few gold nuggets, and some money she had taken from his person. While she had questioned the ethics of taking his things, practicality won the argument.

The dog pushed up against her leg. *He seems to have been well trained by someone, though not terribly well fed.* At this thought, she remembered the quail. Retrieving it, she looked at the dog and said, "Well, buddy, at least we have dinner." He wagged his tail.

Sage debated her options. While her plan for the day had been to fill the last of her gold bags, things had changed. She couldn't free herself of the stench caused by her contact with Nelson. She wanted a bath. She needed a bath.

"Okay, buddy, let's head home." As she spoke she noticed she kept calling him buddy. "How about it, boy, shall we call you Buddy?

Buddy wagged his tail.

"Okay, Buddy it is.

10

Before anything else, Sage grabbed the bar of lye soap and headed for the river. Until now, she had heated a pan of water for sponge bathing, but this odor called for drastic measures. If Phoenix could do it, so could she! She called to Buddy and headed straight into the river, clothes and all. She had survived working in that water for months, certainly a bath couldn't hurt. But somehow a complete dunking seemed different.

"Buddy, come."

The dog stood at the edge of the water looking at her.

She patted her leg. "Come on, Buddy, let's smell good." The cheerful and excited tone to her call had Buddy wagging his tail and pacing next to the river, but he couldn't seem to bring himself to step into it.

With ribs showing, she knew the dog must be hungry, so she had planned ahead for resistance. Pulling a piece of dried venison from her pocket, she waved it and called to the dog.

He stepped into the water, but then backed out.

"Come on, Buddy. It's good!"

The dog couldn't stand it anymore and leaped into the icy water. Sage stood in knee-deep water, no deeper than she had worked in for months. First, a good washing for Buddy. His stench almost equaled Nelson's. Giving him the meat, she hugged him. Using her hands to dip water over him, she lathered him with soap. When a good lather formed, she returned the soap to the cargo pocket of her pants and scrubbed him with her hands. Though she anticipated him attempting to head back to shore, he seemed to enjoy the attention more than he disliked the cold water.

"I'll turn you into a water dog yet." Sage laughed at the obvious enjoyment Buddy derived from the cleansing massage. The poor dog was starved for positive attention. She had no idea how his previous owner had treated him, but it was obvious Nelson had not provided a positive experience for the poor guy.

When fully rinsed, Sage led him back to shore. "Shake, Buddy." The command had not been necessary. The dog seemed to take great delight in sending water flying for yards. When he finished, Sage used one of her towels and rubbed him until his coat was nearly dry. Taking out a few more pieces of dried venison, she laid them out for him and headed back into the river.

Still clothed, she waded into deeper water this time. Removing the soap from her pocket, she scrubbed her clothing with a flourish, then dipped into the water to rinse. After a quick trip to the shore to wring out and deposit all of her clothing on a nearby rock, she returned to the shallow water with the bar of soap. She got a good lather going over her entire body and then her hair. Tossing the soap to the bank, she headed back to the deeper water. Despite the cold, it felt heavenly. Before rinsing her hair, she scrubbed it with vigor. After a thorough rinse, she headed for the river bank, grabbed the second towel and dried before wrapping the towel around her head.

Dressed in warm, dry clothes and with her hair combed, Sage cleaned up, hung up, and put everything away before working on the quail. Squeaky clean felt so good. It made no difference how many sponge baths she took, they never made her feel this clean.

Buddy napped near the fire. It was nice to have a companion, someone to talk to other than herself.

One thought kept running through her mind, and she couldn't shake it. *How did Nelson sneak up on me? In the quiet of the snow, every footstep sounded like a small explosion; I should have heard him! I know I was focused on the quail, but after losing all focus the day I found the gold deposit, I know I wasn't so intent on the birds to have closed off the world around me. He had to have been lying in wait to ambush me. There's no other explanation. Still, I must increase my awareness. If I had, maybe a man would not have died today.*

Attempting to shake the thoughts from her mind, Sage turned her attention to food. For months, her meat consumption had been either dried or in soup; she looked forward to the fresh meat. With the quail fully dressed, she ran a green stick through it and propped it on rocks above the fire. As it cooked, Buddy raised his head and sniffed the air. "Soon, Buddy, soon. Don't worry, I'll share."

That evening, after warming her sleeping rocks and placing them back in the tent, Sage called Buddy inside. He seemed apprehensive. Lying down, she patted the space next to her. Buddy slowly crept near and lay down. She snuggled up to him, recalling the dog-night forecast in Montana. She smiled, "Well, Buddy, it must be a one dog night. Looks like they all will be now."

The weather forecasts in Montana during the winter included a report of how many dog-night it would be. If it was a one-dog-night, it would only take one dog to keep you warm. This could go up to a four-dog-night, when it would take four dogs to achieve warmth due to extreme cold. These were the tidbits of information Sage enjoyed learning by living in various locations. Before falling asleep, she wondered at the learning opportunities which lay ahead.

The next day Sage filled her last bag with gold. She also added two more large nuggets, though neither as large as the first one. Buddy created an additional feeling of security, waiting for her on the bank. While there was no evidence in support so far, she assumed he would bark if anyone or anything approached. She hoped.

By the calendar she kept in her journal, the date was February 1, 1848, six days after James Marshall was reported to have left Sutter's Mill headed to Sutter's Fort with the news of the gold discovery. Tomorrow morning she would head for San Francisco.

11

Even with the contents of only one cache the pack was heavy. Too heavy. It was also nearly full. The contents of the newer cache still lay untouched. Reluctantly, Sage decided to leave it and part of the first cache. There was no choice, a second trip was required. Her pack weighed an estimated seventy-five pounds; adding more gold would be impossible and carrying even that weight could result in severe injury. It was seriously over her maximum weight limit of just under fifty pounds for hiking.

Already planning to leave non-essentials due to weight and lack of space, she planned to return anyway. The tent, panning supplies, and any non-essentials would stay. The well hidden tent stayed dry. After doing all she could to eliminate any sign of the camp, she prepared to leave.

"Hey, Buddy, let's go!" she said, attempting to don her pack. The weight of it combined with the attempt to put it on threw her off balance. "Okay, Buddy, slight delay." She set the pack on a nearby bolder, shrugged her arms through the straps, then, making sure to plant her feet solidly under her, tried to stand. Instead she plopped back on the boulder. Buddy paced in front of her, anxious to begin the trip. "Hang on Buddy, I have another idea." This time she rolled to her stomach, put her hands on the boulder, and pushed herself to a standing position. "Yes! Well, Buddy, it may not have been graceful, but it was effective. So come on, let's go." The dog ran to her side, wagging his tail and nudging her hand. With a scratch around his ears, she said, "I sure hope you like to walk, it's going to be a long one."

Buddy must have felt her excitement over beginning this portion of her plan. He kept running up the trail and back to be at her side; at this rate he would walk to San Francisco twice on this one trip. For his sake, she willed herself to relax and spoke in a calm, soothing voice.

"Yea, Buddy, you stay here by me. We'll make this a nice, relaxing little hike. After some nights spent under the stars, we'll splurge on a real bed. How's that sound?"

The dog looked at her with adoring eyes.

"I'm really glad you're with me."

The plan called for avoiding people. She would take a southwest angle, meeting up with the Sacramento River to steer clear of Sutter's Fort. While she enjoyed her stay there, carrying seventy-five pounds of gold around left one a touch paranoid. Though it was doubtful anyone would suspect what she was carrying, it also left her more vulnerable. Agility and maneuverability were reduced, plus fatigue limited endurance. Gold did funny things to people; it was better not to take chances. It would be nice to be shed of the gold and move forward with her plans.

The days were cold, but movement and the extra exertion the heavy pack required helped keep her warm. The nights were colder. Without her ready-made rock bed, she was forced to spend extra time each evening preparing for warmth. This time her rock bed was switched to coals with sand or gravel on top and no digging. While the space blanket, wool blanket, and Buddy would help to keep her warm, the ground was cold and the last thing she needed was to awaken chilled and stiff. From her emergency supplies, she removed the extra large, extra tough, plastic garbage bag, used her Leatherman to slit the seams, and formed a tent over her sleeping area, using a low hanging branch to suspend it and additional rocks to hold it down. Once she reached the valley floor, it shouldn't be so cold.

Food consisted mostly of dried venison and the much appreciated freeze-dried meals. Regrettably, there wasn't as much venison left as she would have liked. Not only had feeding Buddy reduced the supply significantly, but she was embarrassed to admit the excitement of the treasure trove of gold had dissuaded her from more hunting. As long as she could stretch supplies until they arrived in San Francisco, they would be okay. She would stock up while there.

Five days into the trip she came upon the confluence of the Sacramento River and the San Joaquin River. Looking at Buddy, she said, "What now? What should we do?" Before them was water. Not nice little wade-friendly creeks, but real water, a large expanse of water. "With all this weight, there's no way we can swim. I'd be food for the little fish, wouldn't I, Buddy?"

Taking her pack off, she sat on it. Buddy lay on the ground next to her. The last of the venison was in her coat pocket. After giving one piece to Buddy, she sucked on the last piece.

"Bad planning. I didn't think of this." With a look at her companion, she said, "I don't know that we have any choice but to build a raft. What do you think?"

Buddy wagged his tail in response.

As she rose and looked over the water before searching for raft materials, Sage saw something on the water. Watching it draw nearer, she wished she had not left her binoculars in the tent. Finally able to make out the form, relief flooded her.

"Well, Buddy, it looks like we may not need to build that raft after all." She lifted her hand in a wave.

As the ferry pulled nearer, the ferry master shouted, "Hi there! Saw you through my spyglass, thought you might need a lift."

"Yes, we're glad to see you."

As the ferry pulled to the bank, he said, "Afternoon, ma'am, my name's Ford Jefferson Singleton, but folks just call me Ford. Where you headed?"

"Pleased to make your acquaintance, Ford. I'm Sage Brooks. San Francisco. Can you do that?"

"Sure can. You got family there?"

"No, just business."

"Ah-ha, well, I can get you there. It'll cost you two bits."

Sage dug in her pocket for the money she took off Nelson's body and pulled out a dollar coin. "This should take care of it." As the man started to hand her change, she held up her hand, "You keep it."

With a raise of the eyebrows and a smile, he pushed off the bank and they headed for San Francisco.

"This your first time here?"

Sage almost said no before realizing this would be an entirely different San Francisco than she knew. "Yes, it is. Have you been here long?"

"About five years. Business is slowly picking up. Place is growing."

"Sir, I have no doubt if you keep this up, you'll have more business than you can handle. What can you tell me about San Francisco?"

This was just the opening for which he had been looking. He told her about the people, the shops, the docks, the terrain; he seemed thrilled to share anything and everything, though it didn't seem like much. He informed her of where to stay and where not to stay, where to eat and where not to eat, where to purchase goods, he even suggested a church to attend.

Sage liked this man. He was friendly and upbeat, obviously a people person. As they neared the dock, she said, "Well Ford, I'll need ferried back over in a few days, can I count on you?"

"Anytime, Miss Brooks, anytime."

Sage stepped onto the dock and looked around, surprised by how small it was. "Wow, I knew this place grew rapidly with the gold rush, but I didn't realize just how small it was before. Well, Buddy, there must be an

91

assayer, a bank, or something for gold here. First though, let's see if we can find a place to stay."

Following the directions Ford had given, Sage's fascination grew. *What an honor to witness this. Amazing! And to think, a year from now this will be a large city.* In her musings, she almost missed the hotel. It was small and unpainted, like everything else she saw. Not sure whether to open the door and walk in, as she would a modern hotel, or knock, the decision was taken from her when a woman with a broom stepped onto the porch, which ran the length of the front.

With a grasp on the fur at the back of Buddy's neck, Sage stepped on the first step and said, "Good afternoon, ma'am. Are there any rooms available?"

The woman glanced from Sage to Buddy, then back to Sage. "Yes, but I'm not keen on the dog."

Ford had strongly suggested staying away from the only other hotel in town, so with a look at Buddy and a smile, Sage gambled. "I'll pay double if he can stay with me."

"Can you bathe him first?"

"Absolutely!"

"There's a well around to the back. You get him all clean and dry and we have a deal."

"Wonderful! I'm Sage Brooks and this is Buddy. I hear good things about your hotel."

"Glad to hear that. I'm Molly Brine. There's some lye soap around back by the door. Go ahead and use it on him. Do you need a towel?"

"No, thank you. I have one."

"Okay, you come on in when you're done and we'll get you registered."

The small room was sparse, but clean. A bed with a patchwork quilt, a wooden chair, and curtains on the window, nothing more. Mrs. Brine explained on the way to the room that for now there was only one wash stand in the hall, shared by all. She hoped to soon have one for each room. Sage wished she could think of a way to tell her to get them now, before the price of everything went sky-high.

She hated to admit it, but that bed sure looked nice. A real bed, with a real mattress. It was a tough decision. Food sounded really good as well. Deciding she wanted it all, Sage headed out to find the recommended restaurant.

While restaurant was a loose use of the term, the food was superb. Authentic Chinese food, before the invention of chow mien for the American consumer. They refused to allow Buddy entrance, so he lay just outside the door, as she told him. Though Sage wanted to think he was that good, chances were likely it had more to do with the bone the proprietor gave him.

After eating and nearly out of the money she had removed from Nelson's body, Sage knew she must search for a bank or an exchange. Through the loose idea of streets, she found a couple of shops, a livery, homes, barns, a shipping company, saloons, and a school/church, but no bank or exchange of any kind.

What do I do? Do I pay for my needs with gold? Tomorrow. I'll deal with it tomorrow. Right now, I hear a real bed calling my name.

Upon waking the next morning, realization hit. She had carried all that gold all that way, with no place to get rid of it. She was too early in San Francisco's timeline. From one of the side pockets on her pack, she removed a small stuff sack, which held emergency fire starting materials. Placing the materials back in the pocket, she partially filled it with gold from one of the bags containing small pebbles, flakes, and dust. It wouldn't due to carry too much at once, thus tipping her hand at how much she really possessed. First things first, Mrs. Brine.

Locking the door to her room, she went in search of the inn-keeper. "Good morning, Mrs. Brine," she said, sounding more confident than she felt, but determined to see this through.

"Yes, Miss Brooks, it is a lovely morning. I trust you slept well."

"Best sleep I've had in ages, thank you. I would like to pay for one more night, but I'm nearly out of coin." The look of concern on Mrs. Brine's face spurred her on. "I do, however, have a bit of gold with me. Would you accept it in payment?"

"Why of course, Miss Brooks. Now don't tell me you've been prospecting."

Sage laughed. "I certainly won't do that, but I do appreciate the nice place to stay and comfortable bed after

94

traveling for so long." She knew her attempt at changing the direction of the conversation to avoid discussion of how she came to be in possession of the gold was flimsy, but Mrs. Brine obviously took great pride in her establishment and perhaps discussion of it might revise the direction the conversation was taking.

"Why thank you. It's always been my dream to run a hotel, so when Mr. Brine insisted this was the place for us, I made the hotel a condition of agreeing to settle here. This way I have my business and he has his."

"What kind of business does Mr. Brine operate?"

"The livery next door. We thought it would be quite handy, livery and hotel next to one another."

"Sounds reasonable to me. Does he sell horses?"

"Oh yes, when he has them available. Are you in the market for a horse? You be sure and tell him I sent you, since you haven't yet had the opportunity to meet."

"Yes, I believe I will need a horse, and I will let him know you sent me."

Sage paid for another night and headed out to do business.

First, she went in search of qualified workers, upon which her entire plan rested. It wasn't like she could check the yellow pages or search the internet. With a few questions, she was directed to the Navarro home. After explaining her needs, she discovered the four Navarro brothers, Juan, Eduardo, Jorge, and Xavador were known for their skill with adobe. Their home left no doubts regarding the quality of their work. Though the family questioned the location of the job, the assurance that she would pay them with gold, with a small deposit paid before departure, sealed the deal.

With a crew secured, she headed for the livery to speak with Mr. Brine. Seeing inside the livery, her heart sank. She had assumed that most of his stock was inside, since only a couple of animals roamed the corral. But after briefly explaining her needs, Mr. Brine assured her he could supply all she needed by morning.

After a quick breakfast, she stopped at the shops in town, leaving a list of items to be picked up early in the morning and another list of items to be ordered. Seeing Ford at the dock, she headed for the ferry.

"Good morning, Ford."

"Why, Miss Brooks, it is good, isn't it. Pleasant to see you again. You're not leaving already, are you?"

"Oh no, but I plan to leave in the morning. I'll have four men and several pack animals with me. Can you manage that?"

"Yes, ma'am. It may take several trips, but I'll get you there."

"I knew I could count on you. See you in the morning," she said with a wave as she walked away.

Satisfied with her day's work, Sage needed to make two more stops. A quick stop at the general store garnered both a change of clothes and directions to her next stop. Stepping into the barber shop, which also sported a sign indicating both dental work and doctoring were done, the proprietor looked at her in surprise.

"Ma'am. How can I help you? Are you ailing?"

"No sir. What I would like is to enjoy one of the hot baths you advertise on your sign out front."

"But, miss, I've never had a woman in for a bath before. I'm not sure..."

"I assume the bath is in another, more private room, correct?"

"Well, yes." His perplexed tone gave clear indication that he was completely thrown by Sage's unusual request.

"Good. Once the bath is ready, I will require no assistance, so I see no problem. Do you?"

Sage could see the man swallow, his eyes big and staring at her.

"I-I-I suppose not. The water is hot, so it'll only take a moment. I'll get the bath ready." He stopped, turned to her with obvious discomfort, and said, "But ma'am, how will I add more water or pour rinse water?"

She felt sorry for the young man. He couldn't have been more than twenty, looked as though he could use several healthy meals, and demonstrated extreme discomfiture with women. "No problem. Just fill it up and I'll be fine."

Soon he left her alone in a room with a wooden bath tub nearly full of steaming water. It was quite warm, but not too hot. After having Buddy lay in front of the door, she undressed, smiling at the thoughts that must be running through the young barber's head. *Poor guy*, she thought, *I didn't mean to embarrass him.*

She slowly lowered herself into the tub. As water hit the rawness where the straps of the too-heavy pack had rubbed, Sage gritted her teeth, sucked in air, and continued to lower herself despite the pain. When she was seated and had dunked her head she sighed. *Oh this feels good. I think I could stay here all day.*

Next to the tub a towel hung over the back of a chair, with a soap dish on the seat. The soap had a trace of manly aroma, but she didn't care. It felt so good to bathe without freezing. Even better, the water was comfortably hot. She scrubbed her body and hair with vigor before submersing herself fully, ruffling her hair under water to rise it. Then she did something unusual for her, she repeated the whole process. Afterward she leaned her head back against the edge of the tub and relaxed.

When the water began to grow cool, she roused herself and stood. Using the towel provided—it was small, but effective—she dried as she stepped out of the tub. Dressing in her new clothes and braiding her hair down her back, she bundled her dirty clothing in her coat.

"Hey Buddy, we saw a laundry this morning; let's go drop these off and find some dinner."

Buddy stood and wagged his tail, moving close and sniffing Sage.

"I bet I smell quite different than you're used to, don't I? It's okay, I'm still me." She scratched his ears and reached to open the door.

Upon seeing her, the barber's eyes grew big and his mouth hung open. With an encouraging smile from Sage, he said, "D-D-Did you enjoy your bath, ma'am?"

"It was wonderful! Thank you so much. I can't remember the last time I felt this good."

"If I may say, you look very nice, too." His face grew crimson giving the compliment. "Is there anything else I can do for you?" He nervously scratched at his neck.

"Not today. Thank you." Sage left the shop and headed for the laundry.

After dropping off the laundry with the recommended Chinese laundress, who inspected each article as though it had come from outer space, stopping to scrutinize the stretchy sports bra with a bewildered look and an odd glance at her newest customer, Sage headed back to the hotel. Mrs. Brine had invited her to join them for dinner. She liked the couple, guessing they were only a few years younger than her own thirty years. Surprise showed on Mrs. Brine's face as Sage entered the hotel.

"Miss Brooks, you look lovely this evening. The dress becomes you."

"Thank you. I thought it would be more appropriate than what I have been wearing."

"But," Mrs. Brine seemed hesitant and rather out of sorts, "you left wearing your britches, how is it you return in a dress?"

"I purchased it while I was shopping, and then I stopped at the barber shop for a bath."

"By the barber?" She seemed shocked.

"Oh, no. He just filled the tub and left me to it. Buddy lay as guard in front of the door. Don't worry, Mrs. Brine, it was all quite respectable."

Mrs. Brine looked doubtful, but said, "Oh, okay. Anyway, you must be glad to be in a dress again."

Truth be told, this was the first time Sage had worn a dress since leaving her mother's house. "Yes," she said after a bit of thought. "I am."

Sage enjoyed the Brine's company and dinner was a pleasant event. She wished she could warn them of the changes about to occur around them, but she dare not. She appreciated such a pleasant place to stay whenever visiting San Francisco.

The next morning, after retrieving her clothes from the laundry and changing into them, two at a time, she took her mules to the shops to be loaded with the supplies she had purchased, each time returning to the livery to exchange them for two more. By the time all the supplies were loaded, she had eight pack mules fully loaded with supplies.

Since the Navarros had no transportation they could take with them, she had requested five horses. Mr. Brine had only been able to procure three horses but had obtained two additional mules for riding. While at the shops, she added the available riding tack to her purchases. Unfortunately, without enough tack, the mules must be ridden bareback.

Though a stop at Fort Sutter would have allowed for more tack, she still felt it prudent to avoid the fort for now.

At the appointed time, the Navarro brothers appeared at the livery loaded down with tools and supplies. They seemed overjoyed at the prospect of being able to ride to their destination. Finally ready, the little train proceeded to the ferry.

It took three trips to ferry everything and everyone across the water. With it being late afternoon, the group camped. They would leave in the morning.

12

The return trip to Coloma was easier despite the additional people and animals. Riding certainly made it easier than lugging the heavy pack back stuffed with gold. During part of the trip, Buddy rode on top of one of the mule's pack loads, but most of the time he wanted down to run off energy. Plenty of food and warmth added to improved conditions.

The pack train bypassed Sage's campsite and continued on to the area that would become the Coloma town site. Although Sage had pictured in her mind the exact lot on which she planned to build, she found a different 1848 landscape than she had visited in the twenty-first century. Then she remembered, the gold rush changed the area so drastically even the river changed course. *I should have inspected the area before leaving for San Francisco,* she thought. However, choosing a lot required only a slight adjustment.

Located on the hill near what would eventually be the edge of town, the building site served several purposes. In theory, avoiding the center of town made it quieter. It was high enough to avoid flooding issues. Drainage looked good. The close proximity to the town center made it handy. The large lot left plenty of space for additions as well as a garden and animals.

Sage had sketched her plans in the journal she had traded for while still at Sutter's Fort. Now, she shared her sketches with the Navarro brothers. They needed the full picture to enable them to see her vision. She just hoped they would remain to complete the work once they heard about the gold rush. But she had an idea to help assure that, also.

While the brothers erected the tents purchased in San Francisco, created a latrine and a cooking area, Sage took one of the mules and made a trip to her tent back down the river.

She loaded all the remaining supplies from the tent onto the pack animal, then dismantled the tent, loading it on the mule. This time on the other side of the river, in front of the large boulder—her treasure trove—she once again constructed the tent and built a fire ring. Brush filled the small space between her tent and the boulder; under that brush Sage dug two new caches. With the new camp ready for living, she headed back to the old campsite. Removing the remaining gold from the cache, she filled her pack and a second pack she had purchased in San Francisco, put them both on the mule, and headed back to her small tent. After depositing the gold in one of the new caches, Sage returned to the building site. She needed to be ready for the coming onslaught of argonauts in addition to supervising the construction of her building. Staking her claim in the most productive area was an important first step.

For now, she would sleep at the building site and spend part of the day at the claim. Both were of equal importance for her plan to succeed. To keep the Navarros from stopping the build due to gold fever, she needed to offer extra incentive. What better inducement than a readymade gold stash and claim? Of course, her current stash served as her grubstake for the business, but whatever she managed to acquire from now on was pure incentive gold. To this end, the second cache provided space to hold the incentive gold.

While some might think her insane to plan to give her diggings away, Sage planned for the long-term, and if the Navarros profited also, she was happy for them. They were a great group of men from a wonderful family.

Upon returning to the building site, she found the brothers hard at work. They didn't waste any time; that was certain. She had thought to return and have a relaxing evening but they seemed very intent on their labors, so she prepared dinner. While it cooked and the brothers toiled, she planned to dig another cache, this time in her tent.

As she retrieved the shovel from the tools brought back from San Francisco, Buddy excitedly ran from brother to brother. "Buddy, come here!"

Buddy turned to heed the command, and Juan said, "He is not bothering us, if that is your concern."

"That's good to know, but for his safety, perhaps we should not start a habit of him hanging around the construction site."

"Is a good idea." Juan's accent made everything he said seem more profound to Sage's ears.

She hoped to take advantage of her time with the brothers to improve her Spanish. Though she knew some of the language from college classes, maybe this would be the immersion opportunity she needed to develop a working knowledge of the language. It was on her list.

Since waking in Yosemite, she had been so busy with survival and fulfilling her plan, she hadn't thought of her list. *I guess there are several items I'll never have the opportunity to cross off my list now.* She looked up at the sky; *I'll certainly not be getting my pilot's license. That may be one of several adventures I'll miss out on, but on a scale of one to ten, the one I'm now living is definitely a ten!* With a glance at the brothers hard at work, her musings continued, *I will soon own a business; that's one of many items I'll be able to cross off my list. I'll be able to learn some building; that's another item. I already need to cross 'prospecting' off the list. And before long, I should be able to cross 'help others in a major way' off the list. Perhaps it should just remain and I can put check marks next to it as an indication of how many times I've been able to accomplish that particular task.* Her excitement rose as her thoughts continued. She loved it here.

Each day, Sage spent the morning working with the brothers. Afternoons were spent hunting for fresh meat and panning gold. Though she would have liked to see the cache for the brothers grow at a faster rate, she felt it was important to participate in the building process. Not only was she learning a great deal, but in the end she would have the satisfaction of knowing she had helped in the building of her establishment.

As work progressed and she became more adept at it, she revised her schedule, allowing more time at the gold claim. While the building was important to her, so was providing well for the brothers, who had become more than employees, they were her friends.

While each of them possessed a work ethic which was obvious and admirable, their other qualities also spoke well for them. As they taught her, Sage saw ample patience. When it grew too dark to continue working and they finally stopped for dinner, their time spent together showed each brother enjoyed a very individual but distinct sense of humor. Xavador loved to play practical jokes. Juan, though the more serious as the eldest, had an infectious belly laugh. Jorge's humor leaned to the sneaky side. He liked to sneak up and startle the others, at which time he would snicker in a way that reminded Sage of the cartoon dog, Muttley. Eduardo was a sweetheart and often the butt of his brothers jokes. It was all in good fun and it seemed as if he felt honored to hold such a position. He laughed lightheartedly and seemed to enjoy the joke as much as his brothers. All of the brothers sang like angels. As individuals, the beauty of each of their voices made Sage stop to listen, taking in the wonder of such a gift. But singing as a quartet was when their talents sparkled. Though she enjoyed all of their singing, when they harmonized, Sage felt transported to another dimension. What an amazing gift for them to possess and for her to hear.

As the building took shape, prospectors arrived in the area. At first, a few here and there, but soon they came in droves. Sage could no longer remain at the building site. Her claim needed protection. Before staying at the claim, she needed to speak with the brothers.

Around the campfire that evening, Sage began with some trepidation. "The building is going up so much faster than I ever dreamed it could. Your work is beyond reproach. Thank you."

Nods and smiles of appreciation, along with a, "Gracias," thrown in by one of the brothers was the exact response she had anticipated.

"Not only that," Sage continued, "you have become my friends."

More enthusiastic nods in response.

"It is because you are my friends that I feel I must tell you the truth."

Looks of concern pulled at her heart.

"I have not told you everything, and I now regret this. All should have been in the open since our arrival. For this I apologize.

The curious gazes spurred her on. "Surely, you have noticed the large numbers of men arriving in the area."

"Si, we have. You know why?" Juan asked.

"Yes, I do. Gold. There is gold here. This is where I got the gold I gave you as a deposit when I hired you. Guys, there is a lot of gold here. Many, many people will come to get it. This is why I am building in such a strange, out of the way place. I'm planning a business to serve the miners and their families."

The brothers watched Sage with rather puzzled looks before Juan said, "That is a good idea. But why must you apologize for not telling us?"

"Most of the time, when I'm gone from camp, I am panning for more gold. By not telling you, I took the decision of whether to build or prospect away from you. I made that decision for you. That was wrong."

"But, Senorita Sage, we are not miners, we are builders."

"Yes, you are amazing builders. But the gold has the potential to make each of you quite rich."

The brothers looked at each other. Sage had the feeling they were in communication although not a word passed between them.

"While we are happy to work and help our family, our goal is not to become rich. If that happens as a result of doing what we love, we would welcome it. But we are builders, not miners, and have no interest in digging for gold. We wish only to build."

"Do you mean you won't leave the building site to stake a claim?"

"Of course not. We have an agreement with you to build all of the building, not just part of it. What kind of men would we be if we did not honor our agreement? How could we return to San Francisco and look our mamá y papá in the face and tell them we did not finish our job. No, never!"

Sage's admiration of these men increased dramatically. "In the morning, I will leave to stay at the claim. It would be good for one of you to accompany me so you will know where I am. In fact, if you would like to stay the day with me, I will be happy to show you how to pan for gold. If you are in agreement, one of you could come each day to pan with me."

"No, while we do want to see where you are, our job is to build, not pan. I will accompany you tomorrow, but then will return to work on your building."

"Wow. You are, in fact, men of honor. Your mama and papa should be very proud. Okay, in the meantime, all that I have gotten and will get during the building process will be yours."

Once again, Juan spoke, "That is not our agreement. We cannot take more than agreed upon."

"In this matter, I will not argue. It will be a bonus. I have been here for months and have all the gold I need. The four of you are providing a service for which I am grateful. Thank you. As more and more people come to the area for gold, prices will rise. You will need this bonus to pay prices so high you cannot imagine."

"We will think about this."

To Sage, there was nothing to think about. If need be, she would leave the gold at their home in the night. But it would be a while before she must face their decision. For now, she would return to the claim and the brothers would complete their work.

Weeks went by. The second cache at the claim was nearly full. She wanted to check on progress at the building site, but hesitated over concern about leaving the claim alone. With many prospectors in the area, leaving a claim unattended, even for a day, could result in a claim jumper. After a great deal of thought and observation, she determined the solution would be to visit the building site at night, leaving Buddy at the tent to guard her claim. Though fraught with potential complications of its own, this option was the best she could come up with and she would be gone only a short time.

As she unloaded the cache into the two packs late that night, Sage listened for movement. Buddy stood next to her, facing away, as though he knew he was standing guard. Tying the two packs together, she placed them over the mule's back before motioning for Buddy to stay and heading up the trail toward her building site.

The many people coming for gold created a well worn trail, which made it easier to navigate safely in the dark. In the few areas the trail's direction was unclear in the darkness, the LED flashlight she kept in her pocket came in handy. But the need to travel undetected meant traveling in darkness whenever possible.

Astonishment overtook her as she reached the site. There stood a real building! Not part of a building, but a whole building. Roof and all! Excitement coursed through her as the reality that her dream was so close to fruition hit her. Soon. And from the looks of things lately, that was good.

Standing outside the tent she used in camp, which she had insisted Juan use in her absence; she called in a loud whisper. "Juan. Juan. Wake up."

"Senorita Sage?" He stuck his head out the tent opening. "Is everything okay?"

"Yes, I wanted to check progress, but it didn't feel safe to leave the claim unattended during the day, so I left Buddy there and came at night."

"You had a message from town."

"I did?"

"Si, a miner stopped here. Mr. Watson at the Mercantile sent word your shipment arrived."

"Already? Wow. That's good, that's good." She tended to repeat herself when in thought. "This changes things. I had hoped to stay and take a look at the progress, perhaps even help some before returning to San Francisco. A trip that long will also mean I need someone to stay at the claim. Could one of you please stay there while I'm gone?"

"Yes, if that is what you want. You plan to go all that way by yourself?"

"No, I'll take Buddy."

"I could go with you."

"Thank you, Juan, but you'll be needed here. When I return, I'll need to be able to move things into the building. Will it be close enough to complete?"

"Two weeks..." Juan thought for a moment. "Si, it will. With one of us at the claim, it will slow things some, but it should be.

"Good."

While Juan woke his brothers so together they could show Sage the progress on the building, Sage entered the tent and added both packs of gold to the cache under the crate she used as a table. Then thought better of it and filled one pack partially with the gold bags.

"Senorita Sage?" she heard Juan whisper.

Exiting the tent, she explained to him about the cache. She also told him she would be taking a quantity of gold to his family.

"But we cannot accept your gold."

"Juan, this is gold I panned for you and your family as a bonus. Your family will need the additional money once prices rise in San Francisco as a result of all the people and the gold rush." She smiled as she saw the other brothers approach. "Now, show me our building."

The finality with which she spoke made it clear she had no intention of discussing the matter further.

As they approached the entry to the building Sage's jaw dropped as she stared. "It's unbelievable what you have accomplished in so short a time." Inside the large building, under the glow of a lantern, Sage could see the planned rooms come to reality. The kitchen, the large dining room, the shop, the office, and outside, the stairs leading up to many small rooms.

"We need to make many doors and some furniture. We have not yet tried the fireplaces; the mortar is still curing. In the evenings, after it is too dark to work on the building, we use our time to chop wood for the fireplaces, so you will not have a shortage. We also took the liberty of tilling and planting your garden. It is growing nicely."

Sage was speechless. These four men were sons any parent would be proud to have. Actually, by modern standards, three men and a boy. Xavador, at fifteen, worked as hard and well as his older brothers. Sage blinked away the emotion which welled up as she looked at this wonderful building and these amazing friends who had created such beauty, going beyond all expectations, even providing firewood for her use. She would tell their parents what an amazing job they were doing and what honorable young men they were.

13

The journey to San Francisco was not easy. Leading a train of ten mules was more work than she thought it would be, but she needed them for the return trip. The decision to leave two of the horses with the brothers had been good, despite Juan's opinion that she needed to take all of the animals to assure enough packing space for the ordered supplies. She simply could not leave the brothers with no transportation. To have the assistance of one of them would have been nice, but they were needed in Coloma.

Eduardo accompanied Sage as far as the claim, where she stayed long enough to provide basic gold panning instruction. He no doubt enjoyed the process, as he chuckled each time he picked gold out of his pan. After settling him in and showing him both caches, Sage checked the food, water, and bedding on top of the gold in her pack before calling to Buddy and leaving for San Francisco.

Though ordered at low prices, Sage was sure she remembered that during the gold rush, as prices rose, merchants increased the cost to pick up orders. Though she considered the practice dishonorable, she must be prepared. She hoped Mr. Watson would not do such a thing, but she met him only briefly when placing the order. With several months having gone by since her previous stay in San Francisco, there was a very good possibility the city had grown and now offered many more items. If the trail of prospectors she encountered during the trip was any indication, San Francisco would undoubtedly be larger.

As she passed the excited would-be prospectors, they would shout things like, "Hey, you're going the wrong way." Or, "You already struck it rich?" A smile and a single nod of greeting was all the response their banter received. This was one trip on which Sage had no intention of revealing herself as a woman. The last thing she needed was to defend herself against the possibility of someone thinking he had the upper hand because she was the so-called weaker sex. Dressed in the extra set of men's clothing she had purchased when in town, with her hair tucked securely under her hat and a bulk of loose clothing, she gave the appearance of being a man. However, the brothers all agreed that regardless of how many ways she attempted to add a masculine tone to her voice, she failed the test. Best to remain quiet to retain the illusion.

She didn't have long to wait for the ferry. As it landed, four men disembarked, a couple carried plentiful provisions, the others looked as though they simply grabbed a bed role and left. Both reminded Sage of horses champing at the bit, anxious to get going, excited at the future wealth they fully expected. None delayed after going ashore, but immediately headed for the expected pot of gold.

Sage watched them go, and then, turning to the ferry, removed her hat, and said, "Afternoon, Ford. Doing good business, I see."

"Miss Brooks! That is you. I thought I recognized those animals."

"Can you get us all on at once?"

"Sorry."

"Okay, I'll send some of the animals first and pay you extra if you'll see that they get to Mr. Brine's livery before returning."

"It's a deal," he said, and began loading the first of the mules.

Late that afternoon, Sage stepped off the ferry with the last of the animals into a swollen version of the town she had left. While still not large, it had doubled in size since her last visit. However, the energy of the place was transformed. No longer a quiet, laid-back community, it now exuded an anticipatory energy, much like a carnival atmosphere. *If it's like this already, imagine what it will be like next year.*

As she approached the livery, Mr. Brine greeted her with enthusiasm. "Miss Brooks, I heard you were on your way. I've got the rest of your stock all settled in and I'll take care of these for you. The Misses is going to be mighty pleased to see you."

He took the lead from Sage and she barely had time to thank him before he shooed her on her way.

"Come on, Buddy. Bath time. We'll need to get all that trail dirt off you before going inside."

As she washed Buddy at the back of the boarding house, Molly Brine stepped out the back door. "Miss Brooks! I'm so glad you're back. What you did for me was

116

amazing. While I don't quite understand why you did it, I can't thank you enough."

Sage smiled at the young woman. "I'm glad you like them. I assume they all arrived safely."

"Oh yes. And they are so very beautiful! Why ever did you do such a thing?"

"The only answer I have is, I wanted to. You and Mr. Brine made me feel so at home here—you even included me in your family dinner—I wanted to thank you in some way for your hospitality. I knew about the gold, and with business picking up you would need them, so it seemed the thing to do."

As Sage finished Buddy's bath, Mrs. Brine handed her a towel. "Well, this time you'll be staying as our guest for as long as you need."

"Mrs. Brine, I can't do that. I can pay, just like everyone else. This is your livelihood."

"You more than paid for your stay already. And you should call me Molly," she said, leading the way to a vacant room.

"Thank you, Molly. Please, call me Sage."

In the room, Sage saw the wash stand, which included a towel bar, drawer, and cupboard, with a large pitcher, matching bowl, and soap dish sitting on top. The pitcher and bowl were white with blue roses. "They look wonderful! It will be so much more convenient."

"There's one in each guest room. They all look different, but just as nice. I can't possibly thank you enough! It would have been a long time before we could have gotten them. All I know is, you will always stay as a guest in this house. Thank you so very much."

"You're welcome, Molly. It made me happy to do it, and I'm even happier to see you again." Not at all sure why she had purchased the gifts for the Brines, she burst with joy that she had.

"Supper's almost ready and you will, of course, join us?"

"I would love to. Thank you. I'll clean up and be right down."

Sage unpacked her dress, brought for just this purpose. After removing the trail-dirty men's clothing, she poured water from the pitcher into the bowl and then proceeded to bath herself, while telling Buddy, "In a hundred fifty years these will be valuable antiques. But for now they are brand new and I'm actually using them. Wow! I'm not sure how or why I ended up here, but what a privilege to live and experience history." She looked at the dog. "And you. I would travel nearly two hundred years just to meet you, my friend." After running her brush through her hair, she twisted it into a chignon. She wanted to wash it, but that must wait. In the meantime, she headed downstairs to join her host, her friend.

The simple meal was one of the best she had ever eaten. Perfectly cooked fish, melt-in-your-mouth mashed potatoes, and the green beans done to perfection. The best part—the milk which accompanied the meal. Sage savored that glass of milk, her first since arriving in this time-period. Though not cold, she didn't mind. She enjoyed sitting at a table with good food and pleasant conversation.

Never at a loss for words, Molly told Sage of all the changes since the discovery of gold. "The town has grown so much! Who would have thought just a few months ago it would ever reach this size?"

Sage smiled with secret thoughts of what was to come. "I would imagine you are staying quite busy with the influx of people."

"Oh yes. Many nights we're full. Though we have a few guests who stay for days or weeks while they build their local businesses, many stay only one night and then head out to find gold. I assume you've heard of the discovery?"

Sage raised her brow and smiled guiltily. "Actually, I've been prospecting for several months. That's how I came into possession of the gold I used for payment when I visited last time." Sage wasn't sure if the evident shock on the faces of the couple was from the fact that she was prospecting or that she was a woman prospecting.

Finally, Mr. Brine said, "But the gold was only discovered after you left."

"I," Sage struggled for the appropriate word, "happened upon it back in October and thought it might be best to keep it quiet for a while."

"Oh, my. Do you have help? It sounds like very difficult and dangerous work." Molly's concern was as evident as her shock.

"Buddy has been a great help. But other than him, I remained alone until I returned after my last visit here. The Navarro brothers accompanied me back and are nearly done constructing the building for my business."

119

"Business? You won't continue prospecting?" Mr. Brine's curiosity seemed more than idle.

"No. It was never my intention. My sole purpose in prospecting was to obtain enough to start a hotel and cookhouse, with a small shop included."

"But, the gold could make you rich. I've been thinking of trying it myself."

Now Sage understood his odd manner. "Yes, I imagine a few will get rich on the gold. But many, many more will only find hardship, inflated prices, and danger. The real riches, Mr. Brine, are right here. It's the business owners who will profit most from the gold discovery."

"How's that? It can take a full year to make as much as could be found in gold in one day."

"While this is true, the gold is limited. I've been fortunate to be there before others, allowing me to pan for it. Soon, the only way will be to dig. People have only just begun to arrive. As the word spreads more and more will arrive. San Francisco will soon be a very large city. In the end, it will be the business owners who profit from the gold."

"What you say does make some sense, but what if they don't come as you suggest?"

"Look how many have already arrived, and it's only been a few months. Think about it. I used to be alone there; now, there are numerous claims lining the river. Prices on prospecting supplies have already risen and undoubtedly other items will soon follow suit. New fortune-seekers are arriving on a daily basis."

Molly placed a bowl of custard in front of Sage. "But how could it benefit businesses like ours?"

"You've already seen an increase in business, but this will no doubt continue to expand. As prices increase, you will also need to increase your prices. Expansion is one way to enhance your gain."

"That sounds great, but how? It's not like we can open more businesses. We only have the two of us." Mr. Brine seemed at war with himself. The lure of fast money in the form of gold looked tempting, but it was obvious the vision of being a business success held a potent attraction.

"Have you considered expanding what you have? Offering additional services? Having more stock?"

"I'm not sure I know what you mean."

Sage admired what they had accomplished, but it was obvious their entrepreneurial spirit had its limits. Not wishing to be forceful, she did her best to sound thoughtful. "Hmm..." She smiled and gestured around the table. "Molly is an amazing cook, yet your boarders must dine elsewhere. Have you considered serving meals?"

"Become a diner?" Molly's concern was evident.

"No, but you could serve family style meals at the same times you currently do."

"Oh, tell the guests supper is at six or breakfast is at seven and we all eat together." Molly warmed up to the idea. "There could be a separate charge for each meal, since some who stay may not want the meals or at least not all three of them. We've had several guests who come in the evening and leave to go prospecting long before breakfast."

"That's a good idea. Would it be possible to supply to-go meals for them?"

Molly looked momentarily perplexed, then said, "Yes. I do that for Jonathon when he makes trips to local ranches to purchase stock; no reason I couldn't do it for others." Her face took on the glow of an idea. "Sage, when you were here before, you went to the barber for a bath. What if I added a bath for guests to use? For an additional charge, of course." The young woman was on a roll. "Oh, and I could offer laundry services!"

"Now Molly, dear, perhaps you ought to think this through. Laundry is a day-long chore. How could you possibly have time to do it on a daily basis?"

Her brow furrowed as she thought this problem through. Then she smiled, "I won't do it. I will take it to Mrs. Wong's laundry. She can do it and I can charge the guest just a little bit more than she charges me. That way, I provide a service without adding additional work."

Sage was impressed. Molly was really running with the idea. "Perhaps if you let her know you will be a regular, she will give you a price break, thus increasing your profit."

Jonathon Brine smiled. "I've got it! We simply build on what we have. Instead of arranging for horses and mules upon request, I could make sure I keep some in stock for those who are in a hurry."

"Jonathon, you made such beautiful furniture for the hotel. Could you spend more time building furniture? Maybe you could sell it."

"Molly, that's a great idea! Making the furniture for this place was one of the most enjoyable things I've done since coming here. I would love an excuse to make more." He turned to Sage. "Thank you, Miss Brooks, your suggestion may have started something here."

She smiled in response. Looking at Molly, Sage said, "Perhaps while I'm here you could give me some tips about running a hotel. I would imagine you have learned what works and things to avoid."

Talk turned to the running of a hotel and then to the Brines recent chicken acquisition.

"If you're going to start feeding our guests, I better get some more of those chickens. You'll need more eggs." Sage liked the way Jonathon Brine always showed consideration for his wife.

"Would it be possible to get some for me also?" Sage was surprised she hadn't considered chickens before.

"I don't see why not. It's a well-established chicken farm with plenty of chickens. How many do you want?"

"Good question." They went on to discuss the pros and cons of chickens, how many eggs various numbers would provide and what it would take to transport them to Coloma. Together they determined a milk cow would also be a necessity. Mr. Brine told Sage he would keep an eye open for other possible stock while getting the chickens and cow.

Sage enjoyed the chat even more than the food. Waiting for stock would mean an additional day in San Francisco, but that provided the advantage of spending more time with the Brines and enjoying more meals like this, since they insisted she take all her meals with them. Hearing their enthusiasm for expanding their businesses added to her excitement about her own business.

The following day she made arrangements to pick up her order at the Mercantile the next morning. While there, she added additional items to her order. Sage also toured each new shop, picking out items she could use or resell. Then she stopped by the home of Mrs. Jones.

Molly directed her there, saying the woman made beautiful quilts. She did indeed. They were works of art. Beatrice Jones had been injured in an accident on the trip from Pennsylvania, losing the use of her legs. While the stigma of the day sadly considered her an invalid, she refused to accept that label. With no wheelchair to enable independent movement, she was stuck wherever placed until someone could assist her. Despite the inconvenience, this determined woman insisted on doing her part. While her daughters did much of the work around the house, she made quilts, which she sold whenever the opportunity arose. Sage purchased all seven available, vowing to come back for more.

While the beautiful quilts might be somewhat ornate for the men who would populate the American River in search of gold, the women who accompanied them would appreciate the beauty. It was these wives and daughters who Sage wanted most to cater to, assist, and employ.

As she bid good-by to Mrs. Jones, an idea occurred to her. She would speak to Mr. Brine about it that very evening. He made wheels for wagons and buggies. He also made furniture. She would hire him to put the two together and provide a wheelchair for Mrs. Jones.

First, she needed to visit the Navarro's. As prices continued climbing, they would need the gold she brought for them. While there, she suggested they stock up on everything.

14

The next morning, once again dressed in the men's clothing she had worn on the trip into San Francisco, Sage formed her mules into a train. This time it included two steers, a milk cow, two sheep, and a nanny goat at the end. The first mule, the only white one, was known as the "bell mule" due to the bell attached to it as the lead mule. By nature, rather than training, the other mules would follow in a very straight line. The bell mule was already loaded with chickens, caged in baskets artfully positioned in what looked like a very large horseshoe over the mule's back. In all, there were twenty-three mature hens; one rooster; and twelve chicks, old enough to withstand the trip, but still small enough to travel easily. When he had traveled to the chicken ranch to acquire the chickens, Jonathon Brine had taken the mule with him to assure the acquisition of as many as would possibly fit on the mule. A large horse blanket had been applied before the baskets to prevent chafing of the mule's back and sides. The second mule also had an over-sized horse blanket, but only two larger baskets, each containing a piglet. The back of the mule was loaded with the additional supplies she had purchased the previous day, including Mrs. Jones beautiful quilts, all carefully wrapped and secured, with a caged kitten on top.

Leading the train, which included four new mules, to Watson's Mercantile, Sage would have made quite a spectacle, but by thinking ahead, she arranged to pick up her shipment before sunrise, thus avoiding the stares and curiosity of onlookers. The time it took to load the cargo was decreased substantially because Mr. Watson had prepared and loaded the panniers, the bags and boxes used to carry the supplies on the mules. All were made from fabric, with loops to place over the crossbuck, essentially two wooden Xs protruding up from the pack saddle. The loops made them easy to load and unload and the fabric was easy on the mule. In addition, there were four wooden crates which held the glass for the windows of her establishment. While Mr. Watson had equipped the crates with their own loops, they were more difficult to handle than the fabric panniers. Sage did the actual loading herself so she would be assured she could unload and reload the mules each day. With the exception of the mule loaded with the chickens, the load on each was topped by two thin, rolled mattresses.

She hoped to make better time on this trip, with the extended daylight, but the mules would still require unloading each evening. This, she would do in the dark, by the light of one lantern, just as she now did it at the Mercantile. By the time she completed loading and double checked for security and balance, she was exhausted and sweating. It was time to meet Ford at the ferry.

Though she arrived a bit late for their scheduled rendezvous, Ford patiently awaited her arrival. He had arranged for a local boy to stay with the animals at the dock while Sage traveled over with the first group. As they cast off, light was just beginning to cast a dim glow in the eastern sky. The eeriness of riding the ferry in the darkness fascinated Sage, who was always up for new adventures. By the time Ford delivered the last of the animals on the eastern shore, light filled the sky and the stock seemed as anxious as Sage to be on their way.

"Let's go home, Buddy." The dog ran ahead and then returned to remain with the train, checking each animal on a regular basis. Sage had tethered the animals together, so leading them was easy. The mules seemed content in this game of follow-the-leader. About two miles into the trip, Sage heard Buddy barking somewhere in the middle of the train. Stopping and dismounting, she walked back to check on the disturbance. The load on the fifth mule had shifted due to a loosened cinch, creating problems for the mule. "Good boy, Buddy!" After carefully adjusting and cinching down the load, she returned to her horse, mounted, and they continued on their way.

When dark, they stopped for the night. Unloading the mules was hard and took even longer than Sage had anticipated. She left each load piled exactly as she had removed it to make reloading in the morning easier. Though exhausted, after unloading, she headed for the cow and goat, carrying her tin cup with her. They required milking. Other than what she drank and what Buddy and the kitten drank, it bothered Sage to spill the milk directly onto the ground. But the animals needed milking and she had no use on the trail for that much milk. When she completed the task, she lay on her bed roll feeling completely done-in and smelling like a horse, but Buddy, next to her, didn't seem to mind as they settled in for a short night's sleep.

The next morning, she did the milking first thing upon waking, this time saving some in her water bottle for consumption on the trail. Reloading proved to be easier and faster than the previous morning. Though sore from the unusual work and hours on the back of a horse, as well as tired from lack of sleep, she better understood the process of loading the mules, and the organization of the previous night helped. By the time the light showed in the sky, Sage's train was once again headed up the trail to Coloma.

By mid-afternoon the train was well into the trees. Sage knew this could pose potential problems if the loads shifted by scraping against trees or if an animal got spooked and ran around a tree, but so far the journey had been without incident.

Buddy ran ahead then came back to walk with the train. Sage assumed he was checking the trail. She had not only grown to love the dog, but also admired him. He was smart. Someone had trained him well. And he was devoted to her. She smiled as he once again ran ahead. Though unable to see him, she heard him bark and growl.

Alert to possible danger, she pulled her pistol from its holster in her belt. After debating the wisdom of continuing or dismounting and leaving the train, Sage decided to dismount, secure her horse to a tree, and proceed on foot. If Buddy had encountered a bear or other wild animal, it could mean disaster if it spooked the train.

As she gained sight of Buddy once again, she saw his hackles raised as he growled at a disheveled man. "Mornin," the man shouted as Sage grew near. "Saw your

129

mule train comin' and thought you might could use a bit o' help, but your mutt here wouldn't let me get close."

Sage bristled at the use of the term "mutt" in reference to Buddy. She patted her thigh as a signal to him to come to her. Buddy reached her side and in response to a subtle point to the ground, sat. While he appeared relaxed, he remained on high-alert. She trusted her dog's instincts. Though she did not raise it, she held her pistol at her thigh, ready.

The man came closer. "He might be a bit mean, but he seems okay with you."

Once again, Sage found his reference to Buddy irritating.

"Anyhow, it'll be nice for you to have some assistance. We could move the load from one of the animals onto others so I could ride." He ignored the lack of response. "Where you headed? I thought I'd go get me some o' that gold. With all that gear it looks like you don't need no gold, you's already rich." He glared, "Must be nice." Coming even closer, he continued, "Well, let's go."

Though finding it difficult to be civil, Sage responded with as much politeness as she could muster, "Thank you for your offer of assistance, but I have no need."

The man gave Sage a hard look. "You's a woman!"

"Yes."

"Ain't no discussion or assistance needed then. I'll just take that little ol' train myself."

"Really?" The sarcasm in Sage's voice seemed lost on the man.

"Why yes, I will. You're just a woman and can't do nothin' to stop me."

Once again, the man advanced on Sage, only this time his manner made known he had no intention of stopping. Buddy sprang forward, knocking the man off his feet, leaving him sprawled on his back on the ground. Buddy stood growling, with the man's throat between his teeth. Sage could tell he was holding enough pressure to let the man know he meant business, but not enough to cause serious injury.

"Argh, do something! Get this beast off me!"

"Actually, *you* are going to do something. You are going to get up and leave, quickly. If you do not, I will give the command for my dog to have his way. Understand?" The man was not armed and she had no desire to hurt him.

"Yes."

"Buddy, come."

Buddy reluctantly let go of the man and came to stand by Sage.

Standing up, the man looked at her with an arrogant attitude. "I don't need your train. I'm gonna git rich pickin' up gold. I'll soon make you look poor. I'll work for my wealth, not have it handed to me." He turned and strode off through the woods.

Sage watched for a moment before returning to the animals. Profound relief flooded her. Her nerves had been taunt as she had recalled the disastrous encounter with Nelson. But this man was not the lowlife Nelson had been. While he possessed no respect for women, she didn't feel he posed any real danger.

Nevertheless, she learned a lesson. No more pack trips alone. Even if it meant taking one of the Navarro brothers from their work or hiring some other trustworthy person, for safety reasons and to share the difficult work load each morning and night, she would bring an assistant on trips from now on. With the increase of people of all sorts in the area, danger would increase beyond imagination. It wasn't because she couldn't do it on her own, she was doing fine. Being independent meant being smart. An assistant would be the smart thing to do.

15

Sage remained on high-alert due to the confrontation with the would-be gold seeker, but the remainder of the trip was uneventful. Once again Sage was amazed by the rapid, gold-seeking population growth. It seemed as though people were everywhere. Even with the increasing darkness, she pushed on, trusting the animals and occasionally using her flashlight. Knowing the building site was near, she continued. She arrived at her destination a couple of hours after dark.

"Senorita Sage! You are back."

"Jorge! Good to see you." Seeing Juan carrying a lantern toward them, she waved, not thinking that he was in the light, but she was still in the dark. "Juan!"

"Welcome home, Senorita," he said in his calm and reassuring way.

Xavador lumbered up with an ax over his shoulder. She was sure he had grown several inches in the short time she had been gone. "Wait till you see the building, Senorita Sage. It's…"

Juan interrupted his young brother. "First let's get these mules unpacked and give the Senorita supper. Maybe you would like a good night's sleep first. You must be very tired after such a long trip in such a short time."

"Yes, I am. Though I am anxious to see the building, I'm so tired I'm not sure I even want to eat before sleeping."

"I just finished making supper, so you will not need to wait. We will unload the mules for you." Juan untied the goat and then the cow.

"No, I can help. I refuse to be so tired that I shirk my work off onto others."

"I won't argue with you, because I know it will do no good." Juan shook his head as he smiled at her.

Sage removed mattresses and panniers from the crossbucks. As soon as she took one off, a brother was there to haul it away. Before she knew it, the entire load was gone and the animals all secured for the night. *Such good men*, she thought to herself as she headed toward the campfire and food.

Juan moved out of her tent and back into the tent with his brothers, allowing Sage to return to her tent. As she drifted off to sleep she thought, *Soon, we will be sleeping in a real building.*

Waking to the sounds of movement in the camp and still on high alert from traveling, she bolted upright, looked around, and realized she was safe in her tent and the noises were coming from the brothers. Anxious to start the day, she headed out of the tent but stopped when she found a pot of warm water in her way. *What sweethearts!* She carried the pot inside her tent, poured some into the tin cup which was still attached to her pack and set it aside. With a quick removal of her clothing, she used the remaining water to luxuriate in a warm sponge bath. It felt good to rid herself of the dust, grime, and smell of the trail. Then, finding her toothbrush and the baking soda she kept for just this purpose, she used the water in the cup and brushed her teeth. *Much better.*

Dressed and ready for the day, Sage exited the tent, excited at what was to come.

After breakfast, with the sky beginning to lighten, she said, "Let's take a look."

"Not much longer till daylight. Then you'll be able to see well. In the meantime, maybe we should do some milking."

Juan's suggestion startled Sage, she felt bad for forgetting the milking. "Of course. Poor Milkshake and Nanny. I'm so excited about seeing progress on the building, they completely slipped my mind."

Juan held two of the buckets she brought from San Francisco for milking. He just smiled at her.

Having a milking partner was fun. Sage felt much better not having to spill the milk onto the ground. With the four men they should not have trouble making use of it. Fresh butter would also be nice.

After covering the pails of milk with a cloth and sitting it in the shade, Juan said, "Anyone want to see what we've been doing?"

The other two brothers appeared as if from nowhere and all three looked like they had swallowed the proverbial canary.

What are these guys up to? Sage wondered as they walked to the front door of the building. Door was right. It had French doors as the entrance. Beautiful French doors, carved and ornate.

"They're gorgeous! How did you possibly find the time?"

"With a lantern, I can carve in the dark. These gave me something to do in the evenings. I'm glad you like them." Juan opened both doors and oddly, the men preceded Sage into the building, and then stood aside so she could see.

Her hand flew to her mouth and her eyes glazed over as she took in the sight before her. To the right, long tables filled the dining room, each with an equally long pair of benches tucked under it. At the end of the room, a blazing fire added its luminous glow, creating warmth and adding a homey atmosphere. A colorful centerpiece of spring flowers graced each table. Looking to her left, Sage gasped at the sight of the shop, complete with shelves ready to fill with the merchandise she had brought from San Francisco. The sales counter, strategically placed to allow access to both the dining room and the shop, fairly glowed. It was quite obvious a great deal of time had been invested in making it into a thing of beauty.

Juan took her elbow and guided her through the kitchen door behind the shop. Before her was a beautiful kitchen, though it in no way resembled a modern kitchen. Overwhelmed, Sage gazed around the room. The back wall was partially filled by the large, raised fireplace with a small fire burning. A large space had remained to its right for the stove Sage had ordered. To the right of the stove's space, an exterior door. To the left of the fireplace, the oven was within the rock above a huge opening for wood storage, which was full. Xavador pointed to the laid fire to the right of the oven opening, which would heat the oven. Of course, she had seen the fireplace wall before, but it looked so different with a fire and the rest of the room complete. A block island stood in the center for working as well as a couple of "counters" on the far wall under the window. Shelves for storing supplies filled the wall adjoining the dining room. The wash tubs she brought from San Francisco already sat in their place on sturdy frames between two more counters on the wall opposite the fireplace.

Sage was speechless. How did they accomplish all of this in the short time she had been gone?

Juan once again guided her. This time they went back out the front doors and up the steps. Leading her to the door of the first room, he opened it. Sage's jaw dropped. Before her stood two bed frames, each with one of the mattresses from San Francisco. A simple wash stand filled the space between the two beds, ready for a bowl and pitcher. The room, as planned, was small, with only enough room to maneuver, but it was wonderful!

"The other nine rooms look just like this." Xavador's excitement at their surprise for Sage was evident.

She hated herself for it, but couldn't stop the tears which insisted on flowing from her eyes. When she was finally able to speak, all she managed was, "Thank you. But, how?"

"Most were complete and ready to install. Having Sutter's Mill here helped a great deal, though with the gold discovery it is mostly abandoned. We milled much of the lumber ourselves. We wanted to wait until you were gone to arrange everything as a surprise. Since arriving, we spend most evenings working on furniture, counters, doors, and of course, chopping wood." Juan's quiet explanation made it all sound more like a gift than a job. While these men took great pride in their work, his words held a tone of humility. "We have one more surprise, but we took liberty, so if you don't like it, we can redo it."

They all went outside and down the stairs, then around the back of the building. Xavador and Jorge picked up a large slab of finished wood before turning to face Sage and Juan. It was dark wood with carving. Inlaid in the carving was very light wood. The large letters read, "Sage's Place." The smaller letters underneath read, "Hotel, Cookhouse, & Mercantile."

With an intake of breath, Sage's hand flew to her chest. "It's perfect." Then came those despised tears again! Sage had envisioned another name for her business, but at that moment, she had no idea what it had been, nor did she care. *What precious, precious friends I have!*

After Sage recovered from the shock of the many surprises, the three of them went back inside to unpack the panniers. It was like Christmas morning, opening all the supplies, equipment, and goods. Sage realized she had trusted Mr. Watson and had not checked the inventory before it was loaded. *Trust is a good thing, but this is business and I must act in a professional manner. Next time, I'll check them first. Hopefully he will remain trustworthy, but the gold rush may do strange things to people.*

"We will install the glass as soon as we finish unpacking." Juan always thought ahead to the next job.

"But what about the animals? They need a place to live, especially the chickens and the piglets. They can't stay in the baskets."

"Jorge is outside working on temporary shelters for them. They will do until we can build something more permanent."

"In all the excitement, I haven't asked about Eduardo. Have you been to see him?"

"Sí. I was there two days ago."

"How is he doing?"

"He found panning for gold fun at first, but has grown tired of working in cold water all day and misses building. Also, he said there doesn't seem to be as much gold as there was at first."

"Yes, the claim is definitely slowing. I've been panning there for a long time. Perhaps we should go get him and stop prospecting now that the building is complete."

"We don't care for the gold, we just want to build and help you, Senorita Sage."

"You and your brothers are truly exceptional people, Juan."

Sage and Juan took two mules and headed for the claim. As they rode, a disturbing realization dawned on Sage. "I just realized, I've made a terrible error."

"What is wrong, Senorita Sage?"

"I had counted on hiring women and girls who arrived with their husbands and fathers to help me at Sage's Place when I opened, but so far, I haven't seen many women around Coloma. How can I possibly run the place by myself?"

Juan stopped and looked at Sage with a hint of irritation. "Do you think we would not be there for you?"

Sage stared at him in shock. "But you're builders."

"Yes, we're builders. But we also know how to cook, clean, do laundry, make beds, serve meals, and..." he paused, "we could not let our friend down now."

"Oh, Juan, what would I do without you and your brothers?"

"Good question." His laugh sang like a melody.

When they reached the claim, Eduardo sloshed his way out of the water and welcomed them with enthusiasm. "You've returned! Welcome. You may have your pan back. I'm ready to become a builder again."

She greeted him and said, "Actually, we've come to pack up and leave the claim. You've done a wonderful job, but we all have other work to do. We'll leave the gold panning and mining to someone else."

"Good. When will we go?"

"Just as soon as we get the camp torn down and loaded."

Before taking down the tent, they emptied both caches. Amazed, Sage found both nearly full. "I thought the take was slowing."

"Si, it is. But I work very hard. Long hours. I went up and down the river as far as I could."

Sage didn't know why she was surprised at the amount of gold in the cache. *I should have expected it.*

16

Upon returning to the building, the three older brothers worked on installing window panes and building shelters for the animals, while Xavador helped Sage put finishing touches on the business.

When putting the new sheets on the beds, Sage debated about the use of the lovely quilts she purchased from Beatrice Jones. She wanted a nice establishment, but all one needed to do was look outside at the many dirt covered men on the streets to realize reality could well turn out to be something else. After much thought, she determined to place three of the quilts on the beds for now. As guests registered, she would assign rooms according to their soil level. Rooms one through three would go to the cleanest people, four through seven, to the mildly grubby, and eight through ten to the truly filthy. This, of course, called for adjustability. If only filthy people registered, she would precede them to their rooms and replace the Jones' quilt with a serviceable wool blanket. On the other hand, if more clean people registered, she could replace their serviceable wool with a Jones' quilt.

Just as they completed the last bed, they heard through the open door what sounded like knocking on the main door of the building. Sage hurried out and down the stairs. Reaching the bottom of the stairs she saw an older, rather plump woman; she appeared tired.

"Hello! How may I help you?"

"I was hoping to speak to the proprietor."

"That would be me, Sage Brooks." The pride in being able to say this surprised her.

The shock on the woman's face showed, but she soon recovered. "Nice to make your acquaintance; I'm Misses Agnus Flegel. Mr. Flegel is working a claim. When I saw your building, I thought perhaps you may be opening a business and need some help. While the claim doesn't interest me, I am a hard worker."

Sage picked up just a hint of accent in Mrs. Flegel's speech; she thought probably German. "Oh, Mrs. Flegel, I'm pleased to meet you. Yes, I am going to be opening. We are waiting until ready to open before hanging the sign. Please, come in. I'll show you around."

The women entered the dining hall where they could see Eduardo putting the last of the window panes on the back eight-pane window. The matching window at the front of the building was already completed. Mrs. Flegel looked at the fireplace on the end wall, gazed around at the tables and benches, and then turned to see the shop, with its many still-disorganized shelves.

"As you can see, we're still putting things together."

"It's lovely. Your husband does beautiful work."

"Actually, I'm not married. I have a crew of four brothers whom I claim as wonderful friends. They are very talented builders."

"You arranged all of this by yourself?" The woman was astonished.

Unsure how to respond without sounding prideful, Sage continued, "Let me show you the kitchen."

Entering the kitchen, Mrs. Flegel's, "Meine Güte!" reflected her astonishment. She scanned the room before turning to Sage. "This is wonderful, Miss Brooks. Will you be cooking in here?"

Hearing the desire in her voice, Sage's hope rose. "Honestly, I'm not much of a cook. The brothers plan to help me until I find someone. Do you cook?"

With a chuckle, in a voice which intoned the silliness of such a question, the woman responded, "Do I cook!" She smiled. "With a passion. I've been told I'm a marvelous cook."

"Wonderful! What kind of foods do you cook? We'll just be serving family style at the tables, so nothing too complicated."

"While I can cook all of your standard American dishes, I'm also a master at German foods. Whatever you want, I'll cook it."

"We'll be serving three meals each day, will that be a problem? It will mean some long hours."

"I hardly see Mr. Flegel since he started prospecting, so no, it will be no problem."

"Wonderful! When could you start?"

"Would right now be good? I could arrange the kitchen and begin baking bread. Just tell me when you wish the first meal to be served, and it will be ready."

Thrilled with this development, Sage showed Mrs. Flegel the rooms upstairs and suggested it would be nice to have supper that night, even if just for the six of them. She had no idea how long it would take for business to build.

As she left her new cook in the kitchen, Mrs. Flegel busily scurried around, putting things in order. Though hiring in this offhand manner might seem like a risk, Sage felt good about her new head chef.

While she showed Mrs. Flegel around, Xavador unpacked, wiped, and put all the pitchers and bowls on the stands between the beds. Each pitcher, he filled with water. He placed the last pitcher as Sage entered the room. The simple white sets were not as beautiful as the ones Sage had given to the Brines, but they served their purpose.

When walking down the exterior stairs, Sage noticed Juan digging a deep hole. "What's he doing?"

"Digging a well. With all the prospectors, the water in the river is no longer clean, plus a well will be much more accessible."

These men never ceased to amaze her. She also saw Eduardo and Jorge hard at work building a chicken coop.

By mid afternoon everything was organized and ready for opening. While Sage checked on the progress in the kitchen, Xavador made a sign noting meal times, breakfast served six to eight, dinner served twelve to two, and supper served six to eight. After putting it up, he had Eduardo and Jorge assist in hanging the Sage's Place sign above the steps to the main doors.

Almost immediately, customers entered to browse the shop. The gold supplies Sage stocked were selling quickly, as were staple foods, such as flour and coffee. Socks and pants were also good sellers. As Sage weighed the gold used for payment on the scale she had purchased, she was astonished by how quickly this portion of the business took off. She hoped the rest of the business would do as well.

A man approached the counter. "Miss, I'd like a room. Actually, I need three rooms. One for each of my sons and one for myself."

A quick glance told Sage he was new to Coloma. While he showed the dust of the trail, he was clean and well dressed. She smiled, "I'd be happy to give you a room, though each room is set up to accommodate four and I do charge by the person."

"Does this mean we will need to share the room with a stranger?"

"Only if we sell out of other rooms."

"In that case, I will pay for all four spaces. I assume this will mean we'll not be sharing with anyone else."

"That is correct. If you'll just sign the register. By the way, how long do you plan to stay?"

"Just overnight. My boys and I will be moving on to locate a claim tomorrow. While we certainly aren't poor, we thought this would provide an excellent opportunity to increase our fortunes."

Sage hoped the man was not putting all he owned into this operation. She handed him the key and directed him to room three, letting him know they also offered a family-style supper, which would begin serving at six.

By five, the tables began filling with mostly men. There were a few women, a small number of them were obviously prospecting. The others looked very out of their element. A few children were also present.

Panic rose as Sage watched the tables fill. Keeping an eye on the counter, she opened the kitchen door to see Mrs. Flegel putting a large pan of cornbread into the oven. "Mrs. Flegel, I don't know how many you've planned for supper, but the dining hall is already partly full. Will we be able to feed them all?"

She received a knowing smile in return. "I've made enough for an army. I've seen enough of these prospectors to know the only thing they want other than gold is a good, home-cooked meal. I figure we'll be full tonight, and as soon as the word spreads, we'll have lines waiting."

"You're a wonder, Mrs. Flegel. Thank you!"

Sage stepped back to the counter to assist the next person in line, when Xavador started into the building, stopped, looked around, and exclaimed, "¡Ay, caramba!" before hurriedly retreating.

Sage had not completed the transaction before he returned. "The others are washing and will be in soon. What shall I do?"

"We need to collect from those at the tables. We will need a system, but it's too late now." Pressed for an answer to the current problem, she completed the transaction and took out some of the precious paper she had brought for selling. Using a pair of scissors, she cut it into many two inch squares and initialed each. These she handed to Xavador, telling him to collect from all the would-be diners and to give them each a "ticket" to place on the table above their plates.

"But, Senorita, there are no plates."

"Good point. Before collecting, can you please place a plate, fork, knife, and cup at each place?"

"Si." He hurried off, leaving Sage scolding herself for her lack of planning.

Just then Juan neared the counter, followed by Eduardo and Jorge. "What shall we do?"

"Jorge, you go help Xavador; he'll tell you what to do. Juan and Eduardo, check with Mrs. Flegel in the kitchen to see if she needs assistance. If she only needs one of you, the other come back, okay?"

Soon Eduardo returned. "She said right now a third person in the kitchen would just be underfoot, but when serving time comes, she would need me back in there."

"Good. Can you please string a line across the dining area to prevent others from entering without paying first?"

After a quick "Sí" he was out the door, but soon returned with a rope and a few small barrels, which he used to string a temporary barrier. With his questioning look at Sage, she motioned him over. The noise level prevented talking across the space.

"Perfect." She handed him some more tickets. "Create an opening, collect payment, and give them a ticket to place on the table above their plate." She showed him a piece of gold. "It takes a piece about this size if they pay with gold. Later we'll devise something more precise."

Without further discussion, Eduardo took the tickets, doing as she asked.

As six o'clock neared, she grabbed a length of rope from the shelf and closed the shop portion of the business. Later, with an adequate number of employees, she planned to keep it open, but for now, they needed her assistance serving. All of the rooms were booked full for the night and she had sold half of the tents on the shelf. *Where had these prospectors planned to sleep?* She couldn't help but wonder.

Pointing to the corner, Sage told Buddy, "Lay down. Good boy. Now stay." She patted him on the head and scratched behind his ears before heading to work.

She stopped at Eduardo's station. "You seem to have a handle on this, so you stay here. I'll get Jorge and Xavador to help serve and do dishes. At eight you close the doors and let people out as they leave. Then you can help clean."

"Si, Senorita Sage. This is fun."

Sage smiled at him and couldn't help but think, *It would have been if I'd prepared better.*

In the kitchen she grabbed two of the coffee pots, headed back to the dining hall and placed them on two tables. This she continued until all ten tables had coffee. Next, she repeated the process with pitifully small pitchers of milk. *I should have bought two milk cows.* Xavador and Jorge were busy carrying large bowls of beans and plates stacked with cornbread to the tables. The butter, salt, and pepper were already on the tables. Returning to the kitchen, they came back, placing a rice dish on each table. Sage wasn't sure what it was exactly, but it smelled heavenly. By the time Sage carried pans of peach cobbler to each table, all the tables were full and a line was forming along the wall.

Though a simple meal, Sage was amazed at what Mrs. Flegel had managed to put together in so short a time. The woman was a wonder!

As she continued serving, replacing empty dishes with full ones and removing used dishes as each customer finished, Sage kept her mind busy thinking of ways this process could be improved. Many ideas were coming to mind. Instead of tickets, after tonight, upon paying, the customer would be handed their plate, cup, fork, and knife to carry to their place. They needed a receptacle for the customer to place their dirty dishes in, leaving that spot instantly available for the next patron. This would not only eliminate setting tables, but make the whole process more efficient.

Though the temperature outside was quite comfortable, the room grew progressively hotter as more and more people filled it. Sage opened the small back door to provide more air flow. The movement of air was sudden and welcome. This also helped with the odors of many bodies in need of baths, which nearly overwhelmed the delicious smells of the food.

Buddy did not take his eyes off Sage. He remained constantly on guard. If he hadn't been told to stay in the corner, she had no doubt he would have been right next to her all evening.

Jorge moved into the kitchen as dishwasher. Sage knew he needed assistance, but Xavador was needed to help keep the tables clear and loaded with food. Just as she wondered how to handle this, a girl, whom Sage guessed to be about twelve or thirteen, approached her.

"Ma'am?"

"Yes, how can I help you?"

"I don't wish to be bold, but you look like you could use some help, and I would love a job that isn't digging in the dirt."

"Is it okay with your parents?"

"Papa's over there." She pointed to a man standing against the wall. The man nodded at Sage.

"You're hired. Would you rather help serve or wash dishes?"

"I'd like to serve, if that's okay."

"Perfect! Xavador..." She tapped him as he hurried past. "Help Jorge with dishes." She turned back to the girl. "By the way, I'm Sage Brooks."

"I'm Margaret Parker."

"If you can clear empties and reset places, I'll attempt to keep the tables full of food."

Margaret smiled and hurried to clear several places which had been vacated.

By the time the last guest had departed, Sage estimated they had served at least two hundred fifty people. Entering the kitchen with the last of the dishes, she noticed Mrs. Flegel beginning preparations for the morning's breakfast service. She covered dough with damp cloths for rising.

"Mrs. Flegel, you are a wonder! How did you know? And how did you ever prepare so much food in such a short time?"

Mrs. Flegel just looked at Sage and smiled.

"As soon as we've finished here, we need a meeting to better organize. If anyone has suggestions, please come prepared to share them. Also, as much as I appreciate the brother's help, they are builders and should be building. I'll hire more people as soon as possible. I've already placed a "Help Wanted" sign in the window."

17

For an era without electronic communication of any kind, word traveled fast. When Sage came from her tent at four the next morning, a line of seventeen women stood at the door of Sage's Place. A few held onto small children.

"Good morning! May I help you?"

"We're all here about the help wanted sign."

"Wonderful! I didn't realize we already have so many women in our community. Come on in and we'll see what we can do." Pointing to the benches, Sage said, "If you'll have a seat, I'll talk to you in the order you arrived. Give me just one moment."

With that she headed to the kitchen where she found Mrs. Flegel and Juan hard at work. "Looks like I slept in. You should have woken me."

"We are good. Did you see the line?"

"Yes, they are waiting in the dining hall. Do you need help?"

Just then Margaret entered the kitchen. "Oh no, I'm late!"

With a smile, Sage shook her head and looked to Mrs. Flegel.

"Margaret can help us in the kitchen. You take care of your hiring." With that, Sage felt like Mrs. Flegel was in charge and realized, when it came to the kitchen, she was.

"I sent Xavador to milk and the other boys are working outside. Is there anything specific you want done?" Juan always made Sage feel in charge, even when he was building.

"If they could erect something more permanent to separate the dining hall, we could have better control over meals. Perhaps a fence with an opening at both ends."

"Sí, right away." He tapped on the window, motioning to Eduardo to come in.

In the dining hall, Sage noticed a few more women had arrived. After locking the door to assure no one arrived early for breakfast, removing the help wanted sign, and procuring paper and charcoal, Sage asked the first woman to join her at the table nearest the fireplace.

Armed with a list of questions she had written the previous evening, she readied herself. She determined a need of eleven employees. Two positions were already filled by Mrs. Flegel as head chef and Margaret as bus girl. They needed an assistant chef, a kitchen helper, a dishwasher, two servers, a shop keeper, a maid, and two floaters. If she could hire them all this morning, the brothers would be able to return to full-time building.

The first woman was Mary Jane Claus. At fifteen she qualified as more of a girl than woman, but had worked at her grandfather's general store before coming to Coloma with her father. It was just the two of them. Though Sage thought Mary Jane to be ideal for the shop, she made a note and asked her to be seated at the second row of tables. She would decide on the best candidates and make an announcement after interviewing everyone.

The next in line was a strikingly beautiful woman, Camilia Juarez. Soft spoken and shy, she spoke no English. Sage was thankful for her time with the brothers, which gave her a working knowledge of Spanish, or at least a tolerable knowledge. Camilia had come to Coloma with her eight year old sister, Sofia, and three brothers. Her husband had died in an accident a few months before and her brothers insisted it was their duty to care for her. While Sofia liked helping in the search for gold, Camilia did not. She was more the domestic type. Sage made a note next to her name, "Maid."

Sadie Gray was somewhat underdressed and shocked Sage by introducing her desired position. "I can entertain the gentlemen upstairs."

"Thank you, Miss Gray, for coming by, but we aren't that kind of establishment." On impulse she told her, "If you decide to change professions, check with me."

Sadie Gray laughed in a brassy manner, which suggested she wouldn't be back, and left the building. Sage made note of the applicant who took the initiative to let Sadie out and then relock the door.

Next in line was a young woman with small, twin girls who appeared to be about three years of age. "Morning, ma'am. I'm Mrs. Willa Jacob. These are my daughters, Christine and Catherine. I'm a hard worker, and even though I need to bring my girls along, if you hire me, you'll never regret it. They are very well behaved." A few questions soon revealed the reason behind the desperate sound in her voice. "My husband, Farley, was in the river panning for gold. He went too far out and hit a drop-off.

Farley didn't swim. Some miners found his body stuck on a rock about a mile down river. Now it's just the three of us. We had only been here a week so he hadn't found much gold." Sage wasn't sure what position she would put her in, but the woman would have a job.

The next two women, Mrs. Elsie Jonas and Mrs. Ida Reynolds arrived at the gold fields with their husbands and children. The children were all old enough to help with the mining, but Elsie and Ida found the work distasteful as did Elsie's two oldest daughters, Ethel, thirteen, and Myrtle, fifteen, who waited in line.

Mrs. Sarah Huck appeared to be about eighteen with a baby bump just beginning to show. A bit of tactful questioning confirmed that she was due late that year. She seemed well educated and refined.

Mrs. Dixie Washington let it be known, "Yes, *those* Washingtons." She asked, "You do plan to paint and fix things up, don't you?" Then with a look at Buddy, who lay quietly at Sage's feet, pointed at him and said, "And of course, after painting, that filthy beast won't be in here, correct?" Sage wanted to let her go immediately, but had her sit with the others as she finished the interviews.

Ethel and Myrtle Jones were next. They were cheerful, thought her place wonderful, and in general, brightened the day.

Mrs. Ella Landress seemed rather nervous, her clothes were worn thin, as were the clothes of the small girl, Sissy, who accompanied her. Sissy's eyes grew big as she looked around and held tight to her mother's hand. When asked her age, Sissy held up six fingers. "No, Sissy, you be polite and answer the nice lady with words." With a smile from Sage, Sissy managed to speak the single word.

"I'm Susanna Willis," the next girl introduced herself. "My pa said I needed to come and get a job. Said it would give me something to do." She smiled. "I guess he just doesn't notice all the eligible men around here."

The next two girls approached. In halting English one said, "I am Salome Martinez, y esta es mi hermana, Ariana. Work hard. Long hours." Their parents and three brothers were working a nearby claim.

Sage assumed the next girl to approach was with one of the women. With all the confidence of a grown woman she introduced herself, "Pleased to meet you, I'm Belinda Grossman. I may be young, but I'm a hard worker and will do anything you say. Pa and James, that's my brother, have taught me well." Since the death of Belinda's mother and baby brother during childbirth two years previous, she had taken over household chores, "but there's just no house to care for here." She was only nine.

Wilma Freeman introduced herself as a former slave. She had worked in the kitchen until the death of her master, when the distraught Missus set her and her family free. "I has the papers if you wants to see um."

"That won't be necessary, Mrs. Freeman." This aspect of life in 1847 jolted Sage. It hadn't occurred to her before now that slavery was still an active issue.

The next in line greeted Sage with, "Of course you won't be hiring her," with a look at Mrs. Freeman.

"And why would you say that?"

"Well, she's a darkie, of course."

"Actually, I'm pretty sure I will hire her. Thank you for coming." Sage hoped dismissal of the woman without even getting her name would say something to her, though she doubted it.

The next woman had an infant with her. "Ma'am. I'm Juliette Belanger. I know I have a baby, but I would work hard anyway. We really need, uh, I'd really appreciate the job."

After Juliette, a large woman carrying a basket walked up to Sage's table. "Good morning! You sure do have a nice place here. I admit, I'm not so good at cooking and I'm not good at being on my feet all day, but I'm not really here for a job. I'm here to make a proposition. By the way, I'm Dorothy Gamble, folks call me Dodie."

"Nice to meet you Dodie. What kind of a proposition?"

"I may not be any good in your business, but I'm great in mine. I'm a champion with a needle. I can sew or mend anything. I'm fast too. Problem is, I can't afford a building. If you would consider letting me use a corner of yours, I'd give you a percentage of my earnings as rent."

"Dodie, I like the sound of your idea. I'm running out of time to get ready for breakfast though. Could you come back about nine and we'll work out a deal?"

"Sounds good to me. I'll see you then. Nice meeting you!"

Last in line was a disheveled girl who appeared to be about seventeen. She introduced herself as Carrie. Sage was disturbed by her constant fidgets, sweats, the anxiety she displayed, and her obvious chills on a warm morning.

She wondered if this girl was on something. Upon questioning, the girl admitted she "required" Dr.'s Elixir. She claimed it had done wonders for her, but had just run out. Then she asked if Sage carried it in stock. Without even knowing what she was taking, the unfortunate girl had become an addict. Sage guessed the Dr.'s Elixir contained laudanum, an opium product commonly used in 1848. "No, I don't carry such products. I'm afraid I won't be able to use you now, but if you will come back, I would like to talk with you." Sage's heart ached as she watched the girl leave. Through no fault of her own, she had become an addict. If she came back, maybe Sage could help her.

With the interviews complete, Sage stood and announced, "Will the following women please remain? Those I do not name, thank you for coming. Mrs. Wilma Freeman, Mrs. Ida Reynolds, Mrs. Elsie Jones, Mrs. Ella Landress, Ariana Martinez, Mrs. Willa Jacob, Salome Martinez, Mrs. Sarah Huck, Mary Jane Claus, Camilia Juarez, Juliette Belanger, Ethel Jones, Myrtle Jones, and Belinda Grossman." She knew this was more than she had originally planned to hire, but some of these women desperately seemed to need work. The others were so good or in obvious need, how could she not hire them? Besides, better to be overstaffed, than understaffed.

"Thank you for coming, ladies. You may have noticed a few men on staff, but they have only been helping until I could hire employees. Mrs. Wilma Freeman, if you could report to Mrs. Agnus Flegel, our head chef, in the kitchen, she will direct you as assistant chef. Mrs. Ida Reynolds, you may also report to Mrs. Flegel as general kitchen help. First dishwasher will be Mrs. Elsie Jones, assisted by Mrs. Ella Landress. Ariana Martinez, you will join our busgirl Margaret Parker. Mrs. Willa Jacob and Salome Martinez, you will be servers. Mary Jane Claus and Mrs. Sarah Huck, you will work the shop. Our maids will be Camilia Juarez and Juliette Belanger. Ethel Jones and Myrtle Jones, you will both be floaters, filling in wherever needed. And last, but certainly not least, Belinda Grossman, you will serve as our childcare. If anyone thinks they are better suited for a different position, let me know. Of course, all positions must be flexible; if you are not busy and see others who are overloaded, step in and help. If you find you must limit your hours, don't despair, I'll work with you. Just so you know, I am hiring five more people than I originally planned because I think you will all be wonderful for the business. So if problems arise which create a loss of personnel, that position probably won't be replaced. Try to learn as much as you can about each position.

"For those with children, we will set up a corner up front for Belinda to care for the children. Mrs. Belanger, you may keep your baby with you as you work. Also, anyone who would like to eat, meals are included. Please be in the dining room at least twenty minutes before your shift."

"For those employed in the kitchen, follow me. I will be right back to get the rest of you started." She led the four women into the kitchen. After introducing them to Mrs. Flegel, she asked Juan if he could set up a special area for the children in the front of the dining hall. "A fenced area would be nice."

Returning to the dining hall, Sage gave instructions to the bus girls and servers. Since the small shop really wasn't in need of two women, she put Mrs. Huck in charge of meal charges. Creating two places on the counter, each with its own scale, she asked Ariana to move the clean plates, cups, forks, and knives to the shelf under the counter so Mrs. Huck could give each diner a set as they paid. This would alleviate the need to set the tables and make the system much simpler than the previous evening.

Turning to the Jones girls, she asked Ethel to make sure those coming to eat understood where to pay and what to do. She sent Myrtle to assist Belinda with the little ones for now.

"Camelia and Juliette, we already have a few guests who have left their rooms, so why don't we go upstairs and see what needs done."

The breakfast service went much smoother than supper the night before. Though there remained a few kinks to work out, Sage was pleased. Between breakfast and lunch she had the Jones girls start weeding the garden. With so many employees and so much to do, Sage kept a notebook with her to help keep things organized in her mind and make notes of any needed changes. At this point, her main goal was not to be a worker, but to coordinate and make sure everything ran as smoothly as possible. When things settled down, she could assume a more definite position.

Later, Juan informed her the work on the stables, hen house, and pig pen were proceeding nicely. He also had Xavador working on a fence.

"Juan, you built ten wonderful rooms, but we're still sleeping in tents because the rooms are full of guests. That's not what I planned."

"Either you can rent two less rooms, we can build more, or my brothers and I can stay in our tent."

"No, you need something solid. I'm thinking Willa Jacob should be moving her tent here also. She's not prospecting and it's not safe for her to stay on the claim. She's a hard worker and her girls are wonderful. That's a third room I'd like to have. One or two more would be nice, just in case. I could always rent them out if we don't need them."

"You would like us to build five more rooms?"

"Yes. Can you do that? And how long would it take?"

"Not long at all. They would be small, simple."

"Yes, but they do need a heat source."

"No problem. We will make small fireplace, a chimenea."

They discussed location and size. The brothers' tent would need to be moved to make room, but according to Juan, that was "no problem."

Between the lunch and dinner service, Sage spoke to Willa. "You are staying on the claim?"

"Yes. I don't have anywhere else to go."

"Do you feel safe?"

Willa didn't answer.

"What if Juan and one of his brothers accompany you back to the claim, pull your tent down, and bring it here?"

"But…" she didn't seem to know what to say.

"Do you wish to stay at the claim?"

"No, ma'am."

"Good. We'll move your tent here and after the brothers build another set of rooms, you and your girls will have a room." She motioned to Juan. "Can you go with Mrs. Jacob to bring her things back and help her set up here?"

"Si. I'll take a mule and Xavador to help."

Watching them leave, Sage's excitement at the day's progress grew. Everything was going quite smoothly. Turning to the front of the building, Sage noticed Dodie arriving to discuss her proposition.

In short order they had her situated just beyond the counter. Her "shop" would create a nice border to prevent guests from getting in the way of the servers and bus girls. The kitchen door was right behind her area and the staff would enter the dining area through the back "gate." She already had a sign, which Sage added outside the building. She gave Dodie a piece of paper and charcoal for a sign next to her, indicating "mending and sewing done here".

18

Business boomed. As the first such business in Coloma, Sage thought it would do well, but it far exceeded her expectations. The hotel reached maximum occupency every night. The dining hall was packed throughout the serving times. The mercantile was so busy she was running out of products. As word spread, Dodie's sewing business was bringing in more work than she could handle.

Sage needed to make a trip to San Francisco but couldn't take the time. She stared at the nearly empty shelves in the mercantile as they closed for the night when Juan entered through the kitchen.

"Starting to look pretty empty."

"Yes, it is."

"I have a suggestion. I need to check on my family in San Francisco, let them know we are well. Mama worries when she doesn't hear from us. I will take the mules and bring back more stock for you."

"That would be wonderful. But, you will take someone with you, won't you?"

"Si. Xavador is young and Mama frets. He will go so she can see with her eyes that he is doing well. Eduardo and Jorge will continue work on the rooms. They should be complete by the time we return."

Sage looked at Juan, grateful for this wonderful friend. "Thank you. I don't know what I would do without you and your brothers. When will you leave?"

"At first light."

"Then we need to make a list. Is Mrs. Flegel still in the kitchen? We'll need one from her also."

"I asked her to make one on my way in."

She smiled. This was so like Juan. Always looking out for her. While she enjoyed, demanded even, her independence, she had to admit, it was nice to have someone who cared.

The next morning Sage told Juan to take Buddy with them. "He's an excellent guard and he watches out for the mules also. On the last trip he let me know when a load shifted."

"But, who will protect you?"

"I will, Juan. You take him, and I'll be fine."

"Okay. Come on, Buddy, let's go!"

Buddy looked at Juan, then looked up at Sage. He didn't move.

"Buddy, go with Juan." Sage encouraged him.

He nuzzled his head against Sage's leg.

"I don't think he wants to go." Juan spoke the obvious.

Sage squatted and hugged Buddy. "We all have our jobs to do. You need to help get more supplies. With another hug, she stood again, pointed to Juan and in a firm tone said, "Go Buddy. Go with Juan."

Buddy didn't budge. His ears were back and his constantly moving tail was still. He had never before refused to obey an order from Sage.

"He doesn't want to leave you. We will be fine. There are two of us. Let him stay with you."

Sage wasn't sure what to do. *If I let him stay, he may decide he's top dog. But it's quite evident he's determined to stay with me. I must admit, it's awfully nice to be loved.* "Okay, Buddy, you can stay."

At once, Buddy's ears perked up and his tail again wagged. Or rather, his whole body seemed to move with his tail. He nudged his head against Sage, who reached down to pet him.

"Sorry guys, I guess you're on your own."

"Is good."

Juan and Xavador headed out with all the mules in tow and a quantity of gold in pack. The extensive list they carried included items to be ordered if they weren't available. They would also be stopping at Mrs. Jones to purchase whatever quilts she had available. In addition to the list, Sage encouraged them to purchase additional items at their discretion.

As she watched them leave, Juliette approached. "Miss Sage, may I speak with you?"

"Of course. Is there a problem?"

"No, but I would like to make a change, if I may."

Sage looked at Juliette. She was a sweet young lady. Always polite and a hard worker. Though she did need to stop occasionally to care for her baby, she was an excellent employee. "What kind of change?"

The woman looked rather uncomfortable. Sage prompted her, "It's okay, what is it?"

166

"I am an excellent seamstress. Mrs. Dodie receives more work than she can accomplish by herself. She said if you agree, I can work for her. But I do not wish to leave you short."

"That's a wonderful idea! I hired too many women anyway, so it will work well. You start with Dodie today and I'll switch one of the Jones girls to maid duties."

"Oh, thank you, Miss Sage." Juliette's obvious excitement made Sage smile.

"You enjoy sewing very much, don't you?"

"Yes, I do. Before coming here, I always had to force myself to set my needlework aside so I could get my other work done."

Sage watched Juliette sit next to Dodie, who was already hard at work and had obviously planned for the new assistant, by the appearance of a second chair in her shop.

Sage originally thought to add more tables if business called for them. They left space for six more, but with Dodie's shop and the childcare corner, the dining hall was nearly full. As soon as the brothers finished the additional rooms, she would have them build a small building next door for the childcare and Dodie's shop. *In fact, I think I'll have them make it even larger to house the mercantile also. That way, the dining hall can expand even more. It will pay for the cost of the building in no time.* She shook her head in wonder. *Only open a few weeks and already expanding. I knew this would be good.*

A few days later, while Sage placed her breakfast dishes in the kitchen, banging on the front doors echoed through the building. Opening one slightly, she peered at the scruffy man before her and said, "We won't be open for another half hour."

"I'm not looking to eat. At least not yet. I had a run-in with a grizzly and thought you might be interested in buying him. I can't begin to eat all that meat before it spoils and don't have time to process it."

"You killed a bear?"

"Yep. It was him or me." With a toss of his head he indicated the current whereabouts of the bear.

Sage looked toward the designated direction and saw a mule with a travois attached. A huge bear lay on the travois. Even dead, the sight of the massive beast sent a shiver down her spine. "That's definitely a bear." Thoughts of the large quantities of meat which could fill the rapidly declining brine barrel prompted a quick response. "What do you want for him?"

The two haggled over price for a moment and came to an amount which pleased them both. It also included a month of free meals for the man, who introduced himself as George Frist. He hauled the bear to the back of the building, where Sage planned to use her day to dress him out. Seeing the bear being hauled into the compound, Buddy barked wildly.

"Buddy, quiet!" Buddy obeyed Sage's command instantly, but the growl and barred teeth said he still wasn't happy with this development.

With the help of Eduardo and Jorge they heaved the bear onto the table the brothers had made and placed outside the back of the kitchen door for just such work. Sage gave thanks for the table. The job ahead would be a far more difficult, dirty, and back-breaking on the ground.

"We can prepare it," Eduardo offered.

"Thank you, but I can do it. You work on the rooms. It looks like they're nearly done."

"Sí. Just another day and we can move in."

"A day! Ah-h, that sounds wonderful. Thank you for the help with the bear."

As he walked off, Sage heard him say, "De nada."

Buddy continued a low, deep growl. Though he seemed to sense Sage was okay with the bear, he obviously had his doubts.

Mrs. Flegel's excitement over the meat source made her almost giddy. She exhibited confidence in her ability to create a palatable meal from the bear, whose meat tended to be strong tasting and chewy. Low supplies meant anything was welcome. They had already been forced to butcher one of the steers, and it was almost gone. Now that the garden produced in abundance, the meat should stretch farther, but hordes of people consumed a lot of food.

Sage hoped Juan would be able to find a meat grinder in San Francisco. She had ordered one, but it had not yet arrived. It was quite new as inventions go; she hoped they might have one. A friend in Montana said grinding bear alleviated the tough quality of the meat. Grinding also served as an excellent meat stretcher.

169

Before beginning work on the bear, Sage went to her tent and changed. She had taken to wearing dresses except for when doing work not suited to a dress. Considering the year, it appeared more appropriate, especially for a business woman. Strangely, she found them quite comfortable.

Buddy stayed with the bear, the low growl still resonating from deep within him.

After changing, Sage returned to the bear. Never having skinned a bear before, Sage thought for a while. She wanted to keep the hide. It would be perfect over or even in front of the fireplace in the dining hall.

The repulsive odor of the bear reminded her of Nelson. At this thought, her stomach churned and threatened to revolt, as it did any time she thought of him. Despite it being self-defense, accepting the taking of a man's life eluded Sage.

The bear lay on his back. Sage sliced down the center from his head to his groin. Then she cut out from that slice to his arms and then his legs. Slits around the neck, hands, and feet brought her to the peeling point. As she slipped her fingers under the hide to peal it from the meat, she could feel the warmth still remaining in his body. George Frist said he killed him that morning when he came out of his tent and found the bear rifling through his provisions. From skinning deer, she knew the hides came off much easier with the animal still warm, so was thankful Frist brought it early. As she pulled on the hide, she ran her knife between it and the meat to help disengage the hide. She kept at it, attempting to block thoughts of the stench as she worked. Her fingers, arms, and back ached, but she did her best to disassociate her mind from the pain. Finally, with a final slice and pull, the entire front of the bear was skinned.

Standing back, she looked at it and a shock reverberated though her. Without the fur coat, the body looked like that of a person! That did it. Sage ran to the outhouse and lost her breakfast. Afterward, she leaned against a tree and breathed in the fresh air, willing herself to relax. Buddy nudged her, his concern for her well-being apparent. Sucking in a deep breath, she pushed off the tree, got a drink of water, and returned to the work table.

Determined to disassociate herself from her work, she continued. Quartering the bear allowed for removal of some of the weight. She cut off a few pieces and tossed them to Buddy. Finally, after more than two hours of grueling work, the hide was removed and the bear lay in several pieces on the work table, ready to bone and butcher into workable meat.

Through the long day, Buddy lay in his favorite spot next to the kitchen door, stuffed with as much bear meat as he could eat. Blood covered Sage. But by day's end, the old guy's meat filled a brine barrel and Mrs. Flegel's bear supper filled many bellies. Though a repulsive job, Sage gave thanks for the provision. She stared at the hide, which she had placed in a barrel of water to soak in preparation for tanning.

That bear made a delicious stew. An amazing cook, Mrs. Flegel could probably make shoe leather taste gourmet! Sage sat in the dining room after closing enjoying her first meal since that early morning breakfast. Light, fluffy biscuits accompanied the meal. Peach cobbler, made from the last of the canned peaches, provided a great end to her day.

How does the woman do it? Most days she works eighteen hours. Wow. I hadn't thought of that before. Maybe I should consider changing things. Let her split the cooking times with Mrs. Freeman and give them each an assistant. All of the other employees worked shorter hours, with breaks between meals.

Picking up her empty dishes, Sage headed for the kitchen where she found Mrs. Flegel kneading bread dough. The woman looked as though she kneaded in a meditative state, which included a rhythm that almost held a musical quality. Then Sage realized the chef was humming an oh-so-quiet tune.

Sage watched as Mrs. Flegel finished kneading, put the dough in a bowl, covered it with a damp towel, and placed it to rise on the mantle above the fireplace next to several other bowls of rising dough. When she turned and saw Sage watching her, she said, "Kind of like putting my babies to bed, if I had any."

"You looked like you were really enjoying yourself."

"Yes. I've never been so happy. It is pure joy to cook for so many. Mr. Flegel says he thinks my cooking's even improved with my contentedness. I think he also likes being left alone to find his gold," she said conspiratorially. "Truth be told, I think he likes having such nice meals brought home to him without the worry of getting supplies." Her smile spoke of her lighthearted feelings for her husband.

"Mrs. Flegel, it just occurred to me, you've been working eighteen hour days, seven days a week. I'm so sorry! I've been so excited about all that is happening, I didn't stop to think. But I have now, and thought perhaps you and Mrs. Freeman could each take a shift and we could give each of you an assistant or two."

"Now Miss Sage, while I wouldn't mind having another assistant in here, maybe someone we can train—it'd be good for them—don't you be taking any of my kitchen time away from me! I've never been happier. This is what I love to do. I have finally found my place in this life. If the good Lord were to take me tonight, I'd die a perfectly content woman. Unless you take my kitchen away!" Her scolding included a good-natured frown.

Sage was in awe. "You really feel that strongly about what you're doing?"

"Oh my goodness, yes. I've always loved cooking. Truth be told, I wanted a big family just so I could spend a lot of time cooking for them. But God must have known that was the only reason I wanted children, so he didn't see fit to give them to me. This is even better, since I don't have to stop to care for any of our diners."

Sage chuckled. "Okay, I won't mess with your kitchen. Did you have anyone in mind to train?"

173

"Yes. Margaret. She's a hard worker and seems to love helping in here. She comes early nearly every day just so she can help prep the food. I see the way she handles it and I think she may have the passion."

"I'll talk to her in the morning." Sage started out the door before stopping to look at the chef who was already cleaning the mess from the bread making efforts. "Mrs. Flegal?"

"Yes?"

"Thank you." The warmth contained in this simple statement conveyed the depth of feeling Sage intended.

"You're welcome, Miss Sage. You sleep well. And thank you."

Sage smiled at the woman with a nod and headed for her tent.

19

Margaret's ecstatic reaction when told Mrs. Flegel wanted to train her in the kitchen made Sage's mood soar. "I love helping her! When do I start?

Sage smiled. "Right now."

Watching the excited child rush to the kitchen made Sage remember that what she was doing here provided far more than a business to serve gold prospectors. This provided an income, a life, social engagement, and opportunity for the women either dragged here or who attempted to be supportive of the men in their lives. To see them settled into or find their niche produced pure joy, for both the women and Sage. Seeing Mrs. Flegel, Juliette, and Margaret all settled into positions of passion encouraged Sage to help the others find their delight.

Rotating job functions will offer a cross-training exercise. Not only will it provide a more versatile staff and some variety, but we may find someone's calling. Of course, not all will rotate. Mrs. Flegel would probably serve me for dinner if I tried to move her out of her kitchen!

She began her experiment by rotating three positions. Ella moved from washing dishes to the shop/dining cashier position. That sent Sarah to childcare, which provided an adult in the mix. Though Sage doubted Ethel Jonas would find a passion for washing dishes, it allowed her more experience.

While Sarah seemed to glow while working with the children, Ethel whined about the job change. "Why can't I move to something more interesting, like serving? I hate dishes!"

Upon hearing her daughter's complaint, Mrs. Jonas scolded her. "For shame, Ethel! We are fortunate to have this job. Think about it. If you don't wash dishes, someone else will need to. Who should be doing the undesirable jobs of life? Someone else? What would make that person more suited to such a job than us? Perhaps they don't dress as well, or speak as well, or maybe they aren't as pretty? Why should someone else be required to do unpleasant work instead of us, Ethel?"

Ethel thought about this for a moment. "So what you're saying is, I'm not too good for washing dishes."

With busy hands submersed in the wash tub, Elsie Jonas leaned her head to the side, touching her daughter's head. "You're a good girl, Ethel."

After overhearing this conversation, Sage acknowledged the wisdom of rotating positions. While the ladies may not be happy to rotate into a less desirable position, like dishwashing, it would be nice for them to know it was not permanent. She wondered if anyone ever found a passion for washing endless piles of dishes every day. Since the jobs were all paired, moving only one person from a position left one to train the next.

Heading out the back door, Sage's desire for breakfast soared as the aroma of the baking bread filled the kitchen. Across the compound, Eduardo and Jorge stood in front of the new quarters. Arms crossed, they just stood there looking at it. She hoped everything was okay.

"Good morning!" She called as she neared the two brothers.

"Buenos dias, Senorita Sage. What do you think?"

"Think?"

"Is almost done. We just need the window panes."

"It's done? But I thought you needed today to complete it."

"Sí. But only a little. It grew too dark to finish or we would have finished last night. We can cover the window with oil paper until we have glass, if you prefer."

"No, it's fine as is. How long will it take to make the furniture?"

"Is done and in rooms. We work on it in evenings by lantern."

"I should have known. You are amazing! Thank you."

"We have also made another dining table and benches. There is still space on the right of the fireplace; we thought you would like to add it."

"What would I do without you? Can you put them in the dining hall before breakfast?"

"Sí. We do it now."

As the brothers walked off, Sage got stuck on the question she had just asked. *What would I do without you? While I could do what they do, though definitely not as fast and certainly not as well, it is nice to have the help. I have come to depend on the brothers, not because I can't do what they do, but because we work well together, and it makes life better for all of us. I never really thought of it that way before. Interesting.* As she took one more look at the new rooms before heading back to eat, a sense of peace overwhelmed her.

Sage looked around. Empty shelves dominated the shop. While getting her breakfast, she noticed the abundant space on the shelves in the kitchen. If Juan didn't return soon, Mrs. Flegel's creativity would require magic to serve food to so many. Sage needed a method for obtaining supplies on a regular basis. This would require some thought.

Mary Jane motioned to her. "Sage, this is Mrs. Hanson. She has goods to sell."

Sage looked at the young woman standing before her, pretty, with unusual green eyes. She held a flour sack. "Good morning, Mrs. Hanson. How may I help you?"

"When my husband wanted to come here, I agreed on one condition, that we bring plenty of wool and cotton yarn goods. See, I love to knit. If I'm not busy with something else, I'm knitting. Other than meals and laundry once a week, living here takes almost no time, so I knit my days away. Now I've made so many pairs of socks, my husband couldn't possibly wear them all. I thought perhaps I could trade them for more yarn." She offered a pair for Sage to examine.

"These are very fine socks, Mrs. Hanson. But as you can see, we are nearly out of goods, and I'm afraid we didn't stock yarn at all. However, if you are interested in selling them, I would be happy to purchase all you have."

"That would be wonderful! I still have plenty of yarn, so selling works." She paused in thought and then said, with some concern. "Will you stock yarn in the future? I'm sure I'll run out within a couple of months."

"Though I didn't include it on the shipment arriving soon, it will definitely be on the next one."

The relief on Mrs. Hanson's face was almost comical, while the relief Sage felt at having something new to put on the shelves remained more on the practical side. After coming to terms, 128 pairs of new socks filled a shelf. Sage let Mrs. Hanson know that she would purchase whatever the woman made.

Still, the lack of supplies bothered Sage. As things were, she doubted they would be able to remain open until Juan's arrival. When she returned with the last mule train of supplies, her wildest fantasies hadn't predicted the huge success the business would be. After the breakfast service, she would discuss the matter with Mrs. Flegel.

"If I do my best to stretch what we have, we just might make it. Variety won't be what it has been, but right now the important thing is to get food on the table." Mrs. Flegel's response eased Sage's concern only slightly.

"Would it help if I went out gathering?"

"Some. With all the folks around here, I'm not sure how much you'll find, but at this point, anything helps."

Sage changed into her hiking pants, grabbed her pack, bow, and quiver of arrows, called to Buddy, and set out to gather whatever food she could.

She headed away from the river. With the massive influx of gold seekers—and it hadn't even really started yet—the chance of finding any edibles there were slim. While she needed to come back with food, getting away from the crowds added an advantage.

After being alone so many months while panning for gold, facing the crowds in Coloma coupled with the full dining hall each day, Sage needed a little time out.

It felt good to hike. The business kept her so busy that walking and other forms of enjoyment took a back seat. Buddy, though giddy with excitement, stayed close to avoid alerting potential prey. As Sage walked, she kept her eyes open for edible plants as well as wildlife. Though they planted a huge garden, with the masses of people they fed, they needed more.

Sage inhaled the aromas of the forest as they walked. The warmth of the sun coupled with the vegetation created a smell like no other. The chatter of squirrels in nearby trees garnered Buddy's attention, but Sage drew him back with a simple pat on her leg. She loved this: the sights, the sounds, the smells of the forest. With knowledge, a person could survive off the forest. However, feeding hundreds was a different thing entirely.

Gathering edible foods proved time consuming, but enjoyable. Though not much, every bit helped. If she could get them one meal closer to Juan's return, it would be worth the effort. Her excitement surged when she located a patch of wild strawberries. The tiny fruits wouldn't go far, but Mrs. Flegel would do something wondrous with them. Popping one in her mouth, the juicy sweetness produced a smile. She popped a second, irresistible berry into her mouth.

An hour into the hike, she spotted a deer. While the bear had provided a lot of meat, it was going fast, being their current primary food source. Letting an arrow fly, her aim proved untrue, forcing her to track the buck for some distance before he succumbed to his wound. From behind its head, Sage slit the deer's throat, removed her arrow, and decided to leave it, returning for him on the way back home. Though she would normally have hung the deer high in a tree, in order to save room in her pack for food, she failed to bring a rope. So she lodged him in the low fork of a tree, head down. While this ran the risk that something may take advantage of the free meal, she wasn't yet ready to turn back.

By noon, she carried a pack stuffed with assorted edible plants. Two rabbits, a pheasant, a mountain quail, and two grouse hung from the outside. She continued to hunt and gather during the return trip, placing the foraged food in the saddle bag style pack she brought for Buddy. By the time they reached the area where the deer waited, Buddy's also carried full packs.

Sage approached the deer with caution, pistol in hand. If something had decided to make a meal of it, she would rather be the one doing the surprising. Buddy laid his ears back, froze in his tracks, and barred his teeth in a nearly silent growl. The deer did, indeed, have company. A grizzly bear was just beginning to feed. Just as Sage realized the gentle breeze blew their scent straight to the bear, it turned and started toward them. Anger at the intrusion on its meal turned the bear's face into a terrifying sight. Sage shot. Though hit, the bear kept coming. It closed the distance so fast it created a blur crashing loudly through the timber roaring its intent. She shot again. Just feet away, the strong stench and revolting breath was evident even upwind. Buddy also sounded like a vicious wild animal, bobbing in and out of the grizzly's reach like a prize fighter. He was circling, trying to lunge in for a strike at the rear, but the grizzly kept pace in the circling dance of death, getting closer and closer to Sage with every turn. She was now terrified not only for herself but for her best and most protective friend, Buddy. The unstoppable beast turned out of the spin, changing its focus from Buddy to her, and stood to lunge just as Sage managed to fire three rapid shots straight to the heart, stopping the forward motion. The bear fell at Sage's feet. Buddy pounced on its back tearing at its throat.

Heart pumping at a frightening rate, adrenaline surged to overdose, Sage instinctively backed away, calling Buddy to her with a commanding voice. Looking around to verify there was no further danger, she tried to calm her trembling body. With a focus on her breathing, she took several calming deep breaths, letting each out slowly.

Buddy continued to bark. With his teeth barred, he placed himself between the bear and Sage. Still shaking, she checked Buddy for injuries. Relief coursed through her as she determined Buddy safe and uninjured.

When the shaking subsided, she needed to assure the animal was dead. After telling Buddy to sit, she approached the bear with vigilant caution, aimed directly at the eye, and shot. Though probably a waste of ammo, this was definitely a case of better safe than sorry.

"Buddy, quiet!" The barking ripped at her already frayed nerves.

She wondered what to do next. Though it wouldn't have been easy, she could have managed to get the deer home. But there was no way she could haul them both back to Sage's Place. Even with a travois, the weight prevented her from pulling without assistance. Once again risking her kill, she determined to return with Eduardo and Jorge. With a travois, together they could drag the bounty home. Despite the need for food, she hoped not to find another encroaching diner when she returned to claim her kill.

Hiking back to Sage's Place at a rapid pace, aided by the remainder of the surge of adrenaline, Sage was thankful to be returning. She hadn't been at all sure she could kill a grizzly with her pistol.

When they arrived at the kitchen door, Sage removed the saddle bag pack from Buddy and he lay in his spot next to the door, growling at the table where she had butchered the bear only days before. His hackles had not gone down since their run-in with the grizzly. Though thankful for the additional provision, she dreaded the job which lay before her.

Sage took the packs into the kitchen and unloaded them on a counter. "I trust you can make use of these."

Mrs. Flegel looked carefully though the various items. "Yes, I believe I can. These greens will make wonderful ingredients for a bear stew. I can make soup from those birds and rabbits." Her eyes lit up at the sight of the precious strawberries. "Oh, I know just what I can do with these! There may not be many, but I can stretch them into a sauce to pour over custard. Thanks to the chickens and cow, we have eggs and milk."

"I knew you would find a wonderful use for those. By the way, I'll be bringing another bear and a deer home. I'll head out to get them as soon as I locate the boys."

"The good Lord does provide, doesn't He?"

Sage smiled and went in search of Eduardo and Jorge.

20

When Sage, Eduardo, Jorge, and Buddy returned with the bear and deer, the men insisted on helping to process them. Though reluctant to take them from their work for an even longer period, Sage was happy to have the help. Starting in the late afternoon, the trio worked well into the night completing the butchering process. There was too much meat to fit into the brine barrel. Just as Sage was pondering what to do with it, Mrs. Flegel approached them.

"Mrs. Flegel, is it that late?"

"I suppose it depends on your point of view. To me, it's that early." Though unable to see her clearly in the light of the lanterns, they heard the smile in her voice.

"Plenty of fresh meat today." Sage told her.

Mrs. Flegel indicated the quantity she would need for the day, and they carried it into the kitchen. She asked, "What are you going to do with the rest of it?"

"That's what we're trying to decide. Any ideas?"

"Well, if I had jars and a pressure cooker, I could can some."

"Good idea! I'll add that to our next shopping list."

"But since we don't, have you considered drying it?"

"We considered it as an option, but thought you might not like it as much for cooking." Sage was curious where Mrs. Flegel was going with this.

"Actually, I was thinking of your shop. With the miners busy in their search for gold, they don't always have time for finding food. If you carried dried meats, they could have a ready quantity of food available to them anytime."

"Mrs. Flegel, you're a genius!"

Eduardo and Jorge turned and hurried away.

"Where are you going?" Sage called after them, trying not to be too loud, thus disturbing the guests.

"To make a smoker for drying the meat."

"Now?"

"Sí, we will sleep when all the work is done."

Sage smiled at their response. Though quite tired, she followed their example and continued working. After she had been cutting the meat into strips for some time, Mrs. Flegel brought a mixture of dry herbs and spice to her.

"I thought you might like to rub some of the meat with this. It will add a lot of flavor creating more variety to sell."

"Mrs. Flegel, you are amazing!"

As she watched Mrs. Flegel return to the kitchen, rustling sounded to her right. Her hand touched the pistol in her belt before realizing it was Willa Jacobs exiting her tent to do the milking and gather the eggs.

"Morning Mrs. Jacobs,"

"Oh, Miss Sage, you startled me. What are you doing out here at this hour?"

Sage explained about the hike to find additional food and the deer and bear which required processing as a result. Then something occurred to her. "We were so busy, we forgot to move!"

186

Willa looked at her with puzzlement.

"The new rooms are finished. We were supposed to move into them yesterday. There's one for the brothers, one for me, and one for you and your girls. The other two will be for rent."

"But Miss Sage, we can't take one of your rooms. That would take income from you and I can't afford to pay."

"These rooms were built for our use. We just happen to have a couple of extra right now, so we'll rent those two. Of course you'll move into a room. I don't expect you to pay for it any more than I expect the brothers to pay. If we reach the point where we have more employees living here than we have rooms, I may ask you to share it, but until then, it's all for you, Christine, and Catherine."

Though it was too dark to see, Sage heard the tears in the woman's voice as she said, "I don't know how to thank you. You have done so much for us. I have no idea what would have happened to us if it weren't for you."

"I'm pleased to have you here." Sage wasn't sure what else to say, so she just smiled at the woman, who then headed to the corral to do the milking. Sage saw in the light of the lantern the woman carried that her girls joined her to gather eggs while she milked. They may only be three, but it was a job they could handle.

After closing time three days later, Juan and Xavador returned. Juan had taken the liberty of purchasing four more mules and a wagon for hauling supplies. The wagon, the train of mules behind it, and additional stock behind them made quite a spectacle as they arrived.

"I hope it's okay, but with the way prices have already increased and the speed at which we go through supplies, I thought I should bring as much as possible."

"Of course it's okay! Perfect in fact. I can't wait to see what you brought."

They put the new stock away, four steers, two milk cows, twelve chickens, 20 chicks, and four piglets. As they unloaded the wagon and the pack mules, each item was taken to the general area it needed to be, the kitchen, the shop, the new rooms. Taking a large bundle off a mule, Juan said, "These are five quilts from Mrs. Jones."

"Already? It's amazing she was able to finish so many so quickly."

"I was surprised also. But she explained how she sews quickly and it is all she does."

Seeing another pile of quilts, Sage asked, "What are those?"

"Mrs. Jones told me about Mrs. Greeson, a friend of hers who also makes a lot of quilts. Though, as Mrs. Greeson put it, hers are not nearly as pretty as Mrs. Jones, but they're warm and serviceable. There are eight of them."

"Wonderful! We'll be able to have quilts for all the guest rooms as well as our rooms, plus a few for the shop."

Mrs. Flegel watched the quantities of flour, salt, sugar, cornmeal, and other stables she required being carried into the kitchen. "Our diners will be pleased. They've been asking what happened to all the bread."

"You'll also have more milk and eggs to work with; they bought more cows and chickens." Jorge told her as he emptied another flour sack into the new barrel Juan had brought for just that purpose.

Juan placed the crates containing the windows for their new rooms just outside Sage's room. Next to it, he put another crate. "What is in that one?" Sage asked.

"I see Eduardo and Jorge are working on another building. I thought that might happen, so I brought extra glass."

Since she had asked for the childcare/shop to be built after Juan and Xavador left, Juan's forethought astonished Sage. She explained to him what his brothers were building and told him of the two bears and the attempt to stretch the food supplies while awaiting their return.

"In with the food supplies are many dried fruits and vegetables, as well as canned ones. Plus more seed for the garden so we can keep it producing as long as possible. No one carried a meat grinder, but I did order one. Mr. Watson said your last order should arrive within a couple of weeks."

Sage asked about his family, what prices were doing, the growth in San Francisco, and if he had given Mr. and Mrs. Brine the note she sent.

"Sí. She sent this to you." Juan handed Sage a small package with a note attached, which Sage placed in her room to open when the work was finished.

This was all so exciting! Many of the items replenished depleted supplies, but some of them were new. A few of the items Sage would not have thought of since she came from the twenty-first century. She was pleased there to see two sadirons. Coming from a time of permanent press, it hadn't occurred to Sage that almost everything needed to be ironed to look good. Mrs. Freeman had shown how to use a pan filled with hot coals to iron, but these would work much better.

Sage worked late into the night unpacking the shop items and placing them in an orderly fashion on the shelves. Seeing the shop full again felt good. She hated to raise prices already, but the receipts Juan turned over to her showed that if she did not raise her prices, she would barely break even. Unfortunately prices were only going to get higher in the coming months and years.

She decided then and there to give all of the employees a raise. They all worked hard. While she had put a significant amount of her original gold into this operation, she was also raking it in. What it took her weeks to find while panning, she now made in a single day. The real gold mine of the gold rush truly was in entrepreneurship.

As the brothers built the buildings, Sage had them include several floor safes. Though not safes in the traditional sense, they were hidden storage places for the gold. There were two in the shop, two in the kitchen, two in each of the new rooms built for staff, and even one in the stable. When the new shop was complete, it would include two also. She spoke to Juan about building a barn after the shop's completion, which would include four safes. If robbed, her goal was to assure they only got a very small portion of anyone's gold.

With the gold and miners, came other merchants. Other buildings sprouted up all over Coloma. Not far from Sage's Place, a blacksmith shop was being built. Two saloons, a gambling hall, and a brothel were under construction. Building on another store had just been started. Sage knew it was only the beginning. But it wasn't a concern. While the area currently boasted a few thousand people, with miners' tents dotting the countryside, she knew in the next year, 1849, the real population influx would begin. Competition would not be a factor for merchants. It was the gold seekers who would lose out due to competition.

She felt for them. Many would come so far to find little more than hunger, hard work, sky-high prices, even violence and death. Their dreams of riches and glory would result in only pain and hardship. Though some of the early gold-seekers, like herself, would become very rich, others would only waste their wealth on drink, gambling, and prostitutes. The later an argonaut's arrival, the less chance they would find more than a bare subsistence, if that.

Overall, the miners behaved well while at Sage's Place. Occasionally a quarrel started, but Sage quickly make it known there would be no arguments or fighting in her place. When an obviously inebriated diner decided to question her authority by grabbing her, much to his humiliation and the other men's entertainment, he soon found himself on the floor, a victim of her martial arts training. Escorted to the door, he received the admonition that returning would require an apology and sobriety.

After that incident, Sage thought of all the drinking occurring in and around Coloma. While she knew many would only have a couple of drinks when they took a rare time out of mining, others were obviously alcoholics. Then there were people like Carrie, the girl who had applied for a job. People who had taken an elixir to aid their constitution and unknowingly became addicts. Maybe Sage's Place could somehow be used to help them. After all, that was her profession in the future. It deserved more thought. Maybe start a support group like AA or offer counseling services, or both.

One morning in July, after the breakfast crowd cleared out, Sage noticed a man remained seated after the others left. He looked around the dining hall and appeared to be summing it up. Somewhat uneasy, Sage made her way to him. "Did you enjoy your breakfast?" she asked him with a cheery lilt to her voice.

"Very much, thank you. Best meal I've had in months." He still seemed preoccupied, scrutinizing the place with a purposeful eye.

"Is there something I can help you with? The dining hall is closed between servings."

"Actually, that's precisely what I'm here about." He stood and nodded at Sage. "Please forgive my rudeness. I'm Pastor Robert Witham. You have a wonderful place here."

"Pastor Witham, pleased to meet you. I'm Sage Brooks."

"As in Sage's Place? You are the owner?"

"Yes, that's me. Is there something I can do for you?" He still seemed lost in his thoughts.

"I hope so. I'm here to start a church. Maybe if we can establish one now, some of the evils the lust for gold will bring about will be held at bay."

Sage couldn't help but be leery. Her perception of Christianity had been colored by her mother's legalistic and judgmental ways. "So you think gold is evil?"

"Oh no! Just the lust for it. Gold is just a rock. In itself it is neither good nor evil. In fact, because of its value, it can do a lot of good. But as the Good Book informs us, "...love of money is the root of all evil...""

"Yes, that's understandable. But what does this have to do with me?"

"To start a church, I need a meeting place. I see you have time between meals when your dining hall is not in use."

She looked at him skeptically. "Yes..." She stopped, not sure what else to say.

"I was thinking this would make an excellent place to hold services. At least until we could afford to build a church. You have plenty of space, seating, and it's a wholesome place."

Sage was dumbfounded. Turn her dining hall into a church? "Tell me Pastor Witham, why should I let you use my dining hall?"

The man looked at Sage, studied her. "I notice, Miss Brooks, that not only do you not serve liquor in your establishment, you do not allow people to imbibe nor be obviously intoxicated when here."

"That is correct." Sage was curious where he was going with this line of thought.

"Why is this? Is it merely to keep the peace?"

"While I do like to keep a peaceful establishment, it has more to do with not caring for what alcohol does to people. Not just the social effects of acting in ways a person wouldn't normally act but also what it does to their bodies. I've seen many people whose lives and families were ruined by alcohol, so, though I have nothing against an occasional drink, I don't wish to encourage it."

"I also notice that despite rapidly rising prices, you seem to be keeping yours at a reasonable level.

"I am trying. Unfortunately, as prices of goods rise, so must mine."

"Your server, Mrs. Jacob, told me you are providing a place for her and her daughters to live after the death of her husband."

Concern showed on Sage's face. "Yes."

"I notice also you provide care for the children of your employees."

"I'm sorry, Pastor, but where are we going with this?"

"My point is, Miss Brooks, you seem to be a very caring person. I would suspect you wish the best for the people of Coloma."

"True."

"I happen to believe knowing God and being able to gather with other believers to worship Him is best for everyone. By having a place to gather and the support of other believers, or even just people who wish to avoid the seedier elements of life, is good for everyone. If Coloma having a place to worship might prevent even one person from making a regrettable mistake in their life, it will be worth my trip here. If anyone finds their way to Him as a result, well, I can't ask for more."

Sage looked at the pastor for a while, studying him. "What would be required of someone to attend your services?"

"Absolutely nothing. Of course, I would take an offering, if attendees felt so inclined, but nothing else other than to not be disruptive."

"What if they didn't have appropriate clothing?

"No problem."

"What if they live a sinful life?"

"They would certainly be welcome. Jesus did not come for the righteous, but the sinner. My place is not to judge, but to preach the good news of our Savior."

His statements aroused a cautionary curiosity in Sage. Her only exposure to Christianity had been strict rules and harsh judgments. *Could this guy be for real?* She looked at him. He certainly didn't look like the holier-than-thou crowd she had known. Of course she had learned there were many denominations, all with varying degrees of rules and differing beliefs, but with her exposure being limited to the church her family participated in, she remained apprehensive. Though cleaner and better dressed than the average miner, he still exhibited the appearance of a few days on the trail. No member of her mother's church would have gone in public without washing first. They took the saying "cleanliness is next to godliness" very seriously. *Just as I wouldn't want to judge others by appearance, I shouldn't be judging him by appearance. I suppose I shouldn't judge all Christians by those I have known either. But I need to be sure before considering his proposal.* "What about other races? Indians, Mexicans, Blac...uh, Negros?" She switched to the vernacular of the day. "Would they be welcome?"

"Everyone would be welcome, as long as they were not disruptive."

She studied him, unsure of what to do. This indecisiveness was irritating. "Tell me about you, your beliefs, and your goals for this church you hope to start."

Sage sat and listened to his dream of ministering to the miners and others who came to Coloma. The occasional interruptions from her employees didn't deter him. He gave the impression of being a very patient man whose enthusiasm for his project was, Sage had to admit to herself, rather contagious. It sounded as though he wasn't interested in preaching at people so much as serving them. When Sage questioned him on this, he told her, "The Bible tells us Jesus came not to be served, but to serve. How can I serve Him and do any less?"

The time was nearing to place the food on the tables and let the diners inside the dining hall for dinner, the noon-time meal. Sage considered Pastor Witham for a moment. He seemed to instinctively know it was a time for silence. "Okay, Pastor, we'll give this a try. I can't promise yet that it will continue, but I'm willing to see how it works for a week or two. After that, we'll discuss it further."

The pastor breathed a sigh of relief. "Thank you, Miss Brooks. May I place a sign in front noting that there will be services here on Sunday after breakfast?"

"Yes. Check with one of the Navarro brothers—they're working on the building next door—to see if they have something you can make a sign with." Walking away, she turned back. "Nice to meet you Pastor. I hope this works out as you plan." As a second thought she said, "Help yourself to dinner, on the house." After a pause she continued, "You may as well plan on having all your meals here, at least until we have our discussion."

21

The next Sunday, Sage closed the shop while the church service was in progress. Once the shop was relocated to the new building, it wouldn't be necessary, but it would be rude to ask Pastor to compete with the noise from it. She told her staff they were welcome to attend the service, though they would need to figure a way their work could still get done. She noticed several employees seated, including all the kitchen staff.

Curiosity forced her to peek into the kitchen. How were the breakfast dishes being done? Who was making dinner? Mrs. Freeman came up behind her. "We all came in extra early this mornin' and helped prepare the dinner so it just had to sit on a low fire. Then when breakfast was done, we all helped with the dishes. It's sure nice to be able to gather together to worship the Lord again." With that, Mrs. Freeman took a seat.

As several others, including the four Navarro brothers entered the hall and took seats, Sage watched from next to the kitchen door. A few of the attendees obviously wore their Sunday best, but the majority were still wearing whatever they wore while working. Pastor Witham greeted them upon entering, with all welcomed in the same warm manner. It didn't seem to matter how they were dressed, their cleanliness, their race, or if they might be able to give a larger offering. He appeared genuinely glad to see each and every one of them.

When two middle aged men entered together, one black, one white, who had obviously bathed before coming, Sage had a feeling. After greeting the pastor, they went directly to Mrs. Flegel and Mrs. Freeman and sat next to them. With the familiar and pleased manner in which they were welcomed, Sage assumed this was Mr. Flegel and Mr. Freeman. Despite the months the women had worked for her, she had yet to meet their husbands.

Pastor Witham strode to the fireplace and turned to face his congregation. After welcoming everyone and leading them in prayer, he announced a hymn. "Let us sing *My Faith Looks Up to Thee*."

The voices rose in a beautiful concert of song. Though Sage was familiar with the hymn, she didn't know the words. It was nice to hear music again. Despite an occasional off note by one of the less than gifted singers, and even without instruments, it sounded beautiful. She did notice, though, that she was not the only one who wasn't singing. There were others who either didn't know the words or weren't inclined to sing.

Pastor then made announcements. This surprised Sage. She hadn't thought there would be much to announce at the first service. Proving her wrong, the announcements took some time. Pastor Witham let it be known he would like to begin a mid-week Bible study and anyone interested should let him know. He asked if anyone knew of neighbors in need of assistance of any sort, please notify him. Then he made it clear this was not just for physical needs, but mental and emotional needs also. If anyone struggled in any way, he wanted to be there for them. He included a happy birthday to Mr. Davon Green. Mr. Green waved to the rest of the congregation. *How did he know this?* After a few other announcements, Pastor Witham thanked Sage for the use of Sage's Place to hold their services. Then he explained how he hoped to soon build a church. This, of course, would depend on availability of funds.

He opened his Bible, explaining he would be teaching today from the book of James. He especially liked James because he spoke boldly, simply. His teaching surprised Sage.

He then asked the children to come to him. Eight came forward. They sat on the floor with him and listened to the story of Jesus healing the blind man. Pastor told the story in a way easily understood by children. His gentleness and affection for them encouraged Sage.

With the children settled back with their parents, he explained how he would first teach from the Bible and then preach his sermon, which may or may not be associated with the Bible passage he had just taught. He began his sermon with a story about himself.

Sage listened carefully. She had never heard a sermon delivered in this manner. At the church she had attended with her mother, Reverend Carmichael didn't speak during his sermons, he yelled. His messages were full of what not to do, how this would condemn you to hell, watch out for that. They were frightening to Sage as a child and when she grew older, they made her angry. Where was the love? Where was the service? Where was the caring?

As the story of Pastor's youth ended, giggles could be heard around the hall. It was an amusing story, which he followed by telling of the lesson learned from his experience. "Just as I literally fell and became covered with filth, we fall in our walk with Christ. But with his assistance, we are able to rise, cleanse, and go forward with Him again.

Sage could see heads nodding.

"But," he continued, "what about our neighbor? You know the one. The one living that sinful life. The one who walked into the bordello last night? The woman in that establishment? The man passed out from drink? The one whose greed has consumed him? The one who cheated on his wife? The one who killed? Can they be cleansed?

The congregation sat still, no heads moved.

"John chapter eight, verse seven tells us, '...He that is without sin among you, let him first cast a stone...' and Matthew chapter seven, verse one says 'Judge not, that ye be not judged.' But Pastor, you might add, those are really bad sins. Yes, their consequences can be dire, but James chapter two, verse ten tells us, 'For whosoever shall keep the whole law, and yet offend in one point, he is guilty of all.' Did you hear that friends? All. Guilty of all. I submit to you, we must not just turn away from our sins, but we must turn away from our judgment of others. If the adulterer walks in that door, he should be as welcome as I. If the courtesan enters, she too, is welcome. For Second Peter chapter three, verse nine says that 'The Lord is...not willing that any should perish, but that all should come to repentance.' He does not tell us that only those with small sins are welcome to repent. He does not tell us that we should decide their fate. He does tell us that if we have sinned by the smallest degree, we are just as guilty as the vilest of offenders. And just as we can repent and become clean from our sins, so can that vile person. While it is true the consequences are quite different if one steals a cookie than if one steals another's horse, both acts are sinful. Both can be forgiven. By God. My question to you is, can *you* forgive both? Can you forgive those harsh, inexcusable sins as you would forgive the theft of a cookie? My question to you, my friends, is this, if God can forgive, who are we to say it is unforgiveable? Are our standards higher than His? Are we greater than Him?" He paused. "Jesus gave us a new commandment, '...love one another.' He did not say to love only the righteous. He did not say to judge one another. He said to 'love one another.'"

As Pastor Witham spoke, Sage listened with fascination. She had heard many sermons, but none like this. While his message included the negative, don't be judgmental. His positive points within the message were overpowering. Forgive. Love. Welcome all. Sage could hardly wait to hear him talk next Sunday. She was also anxious to observe his ways throughout the week.

Sermon complete, Pastor Witham announced another hymn. Afterward he thanked everyone for coming, inviting all to return next Sunday. Then he said, "Anyone wishing to make an offering, the young lady next to the door," he indicated Margaret, "is holding a bag in which you may place your offering." He then prayed a closing prayer and gave a blessing on all.

Sage was surprised. At her mother's church, the offering had been a very public thing, with all able to tell if you gave or not. They even listed offering amounts in the church bulletin. Sage liked this new method of offering. Not only did it mean no pressure, anything given was freely given, it also meant the amount was between the giver and God. No one, even Pastor Witham, knew the amount.

A sudden idea struck Sage. She spoke before anyone left. "The congregation is welcome to dinner, on the house. If you would like to stay, just come on up, get your place setting, and visit until the meal is served." While the majority of the congregation were employees and would eat free anyway, the others seemed excited at the prospect. Their meal was served early, at the time the employees usually ate before allowing diners into the hall.

Sage sat across from Pastor Witham, whose eyes sparkled as though he had just won a coveted prize. "Thank you, Pastor, for your message."

"Am I doing okay?"

Sage suddenly felt as though she were judging him, "I'm sorry, by making this a trial, I hadn't meant to judge."

"Miss Brooks, you were right to be careful. Just because I say I preach the Word, doesn't mean I do. There are many out there who claim to be of God, but are not. The Good Book warns us of this."

She breathed a sigh of relief. "Thank you."

Mr. and Mrs. Freeman and Mr. and Mrs. Flegel sat next to them. Mr. Flegel was a jolly, likable man, perfectly suited to Mrs. Flegel. Sage saw the way they looked at one another; their eyes sparkled whenever one glanced the other's way. She knew from previous conversations they had been married sixteen years. What a blessing to have such an obvious affection after that long. Mr. Freeman was a quiet man. He mostly observed and listened. But Sage soon learned he had a warm, rolling laugh that made her feel good just hearing it. When he finally spoke, she realized who he reminded her of, James Earl Jones, the future actor. Not only did he look a great deal like the actor, his voice had that same distinctive, deep, calming quality to it.

This is nice. Why has it taken so long to meet these people? Sage wondered to herself. Of course, she knew the answer. They were all busy. The men were prospecting. The women were running Sage's Place. It was nice to have this time to gather together and enjoy each other's company for a while.

The next week's service went just as well. There were a couple of new people, for which Sage was glad. She once again invited the congregation to stay for dinner. After they were done and the regular diners were seated, Pastor helped clear the tables as people left. Initially planning to tell him it wasn't necessary, Sage decided to let it go. When all the diners left, he approached her.

"I believe, Miss Brooks, our two weeks is up."

"So it is. Do you feel things have gone well?"

"Yes, I do. Did you notice the new people at the service this morning?" He seemed excited.

"Yes, I did."

"The question, Miss Brooks, is, do you feel things have gone well?"

Sage looked at the pastor. She saw the hope in his eyes. "Let's have a seat." She motioned to a nearby table. "I hear you've been making your rounds among the miners."

"Yes, I have. While many are finding a great deal of gold, others aren't so fortunate. They are living in harsh conditions, with almost no food. Some have fallen ill. I try to help where I can."

"This is what I've heard. They say Pastor Witham truly cares. I like that. Will you please stay and continue to hold services in my dining hall?" She made it sound as though he would be doing her a favor.

"Oh, thank you, Miss Brooks!"

"There is a condition, though."

He seemed to hold his breath as he looked at her. "Yes?"

"You take one of the mules out with you when you go among the miners. I will have Mrs. Flegel fix food you can take with you, and when you find those who are hungry, feed them."

The pastor's smile was bright as he looked at her. "I knew you were a good and generous woman, Miss Brooks, from the moment we met."

She smiled. "Oh, one more condition."

He looked concerned.

"You really must stop calling me Miss Brooks. My name is Sage."

"Miss Sage it is then."

"Please, just Sage. Would you like me calling you Mr. Pastor."

He laughed. "Actually, the equivalent would be Mr. Robert or Pastor Robert. But if you insist, I will call you Sage if you will call me Robert. It would be a treat. Ever since I became a pastor it seems like my name's been changed to either Pastor or Preacher."

They laughed and Sage asked, "Where have you been staying?"

"I have a tent up on the hill. It's quieter and I can look out over the river."

"Please accept a room. I have quarters in the back for employees and would be pleased if you would take one."

"I'm not sure..."

"Come, I'll show you."

The two walked out the back door to the fourth room. Sage opened the door and Robert peered in.

"This room sleeps four."

"Yes, but you don't have to share it. We could move one of the beds out to room for a desk on which you could write your sermons."

"What are you currently doing with this room?"

"Since it hasn't been needed by any employees, we've been renting it out."

"I will move in here if you will continue to rent the other spaces. How many normally sleep here?"

Sage gave him a questioning look. "Four."

"Okay. With me here you can still rent to three."

"But..."

"No buts. It's the only way I'll move into it."

"Okay, under one condition."

"You like conditions, don't you," he said with a grin.

She gave him a look, and then continued. "All of the rents from those three guests go to the church building fund."

"Now that's a condition I can handle! I'll move in today." He looked again at the room. A puzzled look came upon his face.

"Is there a problem?"

"I made a wooden trunk in which to store my personal things, but I'm not sure it will fit. While I have no doubt it would fit at the end of the bed, it wouldn't be possible to get around the bed."

"Don't worry about that. You fit it however you need to and the maids will deal with it."

"I won't need maid service."

"Ah, but since you insist on sharing your room with guests, they do, so I'm afraid you are stuck with maid service." She gave him a sly look and headed back to the dining hall.

As she crossed the compound, Juan called to her from outside the new building. "Miss Sage, come see."

Sage smiled at her friend. She had encouraged him to drop the Miss, but he said it would not be appropriate and continued the practice. She couldn't help but wonder if the inappropriateness was due to him working for her or if it had to do with the racial difference. She hoped it was because he was working for her.

"It is done."

Sage looked at the building. The glass was in, the doors were on. Eduardo and Xavador were holding a sign for her inspection that said *Sage's Mercantile*. Once again, not the name she had planned, but she adored these brothers and wasn't about to change it. Inside, an abundance of shelves provided plenty of space for products.

"If you would like, after supper service, we will move the shop."

"Yes, perfect." Sage was astounded. It was wonderful.

"We also have more tables to take the space of the current shop. We will move Mrs. Gamble's shop into her new space as well." They escorted her to the room where Dodie's Sewing Shop had its own entrance and own sign. Then they entered the day care.

"Oh, this is wonderful!" All of the rooms had both a front and a back door. In the childcare room, there were wooden toys and child sized furniture. They had even built a play stove, doll cradle, and a carved miniature lantern. "You never cease to amaze me."

The men just smiled.

That evening, after the last of the diners left, Sage, the brothers, Dodie, Mary Jane Claus, and Pastor Robert moved the mercantile, the sewing shop, and the childcare into the new building. After moving everything, the women worked at organizing the mercantile, and the men moved the new tables into the dining hall where the shop and childcare had been. This allowed for ten additional tables, which meant they would be able to seat one hundred additional diners at once. With the entire public space now serving as dining hall, it necessitated a change at the entrance. They removed the barrier to the dining portion. Diners would now pay and get their dinnerware as they entered the door.

With all the extra space in Sage's Mercantile, they needed additional stock. Sage needed to make another trip to San Francisco. Her latest shipment should be waiting anyway.

The next morning, Mrs. Flegel handed Sage two baskets of eggs. "To sell at the Mercantile."

Sage looked at her, puzzled.

"We have so many chickens, and they are producing so well, we don't need all the eggs in the kitchen today. I boiled that basket, so the minors can have ready-to-eat food, and these are raw. Then she told Margaret to carry a crate to the Mercantile.

A questioning look from Sage brought a response. "I made several of loaves of bread for you to sell also. There's twenty of them. I figured as I have time, I'll just make things here and there for the Mercantile."

"While I'm not surprised you did this, Mrs. Flegel, what surprises me is that you can actually find any spare time!"

Mrs. Flegel just smiled and went back to work.

A timid knocking came at the kitchen door leading outside. Two young girls, about ten years of age, stood there, each with a large basket.

"Good morning, ladies. How may I help you?"

"We picked berries all day yesterday and thought maybe you could use them."

"Berries?" Mrs. Flegel hurried to the door. "Come on in girls. Let me look at those berries."

They sat their large baskets on the counter. Both were full of berries.

"Looks like you have gooseberries, strawberries, and thimbleberries. That's good. They're mixed and there's so many they've squashed each other, but they look ripe. Good job girls! We'll take them. If you get any more, bring them on by." Mrs. Flegel seemed excited.

"Actually, Ma'am, we've got two more baskets just like those back at the tent. We picked all day yesterday."

"You bring those, and we'll take all you've got."

Sage paid the girls for the berries, and said they would receive more when they brought the rest. Mrs. Flegel dumped all of the berries into a large kettle, and returned the baskets back to the girls, who ran off to fetch the other two baskets.

"What will you do with them?" Sage asked.

"At first I was thinking of making jelly. But I think I'll make pies instead. I believe all those hungry miners would appreciate pastry far more than jelly."

That afternoon, Pastor Witham hurried into the kitchen.

"Whoa there, Pastor! You can't just barge into my kitchen. What are you in such a hurry for?"

"Sorry, Mrs. Flegel, but I need a container. A big one!"

"Now what do you need a container for?"

His eyes twinkled. "Honey! I found a hive and I'm going to get us some honey."

"You're goin' to get stung is what you're goin' to do," said Mrs. Freeman.

"Oh no I won't! My granddaddy kept bees and he taught me how to work with them. So you ladies better start planning for honey." He grinned as Mrs. Flegel handed him two large glass jars.

With a raise of his eyebrows, he left the women to their work, both shaking their heads.

Several hours later, he was back. Both jars were brim full of the beautiful, dark golden, sticky substance. It was also covering the outside of the jars as well as Pastor Witham's hands. He smelled like smoke. At the look he received from the women, he said, "I should have asked for a scooping utensil. Anyway, we will have honey from now on. Juan built a beehive box. Together we were able to transfer the queen into the new hive box, along with several honey combs. Of course, the rest of the bees followed her." He raised both eyebrows and grinned. "Then we cleaned all the honey out of the old hive."

The ladies laughed. "Good job, Pastor!"

The honey butter served with the cornbread the next morning was delicious. Sage hadn't thought Mrs. Flegel's cornbread could get any better, but she was wrong. When she added the honey butter, it was better than eating a slice of yummy cake.

22

Sage expressed hesitancy about having the bee hive near the buildings. But Pastor Robert assured her the bees would increase the garden production through additional pollination. Though the garden already produced in vast quantities, the sheer number of people Sage's Place served on a daily basis required more. Plus, if they were to continue to provide a wide range of food, Mrs. Flegel informed them, they would need to put back for the winter. To this end she dried some of what they produced.

The woman was a marvel! She worked hard every day. All day. Though Sage had endeavored to convince Mrs. Flegel to take a day off, she staunchly refused. Because of Mrs. Flegel, Sage anticipated her upcoming trip to San Francisco as a child would Christmas morning. She expected, hoped, her surprise for her dear friend and chef had arrived.

Though she yearned to begin her journey, spurred by excitement at the prospect of filling the shelves in the new shop, Sage delayed her departure in hopes of assuring the new shipment's arrival. Juan and Xavador's trip had provided well, so a delay should not cause shortages in the kitchen. She would leave before that occurred.

Between the constant influx of new miners and the additional one hundred diners each meal, due to the added tables, business increased each day. Sage formulated an idea to increase it even further. Sage's Place would launch to-go meals. Bring your own plate and carry it out full of food. She hoped this would help to eliminate some of the grumbling over wait time for a space at the tables. Though they would not be able to cover the meal, patrons could take it outside to eat. This plan blossomed in her mind and she asked the brothers to build several picnic tables to place in the vacant lot next to Sage's Place. It included several trees and provided an excellent al fresco dining spot. To aid in this new idea, Sage determined to purchase a large quantity of plates, cups, and utensils to sell at the mercantile.

The idea took off. Soon, the picnic tables were full also. To expedite service, a narrow sideboard was set up. On it was the same selection of food and drink found on the tables. After paying, diners could serve themselves and take their meal outside. The disadvantage of this method to the patrons being they were only allowed one trip through. As a result, all but the uninitiated left with plates heaped with food.

The extra work required as a result of the to-go program and the extra tables meant they needed more help. Additionally, harvesting such a large garden, milking several cows, collecting so many eggs, washing linens, ironing, and all the other daily chores took a great deal of time. Once again Sage placed her help wanted sign in the front window.

The line of women at the door the next morning extended even longer than the previous one. Sage spoke to each woman and a few young girls, one as young as eight. While several were easy to dismiss, many left her yearning to hire them all. But she knew that would create chaos. In the end, she hired seven women. After juggling long-term employees to the more coveted positions, she would add two laundresses, two servers, two kitchen helpers, and one general helper.

Jorge and Xavador added another narrow island to the kitchen, providing additional work space. For now, laundry was done outside, but Sage requested a wash building be built as soon as possible. "Oh, while you're at it, could you make it two rooms? I think it would be nice to provide a place to bathe. Can you build a bathtub, or should I order one?" She asked Juan.

"We will build one. But Senorita Sage, who will service the room? You will need a man."

"I'll look for one immediately."

This, she discovered, proved a difficult task. Though the area was predominately men, they came to Coloma for one purpose only, to find gold. Finally, a young man who had accompanied his two brothers to the area, hoping to finance law school, applied. He hated the digging, the dirt, the rocks, everything to do with mining. He was thrilled to assist in the bath. While they awaited the completion of the bath room, Sage sent him to work with the Navarros.

With so much activity about the place, Sage barely noticed a young man knocking on the door between meals. Opening it, she said, "I'm sorry, but dinner isn't for another hour."

He nervously rolled the hat he held clenched in his hands around and around. "I'm not here for food, ma'am. I need to speak with Mrs. Flegel."

"I'm afraid she's quite busy," Sage said as she let him in, closing the door behind him. "Is there some way I can help you?"

"No, I'm afraid, uh no ma'am. See," He was stuttering uncomfortably. "It's about Mr. Flegel."

The way he said "Mr. Flegel" concerned Sage. He had paused before almost whispering the name. "I'll get Mrs. Flegel. You have a seat."

The young man didn't budge.

"Mrs. Flegel, there's a young man here to see you." Sage leaned into the kitchen and called.

"Can you tell him I just don't have time right now? My corned beef is about ready."

"I'm sure Mrs. Freeman can keep an eye on it. Whatever he wants seems important."

"Fine, fine, I'll be right out." She took one more peek before motioning to Mrs. Freeman to keep an eye open.

As she entered the dining hall and saw who awaited her, Mrs. Flegel said, "Why Richard Meyers, what are you doing here?"

The speed of the hat in his hands had increased. Sage wasn't sure that hat would ever be the same, as he was now twisting it. "Mrs. Flegel, I come to get you."

"Why ever would you do such a thing?" Just after saying this, concern crossed the woman's face.

"It's Mr. Flegel, ma'am." His look did not bode well. Sage moved closer to Mrs. Flegel.

"Tell me, what about Mr. Flegel, Richard?"

"He's been shot."

"What! How? Why? Who?"

"Some feller came along and thought he was gonna take all that Mr. Flegel's been working so hard for. Don't know his name, never seen him before. Well, Mr. Flegel laughed at the man, thought it was a joke, a way of meetin' someone I guess. Then the guy pulls a gun, points it at Mr. Flegel and shoots. My brother James, he picked up his rifle and shot the guy dead."

"Oh my, oh my." Mrs. Flegel seemed to be having trouble processing what she had just heard.

Sage held onto her friend. "Richard, is Mr. Flegel alive? Her words were spoken slowly, hesitantly, but with emphasis.

"Yes, ma'am. But he's doing poorly. I come to get Mrs. Flegel."

Sage snagged Willa Jacob as she passed by and told her to get Juan. "Let him know we need Pastor Witham." The urgency in her voice sent Willa scurrying out of the room. Then, to Ethel Jonas, who was now a server, she said, "Ethel, tell Mrs. Freeman we need her immediately."

After a quick explanation Sage accompanied Mrs. Flegel out the front door, down the steps and turned right down the road toward the Flegel tent. They hadn't gone far before Juan and Pastor Witham joined them.

"I was working with Juan today," the pastor explained. "What's happened?"

As Sage told them about the shootings, she saw tears trickling down Mrs. Flegel's cheeks. "We must hurry," Mrs. Flegel said as she picked up her skirt and began to run.

The rest of them ran with her, receiving pitying looks from those they passed. Sage realized word of the shooting had already spread. As Mrs. Flegel stopped near a tent, she looked at another man, who was even younger than Richard.

In response to the wordless question, he said, "We put him on the bed in the tent. James is with him."

Both ends of the tent were open, allowing air to flow through in the heat of the day. Mrs. Flegel entered the tent and knelt next to the bed, which was actually a pallet on the ground.

Blood pulsing from his chest, Mr. Flegel appeared to display a great deal of trouble breathing, causing Sage to assume the bullet had struck a lung.

"Can anything be done?" She asked this of no one in particular.

"We heard tell of a doctor down river some. Joe Bandis, he's down a few tents, ran to see if he could find him." This answer came from Richard's younger brother.

Mr. Flegel didn't seem to be able to talk, but in answer to his wife's heartfelt words of love, he slowly lifted her hand and kissed it. The touching action seemed to take the last measure of strength he had. His eyes closed and Sage could see him mouth the words, "I love you, Agnus." He attempted a breath, but seemed to accomplish nothing more than a horrible squeak. Then he was still. Terribly, heartbreakingly still.

"No, no August, no. Don't leave me." The words spoken by the distraught new widow could barely be heard. It was as though when he died, he took her breath with him. There just wasn't enough in her to make the words fully audible.

Sage's tears came as a torrent. Though she barely knew Mr. Flegel, her love and admiration for his wife was immeasurable. Sage wanted to say the right things, do the right things, but she wasn't good at this. She had no idea what should be either said or done. If anything.

Mrs. Flegel lay her head down next to his, holding him, cradling him. Sobbing, crying, keening for her love, she seemed inconsolable. Then all became quiet. A few sobs were still visible by the shake of her shoulders, but no sound was heard. With time, she sat up, brushed August Flegel's hair to the side, leaned over and kissed his still warm lips, and took a deep breath.

With this, the Pastor seemed to know instinctively that it was time to step in. He held her shoulders and whispered something so only she could hear. Then he said, "Let us pray."

Sage realized there had not even been time for a formal prayer after their arrival. It was as if he had been holding on for the arrival of his beloved.

"Father God, we thank you for the man before us. This good, good man, husband, and friend. Thank you for the blessing he has been. The time ahead will be very hard, Father, for he was much loved and will be sadly missed.

Please hold our dear Agnus Flegel in your loving arms. We beseech you Lord, bestow upon her the faith, strength, courage, and forgiveness she will need in the coming days to weather this most difficult storm. And Father, if you will, lead us, her friends, in aiding her through this most painful challenge. We trust in you, oh Lord. In Jesus name we pray, Amen."

Once again Pastor Robert said quiet words to the grieving widow. After a moment, she nodded. He stepped out of the tent and stood in front of Juan, speaking quietly. "Please bring the wagon." Pastor turned to Sage, who was next to Juan. "If it is okay, we will lay him out in my room."

"We will lay him out in the fifth room." Sage spoke with a dull tone, but with finality. There would be no discussion. Sage then spoke to James in the same empty tone. "I assume someone will give the murderer a decent burial."

"Yes, ma'am."

When August Flegel's body was moved to room five of the employee quarters, the Flegel tent and other belongings were also brought. Though both Willa and Sage tried to convince Mrs. Flegel to bunk with them, she insisted on sleeping on the other bed in room five. "It's the last opportunity I'll have to be near my dear August."

Three days later, after August Flegel had been laid to rest on the hill up from Sage's Place, which Sage assumed would now become the town cemetery, Mrs. Flegel resumed her place in the kitchen. All who knew her were aware she would find comfort in cooking. And cook she did. She seemed intent on making all of her husband's favorites to serve to the miners. Especially desserts. Cake after cake came out of that wood oven. Then there were donuts. Only these donuts had no holes and she called them Kreppel, as her German family had taught.

Daily, Sage saw Mrs. Flegel trek up to the grave, carrying one of her delicious creations. She would lay it on the grave, wipe a few tears, and then return to her kitchen. Each day the offering from the previous day would be gone, eaten by the squirrels, chipmunks, birds, and other grateful critters that were beginning to anticipate the daily ritual.

23

A week after the funeral, it was time to leave for San Francisco. Mrs. Flegel seemed to be doing well, though all the baking had seriously depleted their supplies. *Bake as much as you need to,* thought Sage. Her heart ached for her friend. *I will bring back all the flour I can find.*

Jorge would accompany her. Sweet on a girl, he missed seeing her. While she was young, only sixteen, her father approved of their courtship. At nineteen, Jorge demonstrated extreme maturity for his age, but after so many months of missing his girl, he wanted to verify they were still in a good place. Though letters had been exchanged through Juan's trip to San Francisco, it wasn't the same.

Jorge was the best driver of the three younger brothers. It bothered Sage that she didn't know how to drive a wagon and was determined to learn during the trip. However, she thought it best that she observe for a while, since she had never even ridden on one as a passenger. Juan agreed.

He seemed nervous to see them go. He checked and double checked the wagon, the way the mules were hitched to it, and the mule train tethered to the back of the wagon. "You are a mother hen, hermano." Jorge told him as he and Sage waited for the final check.

"And a safe one, too. You be careful and hurry back. Adios, Senorita Sage. Enjoy yourself while you are away."

Though Sage offered Buddy a ride in the wagon, for now he resisted. He ran with it, checking the mules and marking his territory. Surely he would run out of marking material before reaching San Francisco.

Sage waved at Juan as they drove off. New experiences: riding in a wagon, driving a wagon, and traveling with someone. She couldn't help but be excited. This would be a welcome relief after the stress of the last ten days.

While Mrs. Flegel didn't complain or weep, it was there, always there. Her husband was lost to her and Sage was at a loss for words. This bothered her. After all, her degree was in psychology. This should qualify her for grief counseling. But she was dumbstruck. She could talk to an addict all day long. She could council them, guide them, listen to them. But she was lost when it came to grief counseling.

Thank goodness for Pastor Robert! She thought as she glimpsed him just before losing sight of Sage's Place. He was a genius when it came to speaking with Mrs. Flegel. She always seemed to come away from talks with him doing just a little better. *I need to talk to him about it. See how he does it. Maybe with a bit of insight, I'll feel more comfortable.*

Sage was pulled back from her thoughts when Buddy chased a squirrel. "Buddy, come!" With a dejected look, he walked back to the wagon. "Shame on you! What were you doing? You have work to do. Go check on the mules," she said, with a backward glance. He looked at her with the appearance of being properly chastised, then turned and headed back to the mules. *Astounding,* she thought. *He seems to understand everything I say to him.* "Good boy, Buddy! Good boy." He wagged his tail and seemed to walk with his head higher at the praise.

The trip seemed longer in the wagon. The constant jarring and bumping was not a comfortable ride. She would rather ride her horse any day. While she did have her horse with her, she needed to either observe how to drive or to be driving. By the time they made the return trip, one of them would drive and the other ride the horse to keep an eye on the mules and their loads. She must feel comfortable driving the wagon before it was loaded and Jorge wasn't on the seat beside her.

Other than a few incoming prospectors, who tried valiantly to purchase Sage's mules, the trip to San Francisco was uneventful. It was good to see Ford was still at his ferry, only he had a new, larger ferry. Sage was glad he hadn't succumbed to gold fever. Jorge stayed with the mules while Ford took Sage, Buddy, the hitched team and wagon to the city.

It was no longer the quaint little hamlet she visited initially. San Francisco had grown. While Sage knew it would continue to grow a lot in the next few years, it still amazed her to see it look so different each time she visited.

"Miss Brooks! I hadn't expected you back so soon after Juan's visit. Welcome back!" Mr. Brine's greeting was music to Sage's ears. It was nice to have friends. "I owe you a debt of gratitude. The ideas we talked about when you were here last time are working out just fine. I've never enjoyed myself so much as I am making furniture."

Sage chatted with Mr. Brine, telling him Jorge would be along soon with the rest of the stock. She then took Buddy to the back of the boarding house for a bath. As she dried him, Molly stepped out the back door.

"Sage! I had no idea you were here. Buddy, hey boy, all clean and beautiful as always, I see. Come in, come in. It's so good to see you. Will you be able to stay long?"

Molly's enthusiasm over their visit warmed Sage's heart. "Molly, my friend. It's so good to see you. We'll just be here two nights. We need to get back with supplies. I know it's late in the day, but do you still have a room available?"

"For you, I'll make one. Build it if I have to. Speaking of building, did you notice the addition off the back of the house? We added a bath! I'm cooking for guests also. Just like you suggested. Before Jonathan settles in for the evening, he'll run whatever laundry our guests have to the laundress and will pick it up early in the morning. You're a genius, Sage!"

Sage was bothered. "Molly, how can you make a room? Are you full?"

"We had a gentleman check in about an hour ago. He wanted a private room, so I gave him my only remaining room rather than having him bunk in with one of the other guests. But I told him if the need arose, I may have to move him to share a room anyway. Well, the need has arisen!"

"I don't want to put one of your guests out of his room."

"Now Sage, don't you worry about that. You won't be, I will." She grinned. Then seeing a man descending the staircase, she called out, "Oh, Mr. Butler, I need to speak with you for a moment."

"Yes, Mrs. Brine. How may I be of service?"

"Mr. Butler, this is Miss Brooks. She is a dear friend of mine, always welcome here when she is in town. Since we are otherwise booked full, I'm afraid I will need to move you in with Mr. Owens in room three."

Mr. Butler quickly covered a spark of irritation. "Well, for such a beautiful lady as this, I would be pleased to give up my room. How long will you be joining us, Miss Brooks?"

"Only a couple of nights, I'm afraid." Something about Mr. Butler's slick manner bothered Sage. "And you, Mr. Butler?"

"I'll be staying until I get my business built."

"Ah, a business man. And what sort of business will you be opening?"

He reached down, petting Buddy lightly. Sage noticed Buddy did not wag his tail. Instead, he laid his ears back on his head.

While Sage was just making polite small talk, Mr. Butler's reaction to her question set her on edge.

"Oh my, look at the time. I really must get to a meeting. Mrs. Brine, please feel free to move my satchel into room three." He tipped his hat. "Miss Brooks." At that, he rushed out of the house.

Sage received the distinct impression her question had been shelved, ignored.

"Come on back, Sage, and we'll get you a nice hot bath while I go move Mr. Butler's satchel. I'm sorry if we made him late for his meeting. He seems a very sophisticated gentleman."

Sage wondered about this, but without more information, refrained from commenting.

Once the water was heated and the tub full, Sage thanked Molly. Then, noticing the soap on the holder in the tub, said "Oh, more of the lavender soap. Molly, thank you so much for the soap you sent to me. I wish I had a way of thanking you when I received it. I love it!"

Molly squeezed her friend's arm, "I'm so glad you've enjoyed it," then left the room so Sage could bathe.

At supper that evening, Mr. Butler's eyes shot up at the sight of Sage in a dress. "Miss Brooks, you look quite lovely this evening."

"Thank you, Mr. Butler. I certainly feel better." Sage did not care to engage in an extended conversation with the man, so she hurried into the kitchen to assist Molly in whatever way she could.

The large table, which Mr. Brine made after her last visit, was crowded with guests. The food was delicious and

Molly confided while they were in the kitchen that the food service was a very profitable aspect of their business.

As they completed their meal, there was a knock on the front door. Mr. Brine answered it, and returned to tell Sage she had a visitor. Sage was surprised to find Jorge at the door.

"I thought perhaps you might like my assistance tomorrow with the shopping."

"Thank you, Jorge, but I'll be fine. You enjoy yourself. We'll meet at Mr. Watson's General Store at 4:00 the next morning to load the supplies."

Jorge smiled. "I told Mama you would say that, but she said I must ask anyway. She still thinks I am a child."

Sage laughed. "I think, Jorge, you will always be her child. Are you spending the day with your girl?"

"Sí. We are going for a picnic. She is making the food."

Sage enjoyed the grin the young man wore. "You enjoy yourselves. I'll see you at four."

As she waved him off, she heard the voice of Mr. Butler behind her. "Is he a servant of yours?"

Sage was unable to keep the irritation from her voice, "No, he is my friend. He and his brothers own a construction company and have done a lot of building for me."

"Oh." The judgment in the man's eyes and voice was clear. "And where would that be?"

Sage was not about to tell this too-slick man where they lived. "At home," she said in an obvious manner. *His slick ways and too-smooth speech remind me too much of*

228

Rory, she couldn't help but think as she entered the kitchen to help Molly with the dishes before retiring to her room for the evening.

The next morning, she rose early to assist with the breakfast service. Though Molly kept insisting she was a guest and ought not to be in the kitchen, Sage refused to sit while her friend worked. Plus, remaining in the dining room meant possible exposure to Mr. Butler, which she hoped to avoid.

Sage did not meet many people she didn't like, but when she did, her instincts were usually correct. Struggling with whether she should say something to Molly, Sage finally decided; after all, she hoped a friend would do the same for her. "Molly, have you noticed how Mr. Butler artfully avoids telling us what kind of business he will be opening?"

"I have been wondering what it will be, but assumed he had a reason for not telling us."

"I believe you're right, he has a reason. I need to come out and say this. I don't trust the man. He's too slick and evasive. Please be careful of him, Molly."

Molly studied Sage. "Jonathan said the same thing, but I just haven't seen it. If both of you are cautious, then I'll be cautious too."

After breakfast, Molly insisted Sage not help with the dishes but get on with conducting the business she had come to San Francisco to transact. Mr. Watson was just opening his store as she arrived.

"Miss Brooks, it's good to see you again. Your latest order arrived about a week ago."

"Oh, I'm so glad to hear it. What I'm really wanting to know is, did the stove arrive?"

"Yes, Miss, it certainly did. And I'm sure glad you've come to take it out of my store room. It's a giant of a thing."

"Oh good! Are there people around to help us load it today?"

"Yes, I can wrangle up a few hefty men. I hope you'll have plenty of helpers to unload it."

"Oh yes."

They walked into his back room to look at the stove, and Mr. Watson said, "By the way, your man, Juan, ordered a meat grinder when he was here. I had already ordered some and they arrived at the same time as your stove, so I held one back for you."

"Thank you. Mrs. Flegel will be thrilled. She's been hoping to make bratwurst when we butcher the pig. That'll be when..." Sage stopped. Stunned. The stove before her was beautiful. She thought she ordered an all black stove, but apparently the black and white drawing in Mr. Watson's catalog couldn't portray all the shiny silver trim. The double, side-by-side ovens would come in handy as would the warming shelf above the burners. "Wow!"

"Told you it was big. You got room for that thing?"

"Yes. We planned space for it when designing the kitchen." Despite knowing what it was and that it was expected, Sage was still stunned. Mrs. Flegel would be

230

thoroughly flabbergasted! She had no idea it had been ordered. It was a surprise.

"The rest of your order is in the crates next to it. Did you bring help for loading in the morning?"

"Oh yes. I'm done making solo trips. Too much loading and unloading for one person."

Sage browsed the store, adding several items to her purchases. "Do you have a lot of flour?"

Mr. Watson pointed to a stack of flour sacks in the corner. "Until the next shipment, that's it. Yours is back with the stove and other stuff. You need more than that?"

"I'll take as much as you'll sell me. Our chef, Mrs. Flegel, buried her husband last week and she seems to find consolation in baking. Our guests love it." She spotted a few cans of fruit on the shelf. "Is that all the fruit you have?"

"Oh no, I've got several crates, but they're stuck behind your stove. I've been hoping you'd come get it before the shelf emptied."

"Oh good, I'll need a bunch of that too."

"I got something in on the last ship you might be interested in. Trees."

"Mr. Watson, we have all sorts of trees in Coloma."

"Fruit trees?"

"Nope, we sure don't. Let's take a look."

Sage purchased forty-three trees: apple, cherry, peach, pear, plum, and walnut. While it would take a while for them to produce, it would be worth the wait. They could plant the orchard behind the picnic tables.

Telling Mr. Watson she would be back with the wagon at three, she went to browse the other shops. There were several new ones since her last visit. As she exited his store, she wondered what the large structure being built across the street would be.

Finally, just before time to go back to Molly's for dinner, she arrived at Mrs. Jones' house. The woman was thrilled to see Sage.

"Miss Brooks, this chair is a wonder. How did you ever think of such a thing?" She demonstrated the wheeled chair Jonathan Brine had built at Sage's request.

"I'm so glad you like it, Mrs. Jones. Do you have any new quilts?"

"Oh, yes. Only two, though. It hasn't been long since Mr. Navarro collected the last ones."

"I'll take what I can get. You make the loveliest quilts. My guests love them."

As Sage took the quilts and turned to leave, Mrs. Jones said, "Now you be sure and stop by Mrs. Greeson's. She may have even more for you."

Sage got directions to the Greeson residence and hurried to avoid being late for dinner. Mrs. Greeson did, indeed, have more quilts than Mrs. Jones. Five, to be exact. Mrs. Greeson lived with her grown son and insisted he carry the quilts to Molly's house for Sage.

Sage found the presence of Mr. Butler quite annoying. He added a tension to the gathering which she had never felt in the Brine home before. Several times during the meal she attempted to discover what sort of business he would be opening, only to be ignored, interrupted, or even laughed at. *What is he hiding?* While it may be none of her business, he was staying at her friends' home, and that put her on edge.

After dinner Sage hitched the mules to the wagon and headed to Mr. Watson's to pick up her stove and anything else to be loaded on the wagon. An hour later the stove was loaded into the center of the wagon bed, stretching all the way from front to back. Other items were loaded in and around the stove. No space was wasted. With the load secured with several lengths of rope, Sage pulled away to park the load at Jonathon Brine's livery until time to leave in the morning. It was a slow trip. The mules seemed to struggle on San Francisco's hills.

When she arrived, Mr. Brine's eyes opened wide. "Wow, that's quite a load you've got there!"

"Yes. I'm a little concerned. What do you think?"

"I think I'd better install some additional bracing under that wagon. When we hitch up in the morning, we'd better hitch six mules instead of four. You're going to need to take it easy on the trip back. Maybe take a couple extra days."

"Whatever you say. Do you have any more mules I can purchase so I don't lose the packing space?"

"Afraid not. With all the prospectors coming through, my sources have all sold out. I've requested some be shipped in, but I'm not sure if they'll show or not.

Actually, it's a good thing I'm an honest man; I could have sold all your mules ten times over during the short time you've been here. Had one man offer me ten times the usual price for one."

Sage's eyebrows went up. "Well, I sure do appreciate you not selling my mules out from under me." She laughed. Then with a look of concern she asked, "Are they safe out here?"

"Don't you worry, they won't go anywhere."

Molly said good-by as Sage prepared to leave the following morning. It had been a frustrating visit. With Molly so busy and Mr. Butler always underfoot, it seemed as though they'd hardly seen one another.

Jorge arrived right on time. When Sage asked how he enjoyed the picnic, he didn't answer, but his grin did. The young man was seriously in love. After a moment, he said, "I asked her father's permission to marry."

Sage looked at him, awaiting the answer.

"Next trip to town, we'll wed. I'm going to need to build us a place."

"I'm so happy for you. The barn should be done by the time we return, you and your brothers can start on a cabin right away. You will stay in Coloma?"

"Sí. I cannot leave our business. We still have much building to do. We can't come back here; I think my brother is sweet on Senorita Martinez. Besides, what would you do without us?"

"I've wondered that myself." She didn't bother to ask which bother or which Senorita Martinez.

With two less mules for packing and warned by Mr. Brine not to add one more item to the wagon, it created a tight squeeze fitting everything. But with the sunrise, they headed out. Ford's eyes got big when he saw the load on the wagon. It made for a tight squeeze onto the new ferry, and the weight produced concern, but the crossing was uneventful. Jorge came next with the horse, leading the mule train with two more milk cows, and five steers attached.

It was a difficult trip. There was so much to unload each night, it was as though Sage was alone again. The going was slow through the day, with frequent rest stops required. Finally, after seven nights under the stars, they reached Sage's Place. The trip took longer than when Sage walked to San Francisco.

The dining hall was closed for the evening by the time they arrived. The brothers, Willa Jacob, and Mrs. Flegel all gathered to help unload. It would be another long night.

When they unloaded the wagon enough to see the stove, Mrs. Flegel gasped. Then she began sobbing. Sage was stunned. "Mrs. Flegel?"

The woman embraced Sage in a warm, motherly hug. "My dear, you are a true blessing. My August always

235

wanted to get me a cook stove. He said anyone who could cook like me deserved the best. You, my sweet friend, have fulfilled his wishes."

There was not a dry eye in the group as they stood, admiring that stove, wondering how they were going to unload it and move it into the kitchen.

Finally, Juan said, "I'll be right back with help." He walked around the building as the others watched him go.

After a few moments, Mrs. Flegel said, "Let's get these poor mules unloaded so they can have a well deserved rest." Each of them grabbed a pannier and laid it on the ground. Soon all the pack mules were unloaded and released for the evening.

Just as they were ready to begin unpacking the panniers, Juan returned with six burley men in tow. Sage recognized them all as regulars at Sage's Place.

The men studied the problem for a while. They took turns making suggestions of how best to get it off the wagon. Finally, they decided it called for shear brute force. This was the same tactic the men at Watson's store had settled upon. Jorge parked the wagon close to the kitchen door and the Navarro brothers all climbed onto the back of it. The ladies were admonished to "stay back." The brothers pushed as the six burley guys pulled. More and more stove hung off the end of the wagon. Before it reached the point of tipping, Sage yelled, "Stop!"

Everyone looked at her. "Before it goes further, there are no feet. It's a box. Before you bring it down to the ground, we need several small round logs to act as wheels. The stove will roll over them and as the stove rolls off the back log, it can be moved to the front, allowing forward movement."

The men all thought about it for a moment before a grunt of approval was heard.

"The fence posts we've been making!" Eduardo said as he jumped off the wagon and ran to retrieve some.

Soon, five round fence posts lay side-by-side on the ground behind the wagon. Two more were ready to place in front of the stove. All the Navarros climbed back in the wagon and the burley men waited to heft it onto the rolling logs as it came off the wagon. As the full weight of the stove was being held by the burley volunteers, all four Navarros jumped off the wagon to assist.

Sage was nervous. She watched, holding her breath. *Please don't let anyone get injured.* One man began to bend over to lower the stove. She shouted, "Bend with your knees, not your back!"

Finally, the stove sat on the fence posts. All present breathed a sigh of relief. The man who had bent at his back straightened up with his hands on the back of his hips. Sage hoped he wasn't hurt.

With five men on each side of the stove they pushed it forward. It moved. Soon it was at the door, but the fence posts were wider than the door. The stove blocked the door.

"Wait, I'll go through the front and you can hand me fence posts." Sage rushed to the front of the building. In the kitchen, she asked for the available posts and placed them in front of the stove. The men pushed and soon the stove was on top of the new posts. They handed her more posts. Before long, half the stove was in the kitchen. "Do

237

you think when it comes off the posts you can push it into place?"

One of the men gave a cocky reply. "No problem!"

"Okay, I think we need to stop using the posts so it will go onto the floor."

"It'll scratch your floor."

Sage figured whoever said that had been raised well. "That's okay. It'll be a memory marker." Sage was happy to have it inside with the men all in one piece.

Before long, the stove sat entirely on the floor and the men pushed and shoved it into place. Juan looked at it. "We'll attach the stove pipe in the morning." He thanked the volunteers.

They turned to leave but Sage stopped them. "Thank you so much for your assistance. I don't know what we would have done without you. Wait here for just a moment." Sage stepped into the dining hall, returning with the slips of paper they had used for meal tickets. Using a piece of charcoal from the fireplace, she wrote on each one. Handing each man a slip of paper she said, "This will allow you free meals for a month. Thank you so much."

Nods and smiles were directed her way before the men left.

Turning to Juan, she asked, "How did you find them so quickly?"

Juan sheepishly responded, "The gambling hall."

"Smart thinking. Thank you guys, I know this was a lot of work."

They gazed at the huge stove. It was a beauty.

"I can hardly wait to put it to use." Mrs. Flegel's eyes glowed like a young child anticipating a long-awaited gift.

Finally, they continued putting the rest of the shipment away. When everything had been placed in its general area, Sage left the kitchen to Mrs. Flegel and went to stock the shop. It would be good to have full shelves again.

Sage finished arranging shelves just as the light showed in the sky. *I'd better make sure Mrs. Flegel was able to get the kitchen done before needing to start breakfast,* she thought as she closed the shop and headed for the kitchen. She cut through the dining hall and breathed in the yeasty aroma of baking bread. She skipped supper in her rush to get home the night before, and her mouth watered. The kitchen door gave a slight squeak as she pushed it open, *I'll need to oil that.* Then she gasped at the sight before her.

Sitting on the shelf above the fireplace were several loaves of bread, ready for the oven. In the fireplace oven she could see several more loaves baking. In the large pot hanging in the fireplace, was something doing a slow boil. Then, looking quite content and standing before the new stove, was Mrs. Flegel. There were pots covering the top of the stove, all in various stages of heating. Sage raised her eyes to the stove pipe going through the wall behind the stove.

"What! How?"

239

"It's those Navarro boys. Aren't they the most amazing things you've ever seen? They refused to leave until this beautiful monstrosity was hooked up and ready for me to start cooking. I've got cornbread baking in both ovens as we speak." The head chef grinned, giddy with pleasure.

"Did you get any sleep?"

"Pshaw, who needs sleep with a stove like this? I'm too excited to sleep. I just started baking and cooking. Wait until the others see this. They'll think they're still asleep and dreaming."

Just then Mrs. Freeman entered the kitchen, followed by Margaret. Both stood still, shock at the sight before them preventing communication. Then Mrs. Reynolds entered the kitchen. Her whole face lit up. "Well, will you just look at that. You bring that back with you, Miss Sage?"

"Yes, I did." Sage found her rather nonchalant comment amusing.

"We'll have food just flying out of here with that big ol' thing."

Mrs. Flegel took over. "I'm about to take my first pans of cornbread out of it." She opened one of the ovens and pulled out a large pan of beautiful, golden cornbread and sat it on the island. Then she pulled a second one out of the same oven, placing it right next to the first. Opening the other oven, she pulled out two more, which were every bit as beautiful as the first two. Then, from the counter under the window, one-by-one she shoved four more pans of cornbread batter into the ovens to bake. Turning to her spectators, she grinned. Then, taking the loaves of bread out of the fireplace oven and adding more to bake, she turned back to the ladies and grinned again.

Just then Willa, Salome, and Ariana came in with several buckets of milk and two large baskets full of eggs. The three ladies stood stock still, staring in wonder at the sight before them. By this time Margaret and Mrs. Freeman had recovered from their astonishment and took the milk from Willa and Salome. Mrs. Reynolds gently pried the egg baskets from Ariana's hands, saying, "I'd better save these eggs."

Sage heard a faint knocking at the door of the dining hall. "Excuse me ladies, time to go to work."

Opening the door, Sage was greeted by Mrs. Hanson, who held a bulging flour sack. "Miss Brooks. I don't know if you're ready, but I've brought more socks. Hope I'm not too early."

"Mrs. Hanson, so good to see you again. No, you're not too early. In fact, your timing is perfect. I just returned last night with a new shipment, which includes lots of yarn. The shop is now next door; shall we go take a look?"

In the shop, Sage showed Mrs. Hanson where her socks were kept for sale. "There aren't many here, you must have a storeroom with the rest?"

Sage laughed. "No storeroom. That's all we have left. Even with Dodie next door doing a lot of darning, these men seem to eat through socks. I'll take all you have."

They counted out seventy-eight pairs of socks. Sage was astounded by the speed which the woman knitted.

After placing them in the basket with the other socks, they went to look at the yarn.

"Can I take it all?" The woman asked timidly.

"Of course. I brought it all with you in mind."

They settled the financial aspect of the deal, with Sage paying Mrs. Hanson the difference. There was too much yarn for Mrs. Hanson to carry it all in one trip, so Sage offered to help her. With a word into the kitchen, they were on their way.

The Hanson's claim was in an area Sage had not yet seen. Beyond the sawmill and into the hills a couple of miles. The walk was nice and she saw a few people she recognized from the dining hall. Why she was surprised at the number of tents along the way, she wasn't sure. She couldn't help but wonder where everyone would squeeze in by this time of year in 1849 or 1850.

Various aromas greeted Sage as they walked: campfire smoke, unwashed bodies, the heat of summer on the trees, cooking breakfasts, and many that were unidentifiable. Sage enjoyed it all. *I need to get out and walk more,* she thought. *But how can I go enjoy myself when so many employees work such long hours?* She decided it was time to hire a second set of employees so everyone could have time off. *The weekly pay will need to remain the same so it doesn't hurt anyone financially.*

Before leaving the Hanson's claim, she handed Mrs. Hanson a large chunk of cornbread, wrapped in a towel.

"Why thank you so much. Here, let me find something to put that on so you can take your towel back with you."

Sage hadn't seen Mr. Hanson. She assumed he was one of the many men she saw at the river, working for gold. As she left Mrs. Hanson sat on a blanket and leaned against a tree. She picked up her current knitting project and continued working. Sage was glad the woman had something she enjoyed to fill her time while her husband dreamed of striking it rich.

24

Coloma already presented as a rough, unruly place. Far too many men, with too much gold and no idea how to spend it except on booze, gambling, and women, crowded into the area. Often a night on the town turned a man who found riches into a pauper. The next day he returned to his diggings. This cycle repeated itself all too often. If only they would invest their riches in a business or just go home. Then they stood a chance of retaining their wealth.

On the walk back to Sage's Place, a familiar face caught Sage's eye. Carrie, the girl who applied for a job but an addiction to the elixir containing laudanum prevented Sage from hiring her. Her face and body contorted in pain. Her withdrawal should have been complete long before now.

"Carrie, do you remember me?"

"You're the lady with the dining hall?"

"Yes, I am. Did you ever find your elixir?"

"Yes, a man came though selling some. A different name, but it worked just as good. But I'm out again. Do you know where to get some more? Do you sell it now? It's good medicine. It keeps this sickness away."

Sage asked to sit next to her. After settling in at a level equal with the girl, Sage ventured forth, "Carrie, the medicine is what's making you sick."

"No, I'm only sick when I don't take it."

"I know this is difficult to understand, but you're a smart girl, so I'm sure you will have no trouble. The medicine contains laudanum, an opiate. It's very addictive. When your body is used to having it, and doesn't get it, your body gets angry and sick. You feel better when you take it because your body has what it has been taught to crave, not because it's good for you. Carrie, the medicine is very harmful to your body. It will eventually kill you."

"But I'm only fourteen."

Sage let out a sigh of sorrow. She thought the girl was at least seventeen. "Do you think being fourteen means you can't die?"

"Well, no, but it's not like I've taken this for years and years."

"It doesn't matter. Your body adjusts to having it very quickly and feels the need for it when it doesn't get it. Do you like feeling like you do now?"

"No." Her answer was said in a sad, quiet squeak.

"Carrie, I can help you. Together, we could get you through the sickness of not having the drug. Together, we can find a normal life for you again. If you want to, that is."

"But I like the way it makes me feel. It just keeps taking more and more so I run out really fast and then I get sick."

"That's because your body builds a tolerance to it. When you run out, and your body is screaming for it; that is a sign that the drug is holding your body captive. Carrie, do you want to be captive to the elixir?

"No, I want to stop hurting so much. When I started taking it, I had sprained my ankle and the traveling doctor said the elixir would make it feel better. It did, too. But then I ran out and got sick. I keep getting sick. Over and over. It healed my ankle, it doesn't hurt any more, ever. Why doesn't it heal whatever's making me sick?"

"The elixir didn't heal your ankle, Carrie, time healed your ankle. The elixir just made it so you didn't feel your ankle hurting. It can't heal what's making you sick now, because it's the elixir making you sick."

"Then why do I feel better when I take it?"

Carrie's lack of understanding of the addiction she was trapped in caused them to talk in circles. Sage needed to try a different approach.

"Carrie, have you ever seen anyone who drinks a lot?"

"Yes, my uncle drank all the time. He was angry when he didn't have anything to drink. He died last year."

"Do you think he would have been okay if he had just stopped drinking?"

"Yes. People tried to get him to stop, but he wouldn't."

"Was it drinking that made him sick and caused him to die?"

"Oh, it was drinking all right."

"Well, that elixir is like the alcohol he drank. Just as his body and mind craved the alcohol, your body is craving the elixir."

"Is that why I hurt so bad? Uncle Hyrum said he hurt when he didn't have any alcohol."

"Yes, it is."

"But, I don't want to die! I want to get married and have babies and a home."

"Carrie, you can choose to live. Stay with me for a little while. Together, we will convince your body it doesn't need that awful elixir anymore."

"Okay. Will I feel better tomorrow?"

"I'm sorry to say this, but you will feel much, much worse before you feel better. This won't be easy, Carrie, but it will give you your life back."

Carrie sat, shaking and sweating. Her eyes darted back and forth, looking all around her. "I don't want to feel worse, but I do want to feel better. If ma and pa say it's okay, I'll go with you."

They searched for Carrie's parents. They found her mother outside their tent, changing a baby's diaper. They found her father panning for gold. Sage introduced herself and told them what she had told Carrie. Their shock exposed their ignorance of the elixir being the source of her illness. Like Carrie, they thought it made her better, since she seemed to improve when she took it.

When Sage explained who she was and what she hoped to do, they hesitated. "Could we come see her?"

"Of course. But you need to understand, she will get much worse before she gets better." Sage explained the withdrawal process, about how long it would take, and the importance of Carrie never having another drop of elixir or anything like it.

Finally, after a long discussion, the parents agreed for Carrie to go with Sage. Mr. Edwards insisted on accompanying Sage and Carrie to town. If he felt comfortable with everything, she would be allowed to stay.

As they walked to Sage's Place, the intense withdrawals made it hard for Carrie to walk. Mr. Edwards asked, "You sure you can fix this?"

"You need to understand, Mr. Edwards, I can help Carrie, but it's really up to her. As I told you before, there is an element of danger in the withdrawal. You need to be aware of this. Also, once she is over the physical withdrawal, she will still need to get past the mental state of the addiction, thinking she wants it or needs it. That will be the hardest long term."

"I understand."

After they arrived at Sage's Place, they ate, encouraging Carrie to eat while she could.

Spotting Robert walking across the compound, Sage called to him. "Pastor Witham!"

He smiled. "Good morning Sage."

"Pastor Robert Witham, I'd like you to meet Carrie Edwards and her father, Mr. Edwards. Carrie will be staying with me for a while. If everything works out, she may even work here."

The pastor looked at Carrie with knowing eyes. "Carrie, it is so nice to meet you. I'm glad you'll be joining us. Mr. Edwards. Nice to meet you."

"I understand you're holding Sunday services in the dining hall. My wife and I may join you when we come to visit Carrie."

"I'm very glad to hear that. You'll be welcome."

"We don't have any Sunday clothing with us."

"You don't worry about that, sir. We ask folks to come as they are. We don't stand on formalities, just the love of our Lord."

"That's good." Mr. Edwards turned to his daughter, "Carrie you be good for Miss Brooks, you hear. Don't be a bother. Momma and I will be here to visit on Sunday."

Carrie, covered with perspiration, spoke in a distracted manner. "See you Sunday, Papa."

The pastor took another look at Carrie and said, "I'll walk you out, Mr. Edwards. Sage and Carrie can get settled in."

As they walked away, Sage heard them discussing the services.

"Carrie, would you like to lie down?"

"Yes, please."

Sage settled Carrie onto the bed she had requested Jorge to move into her room. Then, picking up the pitcher and bowl, she carried them out of the room, after letting Carrie know she would return. In the kitchen, Sage exchanged the glass pitcher for a pewter one used in the dining hall and filled it with water. Then she grabbed a metal pot, a metal cup, and a washcloth. These she placed in a bucket before returning to her room.

While walking through the compound, the pastor caught up to her.

"Do you think you can help her?"

"It will be up to her. But I'm sure going to try. She's only fourteen. She had no idea what she was taking or what it was doing to her. This is what I did for a living before coming here. I was very good at my job, but, in the end, it will still be up to her."

"Let me help. When things get really bad, you will need help."

"Thank you, Robert. I appreciate it."

A groan emanated from inside the door of Sage's room. "I'd better go."

The next three days created a blur for Sage. She napped in Mrs. Flegel's room a few times while Robert stayed with Carrie. But mostly, she stayed with the girl. Sage had never really gone through this stage of detox before. At least not to this extent. The nurses and orderlies handled this stage. Sage's participation came before and after the physical withdrawal. Now, her respect and admiration for those brave and compassionate people grew tenfold.

Carrie's screams of pain created agony for those around her. Before long, the room reeked from the repeated vomiting bouts and diarrhea. Nothing Sage did could dispel the odor. But the odor was not the primary concern, Sage focused on helping Carrie get though the worst of the withdrawal. Sage's tears joined with Carrie's as the girl cried out in agony. During the worst of it, Carrie's agitation grew to the point she lashed out at Sage, bruising and scratching her face and arms. Almost constant perspiration soaked the bed, adding to the overwhelming stench. During Carrie's calmer times, they either changed the sheets or threw a blanket on top of the current sheet in an attempt to keep a dry bed for her. When the girl thrashed about from the ache in her bones, Robert helped Sage restrain the girl to prevent her from injuring herself. The horrific process wrenched at Sage's heart. When Carrie's pulse rate raced to an alarming speed, Sage questioned if they were doing the right thing. What if Carrie didn't survive the withdrawals? Though unusual, without medical intervention it did happen. Sage's fear consumed her until the girl's pulse rate slowed.

Robert stayed with Carrie while Sage rinsed vomit out of her dress. For the fourth time that day. Sage wondered where it all came from. The last meal Carrie had eaten was the one they ate with her father when she first arrived. Most of the vomit was probably water. Despite the nausea and vomiting, Sage insisted Carrie drink water whenever she was calm enough. The last thing they needed was for her to become dehydrated.

Robert had been a godsend. Not only had he been vomited on, but he had changed sheets, held Carrie's hair back when she vomited, encouraged her, prayed with her and for her, held her down when she attempted to bolt, and cheered her when she was coherent. He had been there or nearby throughout the entire ordeal. During all of this, Sage heard him muttering constant prayers.

As she reentered the room, he prayed quietly over Carrie's sleeping body. Sage hoped Carrie would stay asleep this time. So far, she had slept for only a few minutes when exhaustion overtook the withdrawal symptoms. When she awoke, the withdrawal symptoms always seemed worse than before.

Robert looked at Sage with a slight smile, and she asked in a whisper, "Do you really believe it helps?"

"What?"

"Prayer."

"Yes, I do. With everything in me. Don't you?"

Silence filled the air. Finally, "I'm confused." Sage filled Robert in on her religious background and how it soured her relationship with her mother. "Now, I just don't know. I've been there for your services. Though the God you speak of wants discipline, He loves us anyway. Why didn't Mom understand that?"

"I can't say for sure, but my theory is, some people need a very strict disciplinary life in order to keep their walk with Him on the right path. They may be afraid that if they veer from that discipline even slightly, they won't find their way back. Of course, with some, it's simply all they've ever known. For others, I think it's an act of devotion to God. While many Christians of our time believe no work of any sort, even making a meal or milking a cow, should be done on the Lord's Day, and I respect their devotion, I don't happen to agree. The Bible tells us the day was created for man, not the other way around. I prefer to do what needs to be done while making it a day of celebration in Him. But each person must decide for themselves, just as each person must decide for themselves whether or not to accept Him into their lives."

Sage said nothing. She needed to think.

"She's sleeping soundly, why don't you go get something to eat and some fresh air. I'll stay."

Sage went outside. After getting a plate of food, she sat against a tree near her room. As she ate, she thought about what Robert had said, about her mother, about the Jesus she had so happily sung about when they first began going to church. She felt conflicted. She had been doing well on her own. After all, in very unusual circumstances, look at all that she had accomplished here in Coloma. But then it occurred to her, she had needed the assistance of others to accomplish this. They may be paid employees, but they were friends also. People who were devoted to her. People she was devoted to. Confused, she put her dishes away, and went to Mrs. Flegel's room for a short nap.

When Sage awoke, darkness filled the room. Across the compound, lights still burned in the kitchen. Hopefully, Mrs. Flegel hadn't stayed up late so Sage could sleep. The fresh night air felt so very good as she walked the short distance to her room. She eased the door open in case Carrie was sleeping.

She need not have worried. Carrie sat, propped up on the bed. Robert mopped her face with a damp cloth.

"Hi, Miss Brooks." Carrie's voice was weak, but they were the first coherent words Sage had heard her speak in three days.

"Carrie! You're awake. You look better."

"I don't know about that. I hurt terribly, and I feel weak as a newborn kitten. But I did keep some water down."

"Good. I'm so glad to hear that. Maybe we're through the worst of it."

"I hope so."

Sage touched Robert on the shoulder, "Why don't you go eat and rest for a while. I can stay with Carrie."

"I'll be back soon." He seemed reluctant to leave.

By the next evening, Carrie's improvement was significant. Sage had helped her bathe earlier in the day and that evening, after all the diners left, Sage and Robert helped her outside to a chair Juan had placed next to Sage's bedroom door. Time to enjoy some fresh air. Sage and Robert sat on the ground near her.

Sage caught movement out of the corner of her eye. Four people walked on the road just past Sage's Place. Looking closer, Juan and Eduardo used a lantern to walk Salome and Ariana home. Ariana held Juan's arm and Salome held Eduardo's. *This must be the romances Jorge referred to.* Sage smiled for her friends. They were good men. The sisters were lovely women, inside as well as out.

A week later, Carrie was up and about. While it would take a while for her strength to return, physically she was much improved. Beginning with the evening the three of them enjoyed the night air on Carrie's first time out of the room, Sage conducted twice daily counseling sessions with her. Bad days required more counseling. It was time for Carrie to begin helping. She needed to feel useful. Staying busy would help her.

Sage kept Carrie with her part of the day; the rest of it found Carrie paired with one of the employees for work. At this point in her recovery, she only performed jobs behind the scenes. Sage did not wish to expose her to possible vulnerable situations. That would come when she was stronger.

Robert once again made his rounds. Most days, using one of the mules, he left in the morning with a pannier of food to distribute to those in need. He also took with him a few blankets, socks, and other assorted items. To those not in dire need, he spread the word of the Sunday services and hot meals at Sage's Place. Mostly, Robert made friends. He was a man impossible not to like.

25

Sage watched as Robert walked away, mule loaded, on his mission to help those in need. *He is so different. He lives his beliefs. There seems to be no judgment in him, only love and concern for others.* She struggled with the conflict between her perception of Christians and his portrayal of Christianity. *Which is the true representation of what a Christian should be?*

What does God want? Does He ask, require even, the strict legalism Mom epitomized? Is His message of love and service what the Christian life is all about, as embodied by Robert? Or, is it as Robert suggested, perhaps different people have different needs in order to remain on the straight and narrow path? How are we to know? With such conflicts, how can the differing styles all call themselves by the same name?

A sudden realization struck Sage; *I'm asking myself these questions as if I believe in God. Do I? I know as a child, I enjoyed the stories of Jesus, his love and miracles, but do I really believe?* In all the years of her rebellion against her mother and search for independence, she never really rejected God, only the harshness of her mother's beliefs, the restrictions, and judgmental attitudes. That was what she associated with the term Christian. That was what she wanted nothing to do with. *I never really gave any thought to what I believe.*

Week after week I am at Robert's Sunday service. While I still stand back by the kitchen, I follow along. I absorb what Robert is saying. I enjoy it! This thought surprised her. *I've even made suggestions for making the service more user-friendly. He now has sheets available with the words to hymns so those who don't already know them can join in the singing. I still offer a fellowship meal after service at no charge. Am I a part of this? Or not?*

Sage was still looking down the path Robert had taken. *Each week, a few more people join the service. Are they there because of a deep, abiding faith? Are they there because it is what good people do? Are they there because of Robert? Or are they there for the free meal? If it's for the meal, but the message speaks to them, is that as good as those who are there because of a deep abiding faith? Or is it even better?* Torn, this struggle felt like a battle waging within her. *Do I believe? Do I want to? How do I know?*

The answers would not come immediately and she had work to do, so with a last look down the path Robert had walked, she turned away, her thoughts focused on the tasks ahead.

The garden produced an abundance of food. They must preserve what they could for the winter months. While Mrs. Flegel had been drying whatever she did not use, and the smoke house the brothers had built was in almost constant use, Sage's last shipment had included glass jars, flat tin lids, and sealing wax for the purpose of canning foods. Sage discovered Mr. Mason had not yet invented his Mason jar and its lid with the built-in rubber ring. Nor had lightning jars been invented, the glass jars with a clamp and rubber ring. Sage thought sure they would be available. But no, they used flat tin lids, which were sealed on with wax, a clumsy and messy process. Sage had also purchased three pressure cookers. She looked at them as though they were venomous snakes, ready to strike at any moment, but Mrs. Flegel was excited to once again have them available; the woman was fearless.

In order to prevent disruption of meal preparation, they built a fire outside the kitchen. The picnic table kept there for employees became the prep table. Though Sage had hired a few additional employees to allow for days off, the entire crew worked on this day. Anyone not otherwise on active duty assisted in prep work for canning.

With berries in full production, the girls who sold them came each day. While most of them had been used for daily meals, Mrs. Flegel reserved the last two days deliveries for preserving. After the girls visit, they would process the berries. They would be quite a treat in the dead of winter.

Sage enjoyed this. She loved looking around at the compound full of people who had become family and seeing all the action. Upstairs, in the back rooms, maids went in and out, cleaning and preparing for that night's guests. In the large garden, three girls were picking the days' produce. Behind the childcare room, the brothers had built a play structure using Sage's drawing of modern wooden play structures. The children played there now. Buddy, who rarely left Sage's side, was there, watching over the children. He seemed to think his duty when they were outside was to guard them, despite the attendants' presence. Out back, the animals appeared content with the new barn, henhouse, pigpen, and fence, allowing plenty of space for them to roam. She heard the faint sound of hammering down the street, where the brothers were building a home for the owner of the other mercantile.

Mrs. Flegel kept checking the canning progress, making sure everything was done correctly, to her specifications. Sage admired her diligence. Mistakes would not only affect the taste, but with concerns of botulism, could be deadly. If a tainted jar was used in preparation of food at Sage's Place, the resulting death toll would be disastrous.

After a thorough check of the preparations, Mrs. Flegel said, "There is a man to see you in the dining hall, Miss Sage."

In the dining hall, Mr. Grayson introduced himself. "The young woman at Sage's Shop said I would need to speak with the owner about carrying my product. Perhaps you misunderstood; obviously I should speak to Mr. Brooks. If you'll just run along and get your husband, I can find out how many bottles of my elixir he would like in his shop."

"Mr. Grayson, I am Sage Brooks, the owner of Sage's Shop as well as Sage's Place. You have no need to speak to my husband, and as there is no Mr. Brooks, that would be quite impossible. You said you are selling an elixir?"

"Well, yes." He pulled a bottle from his pocket. "This magical elixir will cure whatever ails you. From cough, to sprain, to malaise. There's nothing better!"

Sage took the bottle from him and looked at it. "Doctor's Elixir! Do you realize what poison this is? Of course you do! Leave. Never, and I mean never, set foot in this place or any other place I might be again. In fact, I suggest you leave town. Right now!" She walked to the door, opened it, and pointed.

"Well if anyone needs my elixir, it is you. It will calm you. Perhaps a sample bottle, on the house."

"I said to leave."

The thought momentarily crossed her mind to draw her pistol, which was always on her person, to scare him into taking her seriously, but she rejected the idea. While it always worked in the movies, this was not a movie. To draw it would violate every bit of training and every rule she lived by. Since she was not in imminent danger, and did not intend to eat him, it was simply wrong. To do it even once, would teach herself and anyone in sight that the most fundamental rules of firearm safety only apply when you want them to.

Instead, she walked to the door, opened it, and shouted, "Out!"

The man laughed.

Upon hearing her shout, Buddy appeared at Sage's side. A quick assessment of the situation had him barring his teeth and growling ferociously.

"That's what a little independence does to a woman, makes um crazy!" He said, with an angry look as he backed out of the dining hall, stepping off the boardwalk, falling flat on his back.

Sage was furious. After what Carrie had just gone through, she wanted to hurt the contemptuous snake. But the vision of him on the ground before her was something she could not only live with, but would enjoy the memory it made for years to come. A nudge from Buddy brought her back to the moment. "Good boy, Buddy, good boy." She squatted down and hugged him, instantly feeling the calming influence of her best friend.

Sage returned to the canning process, buoyed by the humorous sight of the scoundrel lying in the street. The day was long, as were the next three days. Carrie proved to be an excellent employee, hard working, diligent, and thorough. Though still recovering from her ordeal, she insisted on working as long and hard as the rest of the crew. Staying busy seemed to help.

She wouldn't have any problem with that in the coming weeks. The corn was almost ready to harvest. Already they had picked a few of the earlier ears. The corn field was a large as the entire rest of the garden. It would be canned, ground, dried, and served fresh. The cobs would be used to make corn cob jelly, and then dried for fuel. The husks would be used to make tamales and soup. The silks would make good tea, soup, and fire starter. Even the stalks would be used as fuel. What wasn't used from the garden was either fed to the animals or added to the compost pile. Sage enjoyed seeing how everything was used, leaving no waste.

In the twenty-first century, the three Rs would become reduce, reuse, and recycle. To be "green" would become fashionable. But the waste, garbage, land-fills, and over packaging which would become epidemic seemed to contradict this approach. Consumer goods would be boxed inside boxes. Large plastic packaging would be found for the smallest of items. In contrast, everything in 1848 was used for something. Despite there being no trash collection, it was okay. There were very few items which could be considered garbage. The tins from the canned fruit which Sage purchased were one of the few items which could be considered garbage. But even those were frequently turned into useful items. Men often built small shacks to live in, using cut and flattened tin cans as shingles for roofs.

On the other hand, sanitation could be problematic, with no public sewer systems and few if any codes to assure safe practices were followed. If an outhouse was built too close to a well, river, or other water supply, the result could be tragic. In order to serve the residents, employees, and guests, there were two privies on the compound. At Sage's insistence, a wash stand had been placed outside each one.

Teaching employees about proper hygiene had been interesting. The lack of understanding regarding germs, the bacteria and viruses which make people ill, was a source of frustration for Sage. Ultimately, she resigned herself to giving orders regarding hand washing and other food service necessities. How could people possibly understand something they didn't know existed?

Though it would soon begin again, the canning was complete. Tomorrow, Robert would help with the butchering of a pig. But today, Sage decided it was time for a hike. She needed to get out, to think, to gather herself. As she wrote in her journal of the past few days, she realized the date. September 19, 1848. She had been in this century for one year today.

Shocked by the overwhelming feelings bombarding her, she needed to find a trace of peace and solace by hiking with Buddy. Perhaps then, all would be back in perspective. Sage felt guilty leaving all the work to employees, but her outstanding staff would do fine. After a hike and some sifting of emotions, without a doubt, she would be back to her normal self tomorrow.

While she packed the usual items for a day hike, it occurred to her how valuable those items had been a year ago. She liked to think she would have survived without the pack, but the difficulty level would have increased significantly. Pouring some of yesterday's leftover soup into the thermos, she smiled. One of the best decisions made that day was to stop and get soup, which resulted in bringing the thermos. It made life much easier while on the move and even when living in the tent.

All those months living in the tent came to mind. *It was hard, standing in freezing water day after day. But*

263

look at the results! This place, these people, I love it here. It was all worth it.

Donning her pack, Buddy close at her heels, Sage headed away from the river. The hordes of miners crowding the river banks certainly would not offer the peace and solace needed today. Walking through the woods, the smell of fall in the air, with Buddy close by, she saw in the distance the remnants of a native village.

The Nisenan people would not fare well as a result of the gold discovery. In fact, it would decimate them. They had been a peaceful people, gatherers. Allowing Sutter and Marshall to build a sawmill on their land had led to the discovery of the useless yellow rocks their people had previously ignored, which in turn would bring about the loss of their land, their way of life, and even their very lives. The place the natives called Cullumah, meaning beautiful valley, would, for a time, be devastated as well, as thousands of miners tore it to shreds in search of the yellow rock. This knowledge compounded the rush of emotions and thoughts Sage was already experiencing.

As she hiked, the beauty was lost to her as the colors of turning leaves and the dried grass reminded her so much of life at the commune. This provoked previously untouched thoughts. *While I'm happy, what has this done to my family? They surely believe I am dead. What has this done to them? Mom must have been devastated to hear of my supposed death. We never reconciled. What must it be like to lose a child during an estrangement? Oh, Mom, how did we lose the closeness we once enjoyed? Dad, I miss you. I miss your sound advice. Have you been able to comfort Mom, or are you too lost in your own bereavement? How have my brothers and sisters faired?* Pictures of the games they used to play while still at the commune came to Sage's mind. She missed them. *Why didn't I visit?* The overwhelming realization that she would never see her family again, never reconcile with her mother, never get another hug from her father, slammed into Sage like a freight train. *I've been so busy surviving and building, that I haven't given much thought to what I left behind. How could I not think of what my family must be going through? They didn't even have a body to mourn!* At this, Sage fell to her knees, tears cascading down her face, and mourned for her family. For their pain and loss. For what could have been, should have been, the relationship with her mother.

Buddy, concerned, nudged Sage, worried about his friend. Receiving no response, he kept nudging her, finally poking his head underneath her arm, as if she were hugging him. This action eventually reminded her she was not alone. She put her arms around her friend, hugging him as a lifeline, until at last, the tears slowed.

"Ah, Buddy, my friend, what would I do without you?"

It occurred to her that she had made that same statement a few times lately. About the brothers, about Mrs. Flegel, about Buddy. Despite her longtime assertion that she didn't need anyone else in her life to be happy, the realization that to have others in her life made it even better, was quite enlightening. *Yes, I can survive on my own, I've proven that. I can even live on my own and enjoy*

265

life. But was I truly happy then? Or just satisfied? I derived satisfaction from meeting goals and new accomplishments. But was happiness a part of my life? How often did I smile and laugh? I did enjoy my life, but was I happy?

This startling line of thought brought Sage full circle, back to the whirlpool. *What if I hadn't fallen in that whirlpool? I would be adding to and crossing off my list. Constantly looking for the next adventure. Working long hours just so I could have that next adventure. Oh, I enjoyed my life, and though crossing a goal off my list had been satisfying, it was not fulfilling. Maybe that's why I kept adding to it. Now I'm living an adventure. Even more, like Mom said, maybe I do need others. Not for survival, but for quality, for joy.* "Just like I need you, my friend," she said, giving Buddy another hug.

Would I go back if I could? If I did, perhaps I could fix things with Mom. Imagine, thinking someone was dead for a year, only to have them show up. But, even with thoughts of my family, would I go back? I love it here. I love the people in my life. I'm successful. Better yet, I'm more than satisfied, I'm happy! I love this way of life. Despite the pain falling into that whirlpool undoubtedly caused my family, I would not choose to return if I could. This is home.

26

A distinct fall bite tinged the air as Sage rose the next morning. Though it would warm as the day progressed, the darkness before dawn spoke of fall's impending arrival. The cool air felt good after the long, hot summer. Since they planned to butcher hogs, this provided comfort. Processing all that meat in the heat made her nervous.

Exiting her room, light from a lantern illuminated the table outside the kitchen door. Though she planned to get the unpleasant job of the kill over first, instead she headed for the light to see what was happening. Nearing the table, Robert and the brothers finished the erection of a tripod near the fire, on which a large pot of water heated. Next to the tripod stood a large barrel.

"Good morning! I didn't expect you to join us."

"Buenos dias!" Juan greeted her. "We will only be here for a short time. For the very heavy work. Then in the daylight, we will finish Mr. Rossland's house."

"It's almost done? He must be thrilled. Thank you for taking time to help us." Sage had wondered how she and Robert would handle the large animals by themselves.

They led the hog to the tripod before killing it. The pigs were handled daily and had been trained from their piglet days to lead on a rope, with this very advantage in mind. The tripod was used to suspend the lifeless hog, allowing him to bleed out before the butchering process.

After the bleeding stopped, they moved the barrel under the hog and filled it with hot water. When full enough, Juan stuck his hand into it to check the temperature. Too hot and it would cook the hide, to cool and it would not do its job of loosening the hairs. When they determined the water had reached the correct temperature, which Sage made sure to learn, they lowered the hog into it. They raised it to periodically determine if the hair could easily be scraped. When it could, they scraped. Soon, they needed to dip the hog again. They repeated this process until no hair remained. Then they gutted the hog, with the entrails set aside for sorting and cleaning. Sage noted the method. Then Xavador led the second hog out and they repeated the process.

The whole procedure fascinated Sage. She had never taken part in butchering hogs before. As usual, nothing was wasted. Even the entrails were cleaned, scraped, and would be used for sausage casings. The fat was rendered, providing much needed lard for cooking and baking. Any skin not attached to the bacon would be fried.

As was her habit, Mrs. Flegel checked on their progress regularly, excited at the prospect of making bratwurst.

Sage and Robert talked as they worked. While they had lived closely for some time, they had not spent a lot of time in idle chit-chat. This day allowed time to become acquainted on a more personal level. Sage was surprised to learn Robert had been raised on a farm, so he brought plenty of experience butchering hogs and other farm animals.

268

When it came time to share her past, Sage found herself in a dilemma, how to be honest, yet not reveal the future. "I spent my early years in what you might call communal living. We were distanced from others and everyone worked together for the good of the community. I suppose it may sound odd, but jobs weren't classified for men or women, they were simply done by whoever enjoyed them or had time."

"This explains your unique outlook. You don't shy away from what's thought to be man's work."

"Yes, at least in part."

"And the other part?"

"I suppose you could call it rebellion. After we moved, my mother changed. She insisted I conduct myself as a lady. I was only allowed to do 'women's work' around the house and to care for my younger siblings. She expected me to prepare myself to be a good wife and mother. But I wanted to explore the world. Being a wife wasn't on my list of goals. I suppose I disappointed her as much as she angered me. We stopped talking when I left home."

"Have you ever considered writing to her?"

"Yes, but only after it was too late."

The sadness in Sage's voice spoke volumes to Robert. He was quiet for a moment before he asked in a gentle manner, "Do you believe your mother loved you?"

"Yes." Sage's response was automatic, without hesitation.

"And what about you? What are your feelings toward her?"

As Sage paused, tears welled in her eyes, causing the task before her to swim. "I love my mother. Despite the changes in her, I realize now that she was only trying to lead me in the direction she felt would be best for me. I also suspect if I had not rebelled in such a harsh manner, she may have found a bit of flexibility in her rules. Instead of attempting to discuss the situation with her, I became angry, said 'fine,' and stormed off. Mom never showed anger, either before or after her transformation. She possessed a gentle soul. Her favorite thing to say to her children was 'talk to me,' only I stopped talking." As she said this, tears fell. "Oh, Robert, it was me. I could have stopped the estrangement!"

He drew a deep breath before speaking. "Sage, I doubt the problem was all you any more than it was all her. Yes, I'm sure you contributed. But just as it takes two to get along and listen, it takes two to create a conflict. It sounds like she didn't want to hear your dreams any more than you wanted to pay heed to her plans for you. Being a parent doesn't make a person perfect. It's a constant learning experience. There's a very good chance she learned from her experiences with you and applied them to your younger siblings."

Sage wiped her face on her sleeve, careful not to get blood on her face, and remained quiet in thought for some time. "You are a very wise man, Robert Witham."

"By the grace of God."

"How did your family feel about you leaving the farm to become a pastor?"

"Pop was kind of disappointed for his favorite farm hand to leave, but remained quite proud of me. Momma was pleased as could be. I think she saw it as a feather in her cap. She was quite giddy at the prospect, well, until the day I left home. Her tears flowed from the time we got up until after I left. She said, "It's hard to let my baby go, but God has plans for him.""

"Do you write to them?"

"Oh, yes. I've sent a couple of letters since I've been here. I've told them about Sage's Place and the wonderful services we are having; how God is using us to fulfill His plans."

"Us?"

"Oh yes. By allowing the use of Sage's Place for services and providing a fellowship meal, you have contributed a great deal to His plan. You may not realize it yet, but I believe the Good Lord has a mighty purpose in you."

This left Sage somewhat unsettled. She wasn't even sure what she believed; how could He use her?

"I have told my family about you. I hope you don't mind. Actually, I've told them about many of our family here at Sage's Place."

He continued. "As the population around Coloma continues to increase, and the ruffians become more and more rowdy, I believe Sage's Place will become more and more of a sanctuary. Not just a place to stay and to eat, but a place of peace within a storm of disorder. In many ways, it may be a better sanctuary than the church I hope to build. People aren't afraid to come here. No one feels the need to

271

be a certain person or dress a certain way when attending services at Sage's Place. I'm not sure we'll be able to carry that over to a church building. I discuss these concerns in my letters to my family."

As Robert continued speaking, Sage grasped why he felt God was using her. This remained in her thoughts as their conversation turned to lighter subjects.

Sage laughed a great deal as they talked, which surprised her. Laughing wasn't something that had been a large part of her life. But here, with Robert, it seemed quite natural.

Robert was not only compassionate, generous, and kind, he was lighthearted, amusing, and rather comical at times. An excellent story teller, he could transport the listener to the scene of the story with seemingly effortless narration.

By the end of the day, most of the meat hung in the smokehouse, covered with a mixture of salt and brown sugar. After it cured for three to four weeks, they would smoke it. Mrs. Flegel took the remainder of the meat to the kitchen for the next day's meals and bratwurst.

Even more important than the meat, Sage discovered more than a pastor, she found a true friend in Robert.

27

All four brothers made the trip to San Francisco in October and brought back another load of supplies. This time Jorge also brought back his bride.

Maria Navarro was a quiet girl. Small, but sturdy, she seemed to study everything around her. Perhaps not shy, just not prone to speaking unless necessary. Her eyes sparkled whenever she looked at Jorge, but she did not cling to him. A perpetual slight smile graced her lips, as though she knew a joke to which no one else was privy.

With the arrival of the new shipment, Jorge and Maria's cabin was complete. Small, not much larger than the sleeping quarters, the design allowed future expansion. With one of Mrs. Jones quilts on the bed, a beautiful new pitcher and bowl on the wash stand, and a small, two burner cook stove, it was complete and ready for the newlyweds to enjoy their new lives together.

Thanksgiving would be special. In addition to the usual three meals, Sage's Place planned a special celebration meal between the dinner and supper services. Not advertised, it was by invitation only. For two weeks, Robert handed out invitations to whomever he deemed most in need. With no defining criteria, only Robert's good judgment and kind heart dictated recipients. Over three hundred were expected for the free banquet.

This would not be a traditional Thanksgiving feast. While Mrs. Flegel planned elements of one, such as pumpkin pie, dressing, and yams, they possessed neither the birds nor enough oven space to prepare that many turkeys, so a more practical meat medley would be served. The platters of meat to be placed on the tables consisted of pork, chicken, beef, and bear in gravy.

The kitchen spent days preparing for the extra meal. Its service precluded the usual time between meals for prep and cooking of the next meal. On Thanksgiving day, the entire kitchen bustled with activity, as well as a temporary prep area constructed outside the kitchen door. Everyone helped.

While a few families attended, the dining hall was full of mostly men, reflective of the population of the area. Some made obvious attempts at dressing for the occasion, hair slicked back and newly bathed. Others gave the impression they came directly from the diggings. All appeared quite hungry.

A few stuffed their pockets with some of the more portable foods, like biscuits. Sage rejoiced that they were able to join in the feast. Everyone should have enough to eat. *I just wish there was more I could do.*

In addition to the opening prayer before the meal, Robert called for the diners' attention as eating appeared to slow and issued an invitation to join Sunday services. When he mentioned the free fellowship meal provided by Sage's Place, a few faces lit up. Sage expected to see those faces on Sunday.

Peals of laughter came from people whose lives consisted mostly of work and hardship. Neighbors were becoming acquainted and seemed to be forming bonds that Sage hoped would continue after Thanksgiving. A few shoveled the meal and left, in a rush to return to their claim and become rich. Most ate leisurely, in no apparent hurry to leave, enjoying the companionship and spirit of the holiday.

While Sage had helped serve numerous meals and had seen many people come and go through the doors of Sage's Place, this meal of thanksgiving filled her with an overwhelming sense of peace and satisfaction like no other. Unsure why, she glanced around, nodding and smiling at an occasional wave from a diner. Across the room, Robert appeared to be doing the same thing. Then his eyes locked onto hers. For a moment, neither moved. He smiled and nodded. She smiled back.

Part way through the regular supper service, an older gentleman, scruffy looking, with a graying beard and unruly hair approached Sage. She recognized him from the Thanksgiving meal.

"Miz Brooks, I's Jason Hampton. I been sittin' out on your boardwalk. I wanted a way to thank you for the kindness you offered so many on this day of thanks. Well, it ain't much, but…" He handed her something.

Awe filled her at the sight of the wooden carving in her hand. About four inches tall, the detail was astounding. Eyes glistening with tears of gratitude, Sage touched the man's arm. "It's much all right. It's everything. Thank you.

I'll treasure this." As the man walked away, Sage patted Buddy's head, while looking at the perfect wooden likeness of him.

After closing, the employees and their families shared a late feast of their own. Of course, Robert and the brothers were included. Sage noticed the Martinez sisters were seated with the brothers. Robert sat across the table from Sage and Mrs. Flegel. The atmosphere contained a celebratory vibe, causing everyone to remain much too long, considering the hour they rose each morning. But the sense of satisfaction everyone derived from the success of the day was immeasurable.

Outside Sage's Place, celebrating continued. The crowds and unrest grew daily. Coloma was no longer a sleepy little place. Businesses lined the streets, including another hotel. With several thousand men in the area and very few women, much of the commerce was geared toward relieving the miners of their hard earned gold through disreputable means: drinking, gambling, whoring, and other forms of debauchery were rampant and openly practiced. Forms of violence and thievery grew to be more and more the norm.

Several months before, Sage had insisted employees be escorted to and from work or remain at Sage's place for their safety. It was no longer safe for a woman to walk to alone, especially in the dark. The Martinez sisters,

Margaret, Mary Jane, Camilia, and Belinda all moved into the employee rooms. Edward, the young man she hired to man the bath house, had taken Jorge's spot in the brother's room. With the rooms at full capacity, Sage had the brothers add three more rooms. Her property was full.

No more space existed for building without taking garden, orchard, or stock space, none of which could be done. Though the garden produced abundantly, with all the people they fed on a daily basis, they needed more garden space, not less. Sage hoped manure fertilizing over the winter would increase production.

The bath house was a sparkling success. With two tubs, both were frequently occupied. On busy days or evenings, the water was reused several times before changing. At Sage's horrified expression in response to the idea, others explained this was standard practice for the era. While she ached to change the practice, the practicality behind it meant admitting defeat and allowing it. Despite the stove she had installed in the bath house making things much easier, two baths still required an abundance of water to be heated. It made more sense to add more water than to start over with each bather. Additionally, Edward poured a clean bucket of water over each bather as a rinse when they stood to get out of the tub. This helped Sage feel somewhat better about the practice.

Keeping the garden and orchard watered throughout the hot summer and dry fall, proved quite a chore. Concerned the well might go dry, they hitched mules to the wagon, loaded it with empty barrels, and drove to the river. Using buckets to fill the barrels, they then placed tops on them to avoid losing the water on the return trip. The wagon remained parked near the orchard or garden to allow watering by the bucket.

At the sound of rain on her roof, Sage rejoiced. *This will save a lot of work!* It rained for two days. When it stopped, Sage became aware of a new problem. Mud. The streets, which consisted of nothing but well traveled dirt, were a muddy mess. A moment of panic set in. The wagon provided an extreme advantage for hauling supplies from San Francisco. But as the rains and snow came, only the mules would be able to get though the muck. When the rain stopped, it was time to make another trip to San Francisco. In fact, she would make several trips until the roads prevented wagon transport.

Sage made four trips to San Francisco. Each time she took two different companions and Buddy. Robert accompanied her on one trip. They left after service Sunday and returned late Saturday night so he would be there for Sunday's service. Despite the need to hurry, this trip provided much pleasure. They enjoyed one another's company. Though Sage's feelings for Robert grew, she pushed them aside. After all, he was a pastor and she wasn't even sure what she believed.

These trips were all business, made as quickly as possible. The main goal was to stock as much as possible of dry goods such as flour, rice, beans, and sugar. Prices steadily rose and would only get worse. By stocking up now, it may save her in the long run, but her concern centered not on the prices, but the mud. Though food stores must be her chief concern, attaining plenty of stock for the shop was also essential.

While there on the first trip, she placed a large order with Mr. Watson. As the floodgate of miners opened in the coming year, 1849, shortages would be a problem. She hoped to be prepared. While at Mr. Watson's store, she noticed the completed building across the street, which had been in progress during her last visit. The large, three story building included a sign on the front, which read "Gentleman's Club."

"Mr. Watson, what exactly is a gentleman's club?"

The storekeeper looked decidedly uncomfortable. "Miss Brooks," he cleared his throat, "it's a place for gambling, drinking, and," again he cleared his throat, "uh, women."

"A house of prostitution?" Sage wanted to be clear.

"Yes, miss." Poor Mr. Watson's face nearly matched the color of his red bow tie. He shook his head. "And across from my store too!"

As a thought occurred to Sage, she asked, "Who would open such a place?"

With a scowl, Mr. Watson said, "It's that Mr. Butler!"

No wonder he wouldn't tell us the nature of his business! Molly and Jonathon must be sickened. She thanked Mr. Watson and continued on her way.

Sage also located three cats. While she loved cats, these cats now had jobs, two barn cats and one kitchen cat. They couldn't afford mice getting into the supplies. With such a large stockpile, much of it would be stored in the barn. The kitchen, as large as it was, simply couldn't hold all of it and still allow room to work.

It was wonderful to see Molly, despite feeling like she had time for no more than "hi" and "bye." Sage was thrilled to see her growing large with child. She purchased some lovely baby yarn to have Mrs. Hanson make into a blanket for the baby. In her excitement over Molly and Jonathon's impending arrival, she also purchased various adorable yard goods, taking them to Mrs. Jones, with the request that she make a truly special baby quilt. Mrs. Jones had laughed at Sage's enthusiasm, "You've brought me enough material to make at least ten baby quilts."

On the fourth trip Sage brought a lovely knitted baby blanket as a gift for Molly and Jonathon, whose joy at receiving it reached the point of embarrassment. Mrs. Hanson had dropped everything to create a masterpiece. When Sage asked if she had enough yarn left to make one for Sarah Huck, whose child was due at any time, Mrs. Hanson chuckled and told her to come back in a couple of days.

When Sage picked up the baby quilt from Mrs. Jones, she gasped at the sight before her. Mrs. Jones had created a work of art! Despite Sage's random choice of material, she had worked it together through appliqué and piecing to create a child's view of the city. Animals, buildings, trees, the boarding house, all were there. The roads were covered with an intricate flourish of stitching. When Sage finished oohing an ahhing over the quilt, Mrs. Jones lifted her hand from the stitching which never seemed to cease and pointed to a large braided rug made from the leftover material. "I thought this would be a good use of the leftover material."

"Oh, Mrs. Jones, you are amazing!"

Molly and Jonathon were overwhelmed by the stunning gifts.

On the way home from the fourth trip, the travelers awoke to a light sprinkle of rain. By noon it was coming down in torrents. While it slacked off to a steady pour by the time they arrived at Sage's Place, it continued for two days. The "road" became one large mud bog. While the mules would be able to make it through, the wagon would be going nowhere until it dried. By then, the road would undoubtedly be in such rough condition, a wagon would still barely be able to traverse it.

Though the mud created its own set of problems beyond securing supplies, such as the constant cleaning it triggered, all were thankful the rain eliminated one chore, the constant watering of the garden and orchard. With the rain came cooler temperatures. While the Indian summer had the garden still producing, with the rain they picked it clean. Then the mixture of manure, compost, and, sawdust from the mill was spread on it. By spring they expected the well fertilized soil to create an abundance of produce. Some of the same mixture also fed the orchard.

"Robert, I have a question for you." Sage's focus on her current idea caused her to bypass any small talk.

Robert smiled at Sage. "Ask away!"

"Do you know of anyone, actually, two or three people, who might be interested in working for a hauling service between here and San Francisco?"

"So will you be starting a hauling business?"

"Only if I can find the right people to make it work. I need two or three unimpeachably trustworthy men. Of course, the lure of digging for gold must either not interest them or they have tried it and are over it. Also, they need the courage to stand up to possible marauders."

Robert looked deep in thought. "I'll need to think on this one. Are you in a hurry?"

"The timing will be right when the right partners are found."

"Good attitude. I'll get back to you. Now I have an announcement."

"Sounds serious, what's up?"

"I've just made a deal with the Navarro brothers to begin construction on a church."

"But," Sage hesitated to absorb the news. "I thought our arrangement was working quite nicely."

"It has worked wonderfully! However, there are advantages and disadvantages to it. Many people prefer, are more comfortable really, in a traditional church setting. While they've been understanding and patient about meeting in Sage's Place, some are pushing for an actual church building. The opposite is one of the disadvantages. There are those who wouldn't consider visiting a church, but because the service is in a dining hall, they have joined us. Many of these people return week after week. Some have been baptized and made changes in their lives. I fear we may lose that advantage of gaining new people by meeting in an actual church building. However, a great deal of gold has been received in offering with the objective of building a church. Also, to establish a solid foundational congregation, we need a permanent structure. Another advantage is that it will give you your dining hall back."

"So it can sit empty during that time? I understand wanting to establish a presence, but Robert, so many come to Sage's Place who have said they wouldn't have if the service had been at a church. Plus, there are those who begin coming just to eat the free fellowship meal. Isn't it worth it for them to receive the Word of God? Does a building mean so much?"

"For months I have considered this and prayed over it. What would happen if God were to call me elsewhere? What would happen…"

"Are you thinking of leaving?" Sage could not contain the distressed tone in her voice as she interrupted Robert. The panic of this thought unnerved her more than she cared to admit, even to herself.

"No, but these things do happen. I'm here to establish not just services for now, but a church for the ages. To do so will require an identifiable church building."

Sage said nothing. While she understood the need and desire for a church building, Robert had said many times the true church was the believers themselves. *If meeting at Sage's Place brings more in for worship, why stop?*

"Sage, don't you see, if we build a church building, then you can extend your food service hours. It would be a very profitable move for Sage's Place."

"While it is true that I like making a profit, it is only one day, actually one morning. I haven't expanded my hours in the afternoon or on any of the other six days for that matter. Besides, aren't you the one who insists that to be spiritually fed is of primary importance?"

Ignoring her last question, Robert changed the direction of the discussion. "I think you should."

"I should? What?"

"Expand the service hours at Sage's Place. There are so many more miners here now than when you opened. Every day there are those who are unable to be served because of the limited hours. I think you should increase your service time from two to four hours per meal. Actually, if it's possible, I would say you should just open in the morning and stay open until you close in the evening."

"But that would create incredibly long hours for the staff."

"Then hire more staff. Limit the length of time they work. Break the day into two shifts."

Sage didn't respond. She was fighting an internal battle of her own. Seeing this, with a comforting touch to her arm, Robert left her to her thoughts.

The next morning, after breakfast service, Sage called a staff meeting. With the job rotations, most of the employees had served in nearly all of the positions, so they were well acquainted with each job's duties. The evening before, after closing, Sage had spoken to Mrs. Flegel and Mrs. Freeman. To have their support was essential. Though Mrs. Flegel was a touch leery of the plan, she agreed it would be a good thing for Sage's Place.

Sage explained to her employees that she would be hiring a second shift of staff. "This will allow for shorter work days. Of course, weekly wages will remain the same, so this will not affect your income. I plan to put out a help wanted sign today and hope to have all the additional staff hired tomorrow morning. We will spend the rest of the week training the new personnel in a buddy system. Then, beginning Monday, we will remain open and serving from six in the morning until eight in the evening, except Sundays. On Sundays, we will not open until noon, thus dropping the breakfast service and an hour of the dinner service. We will, however, still serve the complementary fellowship meal after the church service. Sunday's will be a rotating day off, so one Sunday you will work all day, the next you will have a day off."

This announcement was met with considerable enthusiasm.

"Pastor Witham," Sage continued, "has commissioned the building of the first church in Coloma, so our time of the congregation meeting here is limited. My goal is to continue serving the fellowship meal after they begin meeting in the new church building."

As the meeting broke up, Sage remained in thought. She wasn't sure why Robert's announcement of a new church building affected her so adversely, but she couldn't shake the disturbed and disappointed feelings. *Why does it matter so much to me?*

28

The announcement of the church building project at the next Sunday's service garnered mixed reviews. Most of the people were overjoyed. A few seemed indifferent. A small number appeared apprehensive. Many wondered about the fellowship meal.

"We will still be serving the fellowship meal immediately after service."

"But how will we distinguish those coming in from the church service from those who just decide to come for the free meal and skip the service?" Several nodded their heads in agreement when the question was asked by one of the regulars.

A fleeting sad look crossed Robert's face, "Miss Brooks and I will discuss the matter and decide what to do by the time our new church is complete. We must consider, there are several of us who began attending services after hearing of the fellowship meal and as a result have accepted Christ. So I pray we will not rush to exclusivity."

Later, as Sage helped Robert load the mule for his Sunday trek to help those in need, he said, "Perhaps you were right; maybe a church building will result in more problems than it solves."

Hefting a loaded pannier onto the crossbuck, Sage surprised him. "Actually, I believe I was wrong. The comments during service about both the church and the fellowship meal convinced me there needs to be a church built. I have a feeling it will be an immeasurable learning experience."

Robert looked at her with a puzzled expression.

"Perhaps regardless of where services are held, we will become too comfortable. Even in a dining hall. Have we taken the convenience of being able to serve meals in the same place we worship for granted? When we served food after service, the doors have remained closed. It has remained an environment of exclusivity."

Robert's eyes took on a knowing look and he slowly nodded his head.

"Could the fellowship meal be an extension of the service in some way?"

With a sly smile, Robert said, "I believe it could."

"What if we allowed the dining hall to fill after the congregation makes their way into it?"

Robert laughed. "Sage, you are amazing. I believe this little scheme of yours may prove quite beneficial. I think maybe I'd better have the brothers build a larger church."

"Shall we start next Sunday?"

"While I'm out today, I'll invite a few reluctant miners for a free meal." Robert chuckled as he led the mule down the muddy road.

When Robert returned that evening, he shared good news with Sage. "I believe I've found two gentlemen who would make excellent drivers for your proposed mule train service. They will be in tomorrow to speak to you."

"What can you tell me about them?"

"I've been visiting with them on a regular basis for several weeks. They are good, God-fearing young men who realize they made a mistake coming to search for gold. While they have found some, they detest the digging and the conditions. Their goal was to find enough to start a business, but with costs of supplies what they are, they're realizing they may never save enough."

"Do you know what sort of business they hoped to start?"

Robert smiled. "I don't think they knew. They are quite young, only seventeen and nineteen, but they seem quite mature and very ambitious, if excitement counts for anything."

"I look forward to meeting them."

The next morning, Sage found two young men sitting on the boardwalk when she entered the dining hall to start a fire in the fireplace at four AM. As she opened the door, they came to her.

"We're here to speak with Miss Sage Brooks; Pastor Witham sent us," the taller one said.

"I'm Sage Brooks. Please, come in."

"Thank you, ma'am. I'm Lester McRay and this is my cousin, Floyd Landers."

"I'm pleased to meet you. I understand you don't care for prospecting."

"No ma'am. It's not that we don't like hard work; it just seems everything we make goes toward living. That's not what we had in mind when we came here." Floyd shook his head as he talked.

"How much did Pastor Witham tell you?"

"He just said you may have a good job for us." Lester looked excited.

"As you know, with all the mud since the rain began, wagons are unable to get through to Coloma with supplies. Only mule trains can haul supplies now. Do either of you have any experience with mules or horses?"

"Yes ma'am, we both have some experience. Though I have a might bit more than Floyd. But to be totally honest, neither of us have worked with them a great deal."

"Let's go out with the mules to finish talking." Sage wanted to watch Lester and Floyd with the animals since their care, well-being, and lives would fall to these two young men. As they walked to the paddock, they spoke of other things: family, weather, gold, food, and whatever else came to mind. It was important to get to know these young men.

"Do you intend to give up your claim?"

"If you hire us we do. With the rising cost of goods, it's difficult to pull enough out of the diggings to have any more than just the necessities. Not sure how we'll ever save to start a business. Frankly, though we've always liked to stay busy and don't mind hard work, we aren't fans of prospecting. Digging for rocks just isn't as fun as we thought it would be."

290

Sage laughed. *These two definitely didn't catch gold fever.*

To avoid the mud, the three went into the barn and Sage enticed a few of the mules to join them. As she began to speak of their care, she noted when Lester picked up a curry comb and brushed one of the mules. Absently, Floyd scratched around the ear of another animal.

She showed them a crossbuck and how to saddle the mule; then went on to demonstrate the loading of panniers, both canvas and wooden. They expressed amazement at the amount of weight a mule could carry as Sage explained the importance of even distribution and judicious protection against rub spots.

As she spoke, Lester and Floyd listened intently, occasionally asking questions. Unlike many of the men she had come across since landing in this century, they gave no impression of resentment over being taught by or taking orders from a woman. In fact, they seemed to think her a mule expert. Though she had once taken a series of equine classes, before coming here she had never even been near a mule. But then, this life encompassed one new adventure after another.

After their lesson on mules, Sage stood back and watched the two young men interact with their prospective charges. They each spoke in a quiet manner, soothing the animals as they worked with them. When Lester picked up a foot to check the hoof, a form of care Sage had not yet demonstrated, she nodded. Floyd's concern when he found a sore on one of the mules while currying showed empathy for the animal and attention to detail.

Observation of the two with the mules convinced Sage she had found her drivers, though she would need to watch and work with them, getting to know them before sending them on a trip to San Francisco. It would be necessary to accompany them on their first trip. While she harbored no doubt they could and would do a good job with the animals, the position also carried with it the responsibility of transporting great sums of gold to pay for the load. Assurance of their integrity was imperative. Plus, she needed to introduce them to the people with whom they would be working.

Finally, she said, "I would like to try this if you two are in agreement. I had the Navarros build a room in the corner of the barn for you to bunk. You can take all of your meals in Sage's Place." She went on to explain that for now, in addition to room and board, she would pay them a weekly wage. "For the time being, you will be responsible for the care of all the stock, with the exception of milking and gathering eggs. Does this sound acceptable to you?"

Lester and Floyd expressed excitement over their new job and said they would go break camp and hurry back to begin their duties. As Sage returned to the dining hall, she smiled at their enthusiasm.

The next couple of weeks were busy as Sage hired a full shift of employees and also worked with Lester and Floyd. Though men far outnumbered women around Coloma, the line was still quite long for the positions she had available. Because Mrs. Flegel would take one shift in the kitchen and Mrs. Freeman the other, she made sure to include them when choosing kitchen help. It was important for them to feel comfortable with their help.

She spoke briefly to each applicant, asking those of interest to be seated at a table. As time for breakfast service neared, she had finished her initial chat with each applicant, but still had far more seated at the tables than positions to fill. She needed another location to conduct her second round of interviews. After checking for an available room, Sage asked the ladies to follow her to one of the vacant guest rooms upstairs. "Please form a line along the wall outside the room and I will speak to each of you individually."

Sitting on the edge of one bed and indicating to the woman before her to sit across from her on the other, Sage chatted with each applicant in this manner, asking those she wished to remain to form a line to the other side of the door outside the room and dismissing the others. After a chat with each woman, she still had almost twice the number of applicants as positions.

After the breakfast service, Mrs. Flegel and Mrs. Freeman joined her. Each quickly selected their kitchen help from the remaining women.

Just as she was about to begin yet another round of discussions with the remaining applicants, Belinda Grossman came running in from the childcare center. "I'm sorry to interrupt, Miss Sage, but Mrs. Huck's water just broke. The baby's coming!"

"Excuse me. I'll be back soon," Sage told the woman before her. "Belinda, grab a server from the dining room to watch the children and take Sarah to my room. I'll send for her husband and get help."

As Sage headed for the stairs, one of the women waiting in line called out to her. Sage thought her name was Mrs. Elaine Lynn. "Ma'am, my momma's a midwife. Though I haven't ever delivered a baby by myself, I've been helping her for several years. I know what to do. Do you need help?"

"Yes, thank you Mrs. Lynn. Please come with me." Sage was relieved. Though she knew Sarah was due at any time, she hadn't given the very real possibility that she would go into labor while at work any thought. *I guess I fell down on the preparedness level in this situation.*

With a look at Mrs. Lynn, Sage hoped she knew what she was doing. From the interviews, she knew the woman was eighteen, but to look at her she would have guessed her to be a girl of about twelve. She was tiny, maybe four feet, ten inches tall. Her tiny little hands looked like a little girls hands. Everything about her looked like a little girl except her mass of thick dark blond hair she had swirled into a bun. Her attitude, on the other hand, was anything but small. She had the confidence and bearing of a woman twice her age. She carried herself with purpose. And, unlike Sage was feeling at this moment, seemed quite calm and in control. For such a tiny thing, she had a surprisingly low and commanding voice.

After showing Elaine Lynn to her room, Sage rushed to the barn to find Lester and Floyd. She described where to find the Huck claim and asked for one of them to go tell Mr. Huck the baby was coming. Once she was sure

Floyd could find the claim, she hurried back to her room to see Sarah settling in. There she found Sarah, resting comfortably on the bed, Elaine Lynn giving orders, and Salome Martinez, who had been recruited as assistant. "Is there anything else you need before I return to my interviews?"

"No, we'll be just fine here. If we need anything, Miss Martinez seems quite capable." Elaine Lynn had taken charge, no doubt about it. Sage liked her. She would definitely fill one of the positions. This would also aid the people of the community, since they would know where to find a midwife, if needed.

Before returning to the interviews, Sage checked to verify there were enough servers in the dining hall. She would hire and send someone down immediately to cover the shortage. Then she went by the childcare room to assure herself there were at least two women with the children. Finding childcare adequately covered, she returned to complete the interviews.

Even with the excitement and delays, Sage hired the needed staff, including one to cover for Sarah, by the time dinner service was over. The new hires were shown directly to their trainer.

Sage asked the established employees which shift they would prefer to work; although most requested the early shift, there were enough who wanted the later shift that she could count on experienced people on both shifts.

On her way past the kitchen to check on Sarah, a tap on the window got her attention. Mrs. Flegel motioned her in. "Miss Sage, with all the extra personnel, food, and cooking time, we're going to need more space. I was thinking maybe we could enter a store room through what's now the back door and then have the back door go out of the store room. It would provide more prep space in here and make it easy to unload supplies into the store room."

"Excellent idea! I'll talk to Juan and see when they can do it."

"Don't mean to be pushy here, but we really need it done by the time we change to two shifts."

Sage stared at Mrs. Flegel.

"I know, I'm asking a lot. But those brothers, with the way they feel about you, they'll drop everything if you ask them." Mrs. Flegel had a silly conspiratorial smirk on her face.

"As soon as I check on Sarah, I'll go find them." When it came to the kitchen, Sage knew who was in charge, and it wasn't Sage.

When Sage located the brothers, she explained to Juan what Mrs. Flegel wanted.

"No problem. It will be nice to be building at home again." His smile held warmth.

Then she told him when it needed to be complete.

His smile disappeared. "Miss Sage, that is one week."

"Yes, a whole week for one small, little room." Her bright act wasn't working, but she didn't know what to say.

"We would need to stop all work here. Mr. Drummond is expecting his shop to be complete in two weeks."

Sage just looked straight at Juan.

"Okay, your store room will be done by Monday."

"But what about Mr. Drummond?"

"We will finish on time, don't you worry."

As she headed for the barn later that day to work with Lester and Floyd, she noticed the brothers already busy at work on the store room. She felt somewhat guilty, but didn't dwell on it. She would pay them well and continue to provide food and housing for them. Friends helped each other.

Two weeks later, with the store room in place and additional prep space in the kitchen, the continuous service in the dining hall went off without a hitch. Rarely were there empty spaces at the tables. Gold was pouring in. The shorter hours for the staff and time off on Sundays benefited all, since they appeared rested and this showed in their work. Sarah decided not to return to work after the birth of her daughter. The brothers even finished Mr. Drummond's store on time. Now to accompany Lester and Floyd on their first trip to San Francisco.

29

Lester and Floyd could handle the trip on their own, but Sage thought it important to introduce them to Ford, Mr. Watson, Mrs. Jones, the Brines, and others they would be dealing with. With the large amounts of gold involved and the large orders placed, it would be better for everyone if she were to make the introductions.

She explained to Lester and Floyd that they would run things on the trip, but her presence provided for introductions and facilitating an easier transition. Plus, a visit with her friends, the Brines.

Sage and Buddy followed the mule train on horseback. She wanted them in charge, with her there only for questions or suggestions. It started raining the morning of the second day, making the remainder of the trip uncomfortable and muddy.

When they arrived at the ferry landing, an actual dock greeted them. Ford exploited the advantage of increased traffic well. Sage grinned at the sight. When he arrived, Sage introduced Lester and Floyd, noting that they would be working with her and making regular trips between San Francisco and Coloma.

Like Coloma, San Francisco's streets had become mud bogs. The western movies Sage had watched omitted this detail . The roads in them always appeared dry and dusty. Because of the mud, she introduced the boys around before checking in at Molly's. That way she could wash and stay to visit. While she was on a horse and comparatively clean, Buddy was another story. He was a muddy mess.

They left the mules and horses in Jonathon Brine's care. He would let Molly know they would be returning and needing rooms and baths.

Mrs. Jones was doing well, happy to be able to get around with her wheeled chair. A stack of quilts awaited Sage, who let her know Lester and Floyd would stop by later to pick them up.

Mr. Watson expressed delight that Sage had help, but said he would miss having visits. The massive order she placed during her quick four trips had arrived and would take at least three trips to haul home, especially without the use of the wagon. Despite this, she placed yet another order, this one even larger than the last. With the transport service and the population growth around Coloma, being well stocked must be a priority. The increase in hours at the dining hall meant they used even more supplies. Plus, prices were going to get still higher.

When they returned to the Brines, it was nearly time for supper. Lester and Floyd started toward the front, but followed when Sage headed for the back. "The price of admittance for Buddy is a good bath." As they reached the well, Molly stepped out to the back porch.

"Sage! Jonathon said you had arrived. I'm so glad to see you." The baby had grown since Sage's last visit; Molly was getting quite large.

Lester said, "Go, get cleaned up, visit your friend. We can bathe our ol' buddy here, can't we Buddy?"

He wagged his tail in answer, but when Sage headed for the house, he tried to follow. "Stay, Buddy. Stay with Lester and Floyd." Buddy obeyed, but appeared dejected and hurt.

In no time, all three entered the hotel. Buddy clean and happy to be back with Sage, and the boys wet and muddy. Molly pointed them to the bath Sage had just vacated, where towels, soap, and additional hot water waited for them.

The parlor was beautifully decorated for Christmas. Though they had recently celebrated Thanksgiving, Sage had forgotten all about Christmas. It had been years since she celebrated. When she expressed surprise to see such beautiful ornaments on the tree, Molly explained, "They are Jonathon's family treasures. They were carefully packed and brought all the way here. We were thrilled when they were unpacked and none were broken."

Sage's mind whirled with thoughts for Christmas at Sage's Place. Life in the gold fields was harsh. While some got rich, many barely eked out a living. It would be nice to have a wholesome celebration. *I'll need to speak with Robert. No doubt he'll have some ideas. I need to find out if we have singers on staff. A few artists would be helpful also. Maybe I'll see if any of the shops here in San Francisco carry ornaments. We can fit a tree right in the middle of the dining hall without having to remove any tables. It may block traffic, but only a little.*

"Sage, are you okay?"

Molly had been speaking. Sage came out of her Christmas planning reverie. "I'm sorry, Molly. I just got lost for a moment with thoughts of Christmas."

"It's easy to do."

Sage noticed Buddy studying the tree. Then he started to do the unthinkable and lifted his leg. "No, Buddy!" The poor, baffled dog looked stricken. Sage had never scolded him before.

"It must be quite confusing for him to see a tree in the house. You take him out while I put the finishing touches on supper, and then we can chat all evening." Molly seemed more amused by the near miss than anything.

The next day, Jonathon journeyed to locate the beef cattle Sage hoped to take back with them. At his request, she was never gone from the hotel for long. Molly's due date was close and he was a nervous first-time father.

She did, however, slip down to Mr. Watson's Mercantile. She explained her plans for the currier service, giving him far more information than the previous day, information only Robert knew. With Christmas in mind, she also arranged for several extra items to be added to their bounty and this trip's cargo. After purchasing one more item, which she took with her, Sage hurried back to the hotel.

As Sage and Molly sat in the parlor to enjoy a cup of tea and chat for a spell before starting dinner, Sage pulled out a beautiful ornament and handed it to Molly.

"Mr. Watson carries a lovely selection of ornaments and I hoped to add to your beautiful tree." The hand blown glass ball included silver added to the process, giving the glass a brighter, shiny appearance. "The information on the display said it is a new technique. They are hand blown and called kugeln. They come all the way from Lauscha, Germany. I thought they were quite special, just like my friends, the Brines."

Molly blamed it on the pregnancy as tears coursed down her cheeks, which contrasted completely with the broad smile on her face. She hung the ornament in a "place of honor," then gave Sage a quick hug.

A thick, wet fog hung over San Francisco as the trio rose long before the sun to leave the warmth provided by the Brines and load the mules. As they entered the livery, Jonathon surprised Sage with a couple of baskets already loaded on a crossbuck. Inside bunnies scurried. A quick count revealed six in each basket.

"Ten does, two bucks. They mature and multiply fast and should add substantially to your food source. I hope you don't mind. When I picked up the cattle and they told me there were rabbits available, I made a quick decision. Got some for us, too."

"Oh, Jonathon, it's a wonderful idea. They will be a great addition! Thank you."

After tethering the mules, with the cows following—two additional milk cows and ten for beef—Floyd placed the bell on the lead mule and they headed for Mr. Watson's mercantile. Lester and Floyd had used their time wisely the previous day, spending several hours at Watson's, sorting goods and packing panniers to allow the greatest possible load without overloading the mules. Their diligence impressed Sage. In no time, they finished loading and headed for the ferry.

While she would miss seeing the Brines on a regular basis, Sage was not sad that she would no longer be making this trip regularly. It wasn't so much the harshness of the conditions or even the danger involved, it was more the leaving. Sage's Place and the people there had become home and family. She looked forward to getting home.

30

It was good to be home again. As soon as she found Robert, Sage discussed her ideas for Christmas with him. When he just smiled at her, Sage asked if she was out of line.

"Not at all. I love your enthusiasm and generosity." His eyes sparkled. "Sage, have you given any thought to a commitment to Christ?"

"I've thought a lot about it. But I'm still thinking. What I see of your faith and the way you put that faith into action, makes me want to call myself a Christian. But then I just get stuck on that word."

"Do you remember our discussion of the many degrees of faith? How some believers need more rules and restrictions?"

"Yes."

"If a person had problems walking, would you agree it would be good for them to have a crutch?"

"Of course."

"In some ways, I think perhaps the stringent rules can be a crutch of sorts. They can be an aid to serving when a person might otherwise get lost. The other way of looking at it is people want to serve God with everything in them, make Him happy. If they are as good as possible, perhaps it will please God. The rules are an attempt to make Him happy."

"I get that. But wouldn't it make Him happier if, instead of judging others, we helped them?"

"I'm sure it would. But think about it Sage, what are we doing when we hold those rules against them?"

Sage's hand rose to the bridge of her nose. The look she gave Robert revealed a painful battle within her. With her head down, she said, "We'll talk later." She absently patted her thigh for Buddy to follow, and headed for her room to put her things away before bathing.

Aware Robert watched in silent prayer, Sage continued forward.

After a bath and a change of clothes, Sage made sure Lester and Floyd waited a full day before beginning another journey to San Francisco. They were like children with a new toy and wanted to leave the next morning. "You should take a day between trips. This will allow the mules rest as well as you."

Both young men expressed immediately contrition. "It didn't even occur to us the mules would need a rest. We were just excited to get going again."

"I love your enthusiasm! But rest, enjoy a day. Make sure the mules are clean and healthy. You're doing a wonderful job; just don't burn yourselves or the mules out."

They laughed at Sage's odd expression.

Later, when she saw them in the dining hall, eating like they hadn't eaten in weeks, she couldn't help but be thankful for the superb recommendation Robert had made by suggesting those two young men.

Two days later, when Sage saw them off again, she surprised herself by saying a small prayer for their safety. It didn't feel forced; in fact, it felt quite natural. A quick calculation told her they should be back in time for Christmas.

The plans for the Christmas celebration moved along smoothly. A unanimous agreement among the staff spurred the preparations forward. A visit to Mrs. Hanson's tent provided many additional pairs of socks to add to those Sage purchased at Mr. Watson's store and the new shop in San Francisco. Mrs. Flegel refused to leave the kitchen when her shift ended, choosing instead to stay and go into candy cane production. Not to be outdone, Mrs. Freeman came in early to make caramel candies. Robert said he found the perfect tree, but would wait until closer to Christmas before cutting it and bringing it to Sage's Place. Several staff members revealed lovely singing voices and met several times to practice traditional carols. A few, including Carrie, possessed extraordinary art talent. All plans progressed nicely.

Five days before Christmas, Robert brought the tree in after closing. Mrs. Flegel and Mrs. Freeman were working late to make pies for the celebration. Immersed in the spirit of the season, the two chefs sang carol after carol. As they decorated the tree with the ornaments Sage had purchased in San Francisco, Robert and Sage joined in, "The first Noel, the Angels did say…" Hearing the singing, the Navarro brothers, Jorge's wife, Maria, and the Martinez sisters soon joined in the decorating. Carrie and the other artists painted manger scenes and snowy Christmas scenes on the windows. The Jonas girls, Ethel and Myrtle, had begged permission to stay and help with the decorating and would be spending the night with Carrie, who now shared a room with Willa Jacob and her two girls. They worked on a signboard telling of the free Christmas dinner served all day on the twenty-fifth. When each participant completed their job, they strung popcorn to serve as garland on the tree. Though late by the time they trudged off to their rooms, all were excited and pleased with the evening's accomplishments.

Three days before Christmas, Lester and Floyd returned. The following day, they busied themselves digging two very large pits. When complete, they lined them with large rocks, then built a roaring fire in each, using several logs as well as brush to help them burn. While the fires raged, Sage, Robert, the Navarros, Lester, and Floyd prepared the hogs for roasting in the pits. They also dug a third, smaller pit where several large pots of beans, which included fat back, molasses, and brown sugar, would be cooked, creating a luscious side dish.

With Christmas Eve falling on Sunday, Robert planned both a morning and a late evening service, but no Christmas Day service. This permitted them to serve meals to as many people as time allowed on Christmas Day. Just as Jesus came to serve, the Good Lord would prefer they spend their time and resources in service.

Finally, Christmas Day arrived. Nearly all of the staff was on hand for the entire day. A cheery and festive atmosphere suffused Sage's Place. Near the fireplace, several artists waited with paper and pencil, ready to make free drawings for subjects to keep or send to family. Several more artists, seated on the far end of the dining hall, prepared to paint animal faces on children. As each diner entered, they received a plate. In addition to the usual utensils and cup, a candy cane, four caramels, and a pair of socks lying on it.

Sage noted the startled looks on the diners' faces as they sat at the food laden tables. It had been some time since they had seen a spread like the one which lay before them; some had never seen such abundance. Roast pork, beef in various forms, yams, mashed potatoes, gravy, baked beans, several vegetable dishes, dressing, fruit salad, deviled eggs, potato salad, biscuits, fruit cake, custard, peach cobbler, pumpkin pie, apple pie, mincemeat pie, and on every table, a cake with "Happy Birthday Jesus" piped onto it.

Every half hour, a group of four singers wandered through the dining hall singing carols. Then ten minutes after the singing ended, Robert, with his resonating, pastoral voice, read the story of the Savior's birth from his Bible, followed by an invitation to join them at Sunday services and the fellowship meal which followed.

In addition to the sign out front indicating free Christmas dinner all day, there was a sign offering free hot baths all day. Floyd and Lester had agreed to assist Edward in manning the bath house. Occasionally, when the water was emptied, they switched off and female attendants took over, allowing women to enjoy the baths. Then when time to empty the baths again, it was once again the men's turn.

The overwhelming numbers of men made Sage think of the many women in the community's bordellos. How were they spending their Christmas day? She put caution aside, marched out the door, and headed straight to the nearest house of ill repute. Upon arriving, she knocked on the door, determined to follow through. Surprised at being invited in, she saw several scantily clad and rather sad looking women seated in the parlor. With the knowledge that this was the right thing to do, Sage, with confidence and cheer, invited the ladies to the free Christmas dinner at Sage's Place.

One especially scantily clad woman, who lounged with a drink in her hand said, "You do understand who, what, we are?"

"Yes, of course. You are people who need to eat too and should be able to enjoy this day just as any other person. Please, get dressed and come have dinner."

The astonished looks on the faces of the women soon softened into little smiles and nods. As Sage extended her invitation at all of the other houses in Coloma, she received similar responses. By the time she returned to Sage's place, a group of women, dressed in their most appropriate wear, crossed the street to join the festivities. While some of the guests and staff showed shock at their entrance, Sage set the tone by greeting them with sincerity and cheer.

There were people everywhere and laughter resonated throughout the building. Many times diners bowed their heads in prayer before partaking of the meal. As Sage observed the festivities, Robert placed his hands on her shoulders, and said close to her ear, "May God bless you, Sage Brooks. This is a wonderful and generous thing you have done here." She reached across her chest to the hand on her shoulder and laid her hand on his, her eyes moist and her heart full beyond measure.

When closing time came, there were still people in line, so the kitchen kept cooking and the servers kept serving. Despite stopping only briefly to eat that day, none of the staff wanted to see anyone turned away without eating. When they ran out of pork, the chefs served other meats. When the baked beans were gone, they created a rice dish in its place. Finally, at 1:20 AM on December 26th, nineteen and a half hours after beginning the Christmas feast, the last person in line was seated. Long before closing, they ran out of socks to give out, so they replaced them with mittens, then blankets, then, finally, with a nugget of gold and a coupon for a free pair of socks.

Sage estimated they served more than 3000 thousand meals that day. By her reckoning they gave out 1500 pairs of socks, 120 pairs of mittens, 60 blankets, and over a thousand nuggets with promises of socks to come. It had been a very long day, they had been up for twenty-four hours, but Sage was sure it was the best day of her life.

31

The remainder of the winter was busy.

The Christmas dinner had, indeed, brought a few additional people to church services. Opening the fellowship dinner to anyone also encouraged additional worshipers. When the first service was held in the newly built church, Sage wondered if they shouldn't have built a larger building. Her own attendance surprised her. She was no longer there because the service was held in her establishment; she was there because she wanted to be. Though she still had not made the decision to dedicate herself to God, she had come to the realization that, yes, she believed.

Floyd and Lester established a regular schedule for their runs to San Francisco. After Sage's hauls were finished, they took orders from other merchants. At a rate of one dollar per pound, the business made a tidy profit. A month into the business, Sage asked Lester and Floyd to be fifty-fifty partners with her. She would still provide housing and food, but instead of a salary, they would split the profits evenly. Out of fairness, Sage's Place would pay half the going rate directly to the cousins. The two young men were ecstatic. They loved the mules, being outdoors most of the time suited them, they had several new loading ideas which made the travel easier, and it had been their dream to go into business.

On Floyd and Lester's first trip to San Francisco in the new year, they brought back word that Molly and Jonathon Brine had a new son, born January 1, 1849, Randall William Brine. Sage was thrilled for them and looked forward to meeting the little one.

In addition to the news, they brought a small flock of sheep with lambs, at Sage's request. Easter was just around the corner.

In February, Elsa, a girl from the first bordello Sage had visited on Christmas day, came to see Sage. After stating she would like to be a "respectable woman," Sage gave her a job and a place to live. Though the employee quarters were full, Sage had no intention of turning the girl away, so they squeezed her in. In April, another girl from the same place, Windy, was also hired by Sage. Unfortunately, a willing girl always took their place at the house. Due to the crowded conditions in the employee quarters, Sage turned room number one of the guest rooms into an employee room.

With that, Juan said they could add a second story to the employee quarters as soon as weather permitted. Though they had been building through the winter, with the necessity of removing the roof, they needed to wait for good weather.

He followed this with an announcement. He had asked Ariana Martinez to be his bride. As soon as he finished building a house for them, they would make arrangements to be married. A month later, theirs was the first wedding at the new church.

When they were settled into their new house, the brothers built another house. This would be for Eduardo and his soon-to-be bride, Salome Martinez. They also planned to build a third house for their parents and other siblings to move to Coloma.

Then in April, as the garden was being planted, Robert returned from one of his treks with a baby. He explained how the parents had been killed in a claim dispute and the baby was left with no one to care for him. He appeared to be only a few weeks old. Though Sage thought of Sarah as a possibility to care for him, she and her husband, who had struck it rich, had packed up and left to open a business in San Francisco. So, Sage fashioned a bottle and cared for him with help from Mrs. Flegel and the child care center. She named him James, for the simple reason that Robert had been teaching from the book of James the day he found the child.

By July, Coloma had become extremely crowded. Prospectors from around the world were steadily arriving in hopes of finding wealth. But the placer gold, the gold which could be easily obtained by methods such as panning, was nearly exhausted. This meant deeper digging and more advanced and destructive methods of mining were required. Those who came in search of riches were shocked to find exorbitant prices. A shovel which would normally cost them two dollars sold for fifty dollars in the gold fields. The law of supply and demand had taken over.

As Sage watched the mass of people converge on Coloma, the unaffordable prices, the violence, the sadness of people's lives, she realized she had changed. When the idea of beating the gold rush first occurred to her, she thought of how wealthy she could become, which would allow her to experience the world. She had, indeed, become quite rich. But it wasn't riches which now motivated her. It was the people, friends who had become family. She had the ability to help others and had helped many, though it saddened her to see how many did without. She thrived on helping. Though life had become rather repetitive, Sage didn't mind. Adventure and experience didn't call to her as it once had. She loved the stability, having a home, helping others.

Then, one Sunday, as Robert spoke of God's love for us being so strong he even numbered the hairs on our heads, Sage felt moved beyond anything she had previously known. Tears streamed unrestrained down her cheeks. Finally, after years of anger, months of fighting within herself, and multiple denials, she knew. It wasn't a book knowledge in her head, but a heart knowledge. To the very depths of her soul, she knew. She was a child of God. When Robert gave the invitation for new believers to come forward, Sage rose.

She stood. Eyes locked with Robert's, Sage slowly moved to the front of the church. Pools filled Robert's eyes as they held hers. Reaching him, he took both her hands in his and they knelt together as Robert prayed. When he moved on to others who came forward, Sage remained kneeling in prayer. After the service, they made their way to the river to be baptized in Jesus' name.

Sage felt like a new person. Life was before her, not adventures, but life, with whatever it held. Whether it held hardship or prosperity, it didn't matter, God would see her through.

During the fellowship meal, Sage sat with Robert. They discussed her transformation. After the meal and a few words from Robert to the full dining hall, Sage took Robert's arm as they left for a Sunday stroll.

Even amongst the crowds, dirt, and noise, the world seemed to have gotten brighter. It seemed more peaceful. A peace which Sage had never before known.

A few weeks later, Robert came home from his mission trek pale and sweaty. Sage felt the back of his neck. He was hot with fever. It had come on so quickly! He had been fine when he left that morning. She left James with Mrs. Flegel to take to the childcare center and escorted Robert to his room. After instructing him to strip down to his shorts, she stepped out of the room. Running to the well, she pulled up a bucket of cold water and headed back to Robert. With a cloth, she bathed him in an attempt to cool the fever.

For hours she prayed as she bathed him. When Mrs. Freeman came to take over the kitchen, upon learning of Robert's illness, she had Mrs. Flegel stay late and went back to her tent for a bag of medicinal herbs. After making a tea, she told Sage to be sure Robert drank it. All evening, servers brought more tea and fresh buckets of cold water.

Throughout the night, Sage sat with him. Finally, as the sky lightened, he fell into a restful sleep. The fever seemed greatly reduced. Sage cried tears of thanks and allowed herself to doze in the chair next to him. She had no idea when or how it had happened, but the realization that she had fallen in love with this man of God startled her wide awake.

Robert looked at her. "Good morning." He had pulled the blanket up to cover him.

"You gave us quite a scare."

"Is this where you slept?"

"Yes, some."

"Alone all night long with a man in his room?" His weak voice had a teasing quality to it.

"People came and went throughout the night. Plus, the man was somewhat out of it."

"Out of it, you say." He shook his head and smiled at one of her many odd phrases. "People will still talk."

"I don't care. All I care about is that you are better."

"Thanks to you. I'm thinking our Lord has more work for me to do yet."

Sage felt for his temperature again before going to her room to freshen up.

The next Sunday, after service, Sage and Robert once again went for a walk.

When they finally reached a somewhat private area, Robert spoke. "Sage, we have worked closely together for some time now. During that time, my feelings for you have grown to be more than friendship." He stopped walking, turned and lifted a hand to touch her cheek. "I love you, Sage. I love everything about you. Would you do me the honor of becoming my wife?"

For a moment, Sage's heart soared with anticipation. Then reality hit. She could not marry Robert without telling him her history. All of it. Even the future part of it.

"Before I answer, there are things I must tell you. Things you need to know." She went on to tell of her relationship with Elliot. "You see, I can't come to you as you would like, pure as you deserve."

Robert stood quietly for a moment, as though in prayer. "When you accepted Christ, you were made new in Him. Just as you believe others can start fresh, so can you." He stroked her cheek with his thumb.

"You are amazing. Now for the really tough stuff."

Robert's eyes opened wide.

Sage went on to tell him how she came to be here, the year she was actually born, her desire for riches, the whole story. Then she told him of Nelson. "I killed a man, Robert. I took another's life. How can I possibly be the wife of a pastor?"

Robert's gentle eyes held hers. "You defended yourself. If you had not killed him, he would have raped and killed you. I don't believe God would have us just lie down and allow that. Had that man lived instead of you, he would have likely continued in his wicked lifestyle. Instead, God chose to save you, watch you bloom, reach so many hearts, and change so many lives. You see, God's plan is always the best."

"What about the rest? Do you believe me?"

"I admit, your story is implausibly extraordinary, but I believe with God all things are possible. What purpose could you possibly have in making up such a tale? Or should I say tall-tale? Much of what you say explains a few things I have wondered about you." He paused for a long while and looked at her with intensity. Sage grew increasingly nervous as she waited. "Yes, I believe you." He grinned. "Now, tell me more about the twenty-first century. Oh, but first, you haven't answered my question."

"Question?"

He smiled, "Will you marry me?"

Sage looked at him. He was a strong, rugged, handsome man. His dark hair and blue eyes created a striking contrast. He was tall enough to make her, at five-seven, still need to look up. But it wasn't his striking good looks she loved, it was *him*. His gentleness, his caring, his sense of humor, his heart, and of course, his love of God and willingness to serve. She smiled. "Yes. Yes, Robert, I'll marry you." She reached up and touched his cheek. "I love you."

Epilogue

Sage's father, Sky, had done well since going to work in construction. About the time Sage graduated from college, he left the business he had been working for and began his own construction business. Sage's brothers Thyme and Parsley came to work for him, as did Chamomile's husband, Mark. The business did well, allowing enough money for extras, like vacations.

Chervil was not seen for several years. After high school graduation he rebelled, the lure of alcohol, drugs, and parties called to him. Finally, six months ago, he returned home. He looked much older. His body had been racked with the effects of his party life. But he was clean and ready to work. The family welcomed him with open arms. Amaranth, especially, was thrilled to have her son return.

Amaranth continued homeschooling Sage's younger siblings, Samuel, Rachel, Matthew, and Luke. Vacations were seen as learning opportunities for them.

One of these vacations took the family through Sequoia Nation Park, Yosemite National Park, and then on to Coloma, California, the site of Sutter's Mill where a chance gold discovery led to the California gold rush. The children were interested and excited as they read the various plaques describing gold rush days, panned for gold in the American River, dipped candles, made rope, and played games from the past.

Amaranth stopped, and tears welled as they came to a group of buildings. One sign read *Sage's Place*, another read *Sage's Mercantile*. She regretted the loss of her oldest daughter. Her death had been hard, but it had been made devastating due to the estrangement between them. Amaranth had learned a hard lesson. Greatly regretting her harshness, she had since learned to focus on love. She encouraged others in her church to express His love also.

Luke, the youngest, ran to read the plaque on the outside of Sage's Place.

Sage's Place

Opened as a hotel, dining hall, and mercantile
early in 1848, Sage's Place was the first business in Coloma.
Sage Brooks was one of the first prospectors around Coloma,
and used her gold to build a thriving and generous business.

"Momma, her name is the same as our sister."

As Amaranth and Sky approached the plaque and read it, the tears in Amaranth's eyes overflowed. "Imagine, Sky, she had the same name as our Sage."

The dining hall still served meals to tourists just as it had to the miners during the gold rush. The Brooks family sat at one of the tables and enjoyed a meal before looking through the rest of the compound. Sage's Mercantile now sold locally made items and art to the tourists. The employee's quarters had been turned into a multi-roomed museum.

The room which sported a wooden plaque inscribed "Sage's Room" held a bed, desk, trunk, and many photos and historical documents. As Sky and Amaranth started to leave, they noticed a glassed-in outfit of clothing. A very worn, but modern looking pair of pants with zip-off legs, an LL Bean coat, and a pair of LL Bean hiking boots. Next to it was a plaque stating these were among Sage's belongings. Though the family insists they were hers and age supports it, historians are baffled. Next to that, they found a glass-enclosed, framed letter written on old paper using the quill and ink on the desk in the room.

For: Sky and Amaranth Brooks

Dear Dad and Mom:

I don't know if you will ever see this, but in hopes that you will, I left instructions with my grandchildren to turn these quarters into a museum and post this letter.

I know you thought I drowned when I fell off that rock into the river in Montana. I'm so sorry for the pain that put you though. Instead, I was miraculously saved and landed here.

After finding myself in Yosemite on September 19, 1847, I made my way here to find a fortune in gold. While at first I thought I had found the ultimate adventure, as well as the funds to find many more, I discovered something much better, faith in God.

Through the guidance of an amazing man, Pastor Robert Witham, I stopped searching for adventure and began serving God. Eventually, I married Robert. Imagine, me, a pastor's wife!

As the Good Book tells us, "And we know that all things work together for good to them that love God, to them

who are the called according to his purpose." Despite the loss I know you suffered, all things have truly worked for good.
I love you all and have missed you greatly.
With much love,
Sage Brooks Witham

A note below this framed letter stated: "The posting of this odd letter was a condition of opening Sage's Place and its compound to the public."

Next to the letter were several pictures, some earlier drawings and some later photos of Sage Brooks Witham, including one with her husband Robert and their children.

Sobs racked Amaranth's shaking body as Sky held her, tears flowing freely down his sun aged face. The children stared in amazement at their parents.

Soon a gentleman approached. "Are you by any chance Sky and Amaranth Brooks?"

"Why, yes, we are."

"I am Robert Witham, Sage's great-great-great-great grandson. Please come with me; I'll explain everything and tell you an amazing story of a wonderful woman."

It is my hope that you have enjoyed reading Sage's story. Please take a moment and leave a review on Amazon, Goodreads, or your favorite review site. Reviews mean a lot to authors. I do read them and do my best to apply suggestions.

Follow my author page on Facebook at: https://www.facebook.com/groups/834896499939990/?ref=bookmarks

Follow my web page at: http://www.rardledford.homesteadcloud.com/

Continue reading the *Out of Time Series* to learn how other women handle finding themselves *Out of Time.*

Other books in the *Out of Time Series*:

A devoted and loving homeschooling mother of three, Gabriel strives to be the perfect wife, mother, and homemaker her husband expects and requires. Her faith in God and love for her children create solid foundations in a life filled with restrictions, demands, and insanity.

Young, spoiled, and immature, this party girl's lifestyle is all about her. Self-centered, yet without self-esteem, she believes her party life will lead to happiness.